"Please give me a baby..."

Doc couldn't. Francesca "Frankie" Luccetti simply wasn't a good candidate. Doc only wished his strong attraction to her didn't border on surreal. "I'm sorry, our agency has strict rules—"

"But I'd be a good mom."

Doc told himself the hand he nestled under Frankie's elbow was merely for her comfort. That if you got right down to it, offering this virtuous virgin some physical comfort was probably Doc's job.... His husky, honeyed drawl said he was as helpless as the newborn she wanted. "I wish I could give you a baby—"

"Then please, Doc," she whispered back. "Just give it to me."

Somehow, the raspy plea made Doc want to give Frankie so much more. And crying uncle with a soft moan, he swiftly captured her lips with his own....

Dear Reader,

Thanks for all the wonderful feedback on BIG APPLE BABIES! I'm very excited to bring you this third book in the miniseries.

These love stories are set around Big Apple Babies, an adoption agency that is backed by anonymous matchmaking millionaires, one of whom is unmasked in every book. While each romance stands alone, much-loved characters pop up, so we can see their lives progressing. Of course, BIG APPLE BABIES is about far more than babies. So be prepared to meet another sexy Manhattan man with lots of attitude and heart....

I simply couldn't wait to write about pediatrician Winston "Doc" Holiday. As a Texas man in Manhattan, he's an urban cowboy with a combination of city savvy and honeyed drawl that lands him neck-deep in love trouble with a virtuous virgin.

I hope you'll find Doc irresistible, and that you'll enjoy the story's setting in New York's Little Italy, a neighborhood full of old-world charm and romance—not to mention meddlesome matchmakers!

Thanks for sharing all the magic with me as the characters from BIG APPLE BABIES take on lives of their own, and we discover how—no matter where they are—people who were meant to be together always magically find each other and fall in love.

All my best,

Jule McBride

DIAGNOSIS:
Daddy

JULE McBRIDE

Harlequin Books

TORONTO • NEW YORK • LONDON
AMSTERDAM • PARIS • SYDNEY • HAMBURG
STOCKHOLM • ATHENS • TOKYO • MILAN
MADRID • WARSAW • BUDAPEST • AUCKLAND

For my favorite "Doc,"
my uncle John Lawrence Dunlap, Jr., in memory—
he loved to laugh. (God rest his soul.)

ISBN 0-373-16725-3

DIAGNOSIS: DADDY

ABOUT THE AUTHOR

In 1993 Jule McBride's dream came true with the publication of her debut novel, *Wild Card Wedding*. It received the *Romantic Times* Reviewer's Choice Award for Best First Series Romance. Ever since, the author has continued to pen stories that have met with strong reviews and made repeated appearances on romance bestseller lists, and she's become especially known for writing heartwarming romances that are as light and upbeat in tone as they are full of emotion, hopes and dreams.

Books by Jule McBride

HARLEQUIN AMERICAN ROMANCE
500—WILD CARD WEDDING
519—BABY TRAP
546—THE WRONG WIFE?
562—THE BABY & THE BODYGUARD
577—BRIDE OF THE BADLANDS
599—THE BABY MAKER
617—THE BOUNTY HUNTER'S BABY
636—BABY ROMEO: P.I.
658—COLE IN MY STOCKING
693—MISSION: MOTHERHOOD*
699—VERDICT: PARENTHOOD*
*Big Apple Babies miniseries

HARLEQUIN ANTHOLOGY
BRIDAL SHOWERS
"Jack and Jillian's Wedding"

HARLEQUIN INTRIGUE
418—WED TO A STRANGER?

HARLEQUIN LOVE & LAUGHTER
23—WHO'S BEEN SLEEPING IN MY BED?
46—HOW THE WEST WAS WED

Prologue

Almost two years ago

"I can't believe this!" Bride-to-be Marta Straussberg brought her apple red convertible to a shuddering halt at a stop sign, pounded the wheel and shouted, "Fire and damnation!" in a salty way that would have done a sailor proud. "Should I marry him or not?" She was an hour late for her own wedding—and still racing through her old hometown, trying to decide whether or not to grace the chapel with her presence.

"You've only got a minute left to decide, Marta!" Fighting panic, she punched the gas, rounding a corner. Up ahead, a triangular median popped into sharp focus, and a tall white-washed fork at the end of the straight stretch of asphalt pointed in two directions—toward the chapel or out of town.

"I just don't know!" Fresh jets of late-summer air rushed at her face, feeling as cool and gusty as a winter wind in the convertible. As she pressed the car horn to warn any low-flying birds that she was fast approaching, she tried not to think of Doc, who was probably pacing in front of the altar right now.

She was vaguely aware she was driving too fast

and the world was whizzing past at an alarming speed. Everything was a blur—the two birds perching on the roadside's wire fence, the buttery yellow wildflowers bursting from long green grasses and the few puffy white clouds in the clear blue sky. Somewhere beyond the convertible's roar were other sounds— buzzing bees, a gurgling brook, the rustle of late summer leaves in the trees.

Marta definitely wasn't stopping to smell the flowers.

Why had she let Doc talk her into this marriage? Didn't he know she could never give him everything he needed and deserved, not her whole heart...?

"And definitely not with hair like this," she snarled petulantly. Her yellow-blond mass was mercilessly wind-whisked and looked more scrambled than this morning's eggs.

Ignoring how the upturned collar of a black leather jacket she'd slung over her wedding gown flapped incessantly against her ears, she lifted her foot from the tar-gritty clutch and quickly examined the underside, which was as black as soot. Not that she could help it. She'd had to go barefoot, or her toenails wouldn't dry.

Not that she even knew where her satin shoes were.

"They couldn't have run away!" Swiftly unbuckling her seat belt and clutching the wheel with one hand, she leaned and raked through an overnight bag on the passenger seat. For a second, she thought she'd actually found one of the flats, but it turned out to be a scarf with a reptile print. Threading through her fingers with the agility of a real live snake, the delicate scarf suddenly caught the wind, then stretched sensuously in midair, whipping around and writhing, looking for all the world like a floating cobra about to strike.

Under usual circumstances, the fancifulness of the image would have made Marta smile.

But these weren't usual circumstances.

"Oh, no!" she groaned, staring into the rearview mirror as the scarf fishtailed away. Sighing, she downshifted and hiked her wedding gown above her knees—and then she realized her fingernails were still bloodred. She hadn't changed the polish.

Well, if she could say "I do" barefoot, Marta guessed she could toss away a bouquet with ten red talons.

If I'm getting married.

Her gaze bore down on the nearing tall white metal pole and fork in the road, and she told herself that this strange impulse to keep driving probably wasn't everyday jitters. No. Marta Straussberg didn't have common, pedestrian emotions such as that. She was an artist. A unique soul. She lived hard and fast, on the cutting edge of the SoHo art world. These days, with her vibrant paintings selling in galleries in New York, Boston and L.A., she'd become just shy of famous....

But did she love Winston "Doc" Holiday enough to marry him today? And didn't Doc deserve a woman who could love him more than anything? More than her art?

She thought of Doc's big athletic body, how his worn blue jeans were all too tight and frayed at the seams. She could almost see him kick off his boots, take the stethoscope from where it was perpetually looped around his neck, then grasp his hat by the brim and send it sailing across a room, exposing a head of golden curls. She could hear his deep laugh and the teasing remarks he always uttered in that thick Texas drawl. For all his annoying machismo, Doc accepted people just as they were and never tried to change them....

He definitely deserved a woman who could give her whole self.

And that woman isn't me.

"You've got to try, Marta. He loves you."

She was almost right on top of the fork in the road. Her heart was pounding, racing with the impending need to make her decision.

You can't back out now.

She stared straight ahead at the tall white metal pole. The arrows on the fork at the top might as well have read: Loves Me/Loves Me Not.

Or: Marriage/Freedom.

Or: Does She?/Doesn't She?

Marta had exactly one second to decide....

Chapter One

Almost nine months ago

"Take heart!" a woman shouted. "Yeah, you. Cowboy in the worn-out jeans and white jacket. Why don't you stop and smell the flowers?"

Without breaking stride or looking up at the apartment building from which the voice boomed, Winston "Doc" Holiday resituated his bone white Stetson so it wouldn't blow off his head in the breeze, then he switched his black physician's bag to another hand so he could better glare down at his clipboard, double-checking the address. "Where's this Francesca Luccetti live, anyhow?" he muttered to himself.

"Didn't you even hear me, cowboy?" came the woman's voice again. "Surely it wouldn't kill you to smile."

Doc stopped in his tracks, the well-worn heels of his hand-tooled boots digging into the sidewalk. Glancing down at his white lab coat, he scowled, suddenly realizing that the woman had the supreme audacity to be talking to him. Why couldn't strangers mind their own business and quit telling him to smile? Didn't they know it was rude and intrusive?

"There ain't many flowers in Manhattan, honey bunch," Doc drawled under his breath. *And you want to know why?* The voice in his head rambled on, his lazy Texas drawl tingeing the relentless mental harangue that had been continuous since his fiancée had died. *Because fate is sometimes merciful, baby doll. That's why. And anyhow—unlike yourself—most New Yorkers take great civic pride in being counted among the most hostile citizens on this planet.*

In fact, the only nice thing anyone's ever said about us is that people in Paris can be even worse. Which means the last thing most of us mean Manhattanites want to do is smile. We wouldn't stop and smell the flowers even if there happened to be any. If you want my humble opinion, flowers are only good for one thing. Making little kids miserable when their allergies kick in. And believe you me, I should know about such ailments, 'cause I'm a bona fide, certified, grade-A, prime pediatrician. One who's ailing from a broken heart himself....

The woman added, "Have a nice day, cowboy!" She delivered the line the way every happy person did, in an unnerving singsong tone.

Boy, she was a pistol. What *was* her problem? "With an attitude like yours," Doc muttered, "I can't believe you haven't gotten yourself shot in this neighborhood." Once again, Doc's mind kept right on spinning. *And please. If you really feel you must carry on so cheerfully, don't try to pawn that grating attitude off on the rest of the human race. That's my position, baby doll.*

"A grown man," Doc added in a righteous whisper, "is entitled to his own unhappiness."

For a second, he felt marginally better. After all,

there was nothing like an angry bad attitude to save a man from serious depression. Still, Doc was starting to wish he hadn't gotten quite *this* angry after Marta died. *I'd like a second's peace,* he thought. *Just once in a blue moon, I'd like a reprieve in which this angry mental ranting would stop. Would that be too much to ask?* Nowadays, one hundred and ten percent of the time, the lid of Doc's head was like the banging top of a pressure cooker that was just about to explode. He guessed that's what happened when love completely destroyed a man's life.

It didn't help that his sex drive had died right along with Marta. And that had been more than a year ago. Which meant Doc was starting to feel downright emasculated. In a year, he hadn't felt so much as a twinge of arousal. Another month down the road, and Doc would forget he *had* a male organ. It was hard to believe he'd ever counted himself among the last of the red-hot lovers.

Unable to help himself, he glanced up, toward the window from which that female voice had come, just in time to see a mass of piled jet black hair disappear inside.

He blew out a long-suffering sigh and kept walking. Even though he was still within spitting distance of city hall, he'd hit Mott Street, near Mulberry— where Little Italy bordered Chinatown. Italian flags blew from windows, and old men in black suits sipped espressos at sidewalk tables shaded by green umbrellas. Some tourists sucking on Italian ices ambled toward a red pagoda in Chinatown, heading for where straight streets gave way to curving alleyways and fish markets with aquariums full of live lobsters and eels.

Doc's eyes settled on the Woo Long Chinese Bakery at the corner. In spite of himself, he smiled, loving the jumble of Italian *cannoli,* fortune cookies and American-style wedding cakes. No matter how bad things got, Doc—a Texas transplant and urban cowboy—could still rely on the endless stimuli this wild, wonderful city offered. It was the only place he'd ever felt truly at home. Here, he could charge down hospital corridors, saying "ain't" and swearing like a sailor. He'd even delivered a baby once while wearing swim trunks, a Stetson and spurs.

Nobody had even looked twice.

Now he swallowed hard. Why was he torturing himself, staring at Woo Long's wedding cakes? His eyes trailed over the sign reading Woo Your Bride With Woo Long Cakes! Even now, he just wished he knew where Marta was headed on their wedding day—to the church or out of town.

"Wedding cakes," he suddenly growled, fighting painful emotions and jump-starting the usual righteous harangue that was calculated to hold them at bay.

This was all Francesca Luccetti's fault. If not for her, Doc wouldn't even have seen those fool cakes. But the woman wouldn't take no for an answer and she had her heart set on adopting a baby....

Oh, Doc had read her file. Twice, in fact, since he was so appalled. Each time he'd wondered what the woman was thinking. She had no money. No college degree. No skills. No husband. She didn't even have a boyfriend. And she was living in a miserable rundown excuse for an apartment, judging from the look of her block. Even more unpromising, Francesca Luccetti had just had a heart transplant a little over a year ago.

"And she really thinks a reputable agency like Big Apple Babies is going to allow her to adopt?" Doc shook his head. "Sorry, Ms. Luccetti," he murmured as he scanned the street for number 204. "As bad as I might feel about it, you don't have a snowflake's prayer in hell of becoming an adoptive mother."

On the upside, the Luccetti case *had* given Doc extra work. He'd rushed straight here in his lab coat after inoculating fifty toddlers. While he didn't look like a caseworker—they wore dark suits and ties, not stethoscopes around their necks—it didn't really matter. This visit wasn't nearly as official as Francesca Luccetti believed. It had already been decided: she could not be given a baby.

Doc felt a surge of pity. He hated crushing someone's life dream of having kids. After all, there'd been a time when he'd wanted kids more than anything in the world—a dream he'd given up since Marta hadn't wanted children.

Well, at least all this extra work helped keep his mind off his love life. Or lack thereof. Between pediatric shifts, Doc was helping run an adoption facility for teenagers. And when it came to these preadoption interviews, everybody at Big Apple Babies agreed Doc knew how to let the hard-luck cases down easy. It was why Francesca Luccetti had been assigned to him. His job was to go over her interview with her and then, without breaking her heart, tell her she'd never be a parent. Unfortunately, she'd already done a phone intake with Ethel Crumble, a soft touch, which meant Francesca still thought she had a fighting chance of getting a child.

"Francesca," Doc drawled, still scanning the street, "which of these dumps is yours?"

It turned out to be the dusty, yellow-brick walk-up right across from the Woo Long bakery. The same building that housed the woman who'd told him to smile. With Doc's luck, the black-haired woman in the window *was* Francesca Luccetti.

Doc shook his head. No. Even he wasn't *that* cursed.

He rang the buzzer of 204. When there was no answer, he checked the rustling papers on his clipboard again. Sure enough, a note read, "Doc—downstairs buzzer doesn't work. Call her from the Woo Long bakery and she'll let you in."

Doc glanced over. Sorry. But he wasn't getting anywhere near those wedding cakes. Fortunately, the lock on Francesca's lobby door was no more operational than her buzzer, and when Doc pushed, the door creaked inward. He shook his head in disgust. "No locks on the doors. No bars on the windows. And this woman thinks Big Apple Babies is going to hand her an infant?" Whose reality was Francesca Luccetti living in, anyhow?

"Apartment 2F," Doc said, reading off the clipboard.

As he neared the apartment, he heard music, then a woman's off-key humming. "Neil Diamond?" he drawled with a groan. "Aw, baby doll. Not Neil Diamond. Anything but Neil Diamond."

It was "Song Sung Blue."

He knocked on the door of 2F. And then he realized it was open, just a fraction.

Was she crazy? he fumed. She was living five blocks from the criminal courthouse where buses released convicts from Rikers Island prison every day.

Didn't she know some major creep could walk right up here from the street?

Doc's eyes cruised down the door. She had locks. Why wasn't she using them?

And why wouldn't she answer?

He guessed she couldn't hear him knock. Who could hear *anything* over that blaring music? In the one blessed heartbeat of sweet silence between "Song Sung Blue" and "Beautiful Noise," Doc tried pounding again.

Nothing.

Shoving the clipboard under his arm, he resituated his physician's bag and grabbed the doorknob. Then he tried simultaneously holding the door in place while he pounded on it, shouting over Neil Diamond, "Howdy? Anybody home?" When that didn't work, he got concerned and simply pushed open the door.

He wished he hadn't. He wished he'd called from the pay phone at the Woo Long bakery, the way he was supposed to. Or, since his primary job responsibility was really as head pediatrician at Big Apple Babies, that he'd never agreed to come here at all.

Because the woman—who wasn't exactly any man's idea of a fairy-tale princess—was prancing around the barren room, her eyes tightly closed, clutching an up-ended sponge mop to her chest and obviously pretending it was a man. She had alabaster skin, as pale as Snow White's before the Prince's kiss, but it looked as if it had been dusted with rose powder. And judging from the whimsical smile playing over her lips, Doc figured the lady was having herself a doozy of a fantasy.

Great, he thought. *A woman dancing with a mop.* He remembered this from English classes he'd taken in college. Yeah, this was the classic, age-old metaphor for romantic fantasy. And after just seeing those fool wedding cakes at the bakery, this was all Doc needed. Even worse, the woman had to be the one who'd told him to smile. Surely, no one else in Manhattan was living in this kind of happy-go-lucky fantasy world.

Dancing, Francesca Luccetti—at least he assumed it was her—definitely reminded him of Cinderella. Not that he meant to offer any glass slippers.

All Doc had was his cowboy boots, and his first impulse was to dig in his heels and run.

Trouble was, his hand-tooled Tony Llamas were glued to the spot, seemingly held there by a supernatural, unseen force, as if the threshold of her apartment really had opened onto a fantasyland. But his inability to move had nothing to do with the fact that Francesca was obviously fantasizing about Prince Charming.

No, Doc was held spellbound by something far more disturbing.

The second he'd entered the apartment, he'd felt a sudden, unmistakable drop in the room temperature. Cool tentacles had curled through his veins, and the golden-blond hairs at the nape of his neck had prickled. His muscles tensed, making his rigid thighs turn as smooth and hard as glass, and the thick veins in his arms popped up like ropes. And all because he could swear his deceased fiancée, Marta, was in this very room.

She wasn't, of course.

It was nothing more than a strange trick of imagination.

But Doc felt her presence—a certain, recognizable

vital hum of her energy that vibrated and radiated around Doc like a magnetic field; in its wake, he felt a strange, blessed wash of peaceful silence. At least until his heart started thudding against his ribs, and he drew in a breath so sharp it hurt his lungs.

Not that Francesca Luccetti heard.

She kept dancing, tilting her head backward as if for a kiss. Which was just as well, because Doc had gone into a brand of shock he'd never encountered in any medical book. His hand slid inside his lab coat, over a chambray shirt. He touched his washboard-flat stomach where the muscles had clenched, then his eyes darted around, trying to pinpoint what in the room had reminded him so strongly of Marta. The feeling was so intense; it just wasn't…natural.

It wasn't the music; Marta had played fifties rockabilly. And it wasn't a perfume. All Doc smelled was fresh paint and Pine Sol. Apparently, Francesca was just moving in. No pictures were hung, boxes were stacked against a wall, and what looked like second-hand furnishings were sparse. His gaze lingered on a sleeping alcove. It was the one area of the studio apartment she'd finished decorating. Right inside a square archway was a large bed with a frilly, dainty dust ruffle and white spread.

That wasn't what reminded him of Marta. The SoHo loft they had planned to share, and where he now lived, had been very contemporary, with art everywhere and not a thread of lace.

This woman's outfit didn't remind him of Marta, either.

Marta had favored expensive, flashy clothes, low-cut French blouses that showed off hints of vibrantly colored underwear. Francesca—Doc finally forced himself to ignore the mop and take a real good look at her—wore girlish, round-toed white flats and a practical knee-length navy skirt. Tucked into the skirt was a stiffly pressed pink blouse with short cuffed sleeves, and when she whirled breathlessly around again, Doc glimpsed a no-nonsense white bra through the cotton. No suggestive cut. No lace... With a start, Doc noticed the tiny gold cross hanging demurely at her throat, and he lifted his gaze.

She did have an interesting face, with a wide forehead and well-spaced eyes heavily feathered with jet eyelashes. Piled high on her head were thick black curls; worn down, he figured the hair would have hung, like Rapunzel's, all the way to her knees. A colorful elasticized band was wrapped around her head so that knots of color peeked through the strands of hair. Hair that, when Doc did a sudden doubletake, seemed to flow like jet ink. Hair that, beneath his fingertips, might feel as soft as soapy water on a baby's back.

Hair—the thought came right out of the blue—that Doc desperately wanted to release and pull down. His lips parted slightly in protest.

Oh, for the past few months, he'd *wanted* to feel attraction toward women again. But not right now. Not like this. He hazarded a glance at her blouse again, and felt a rush of relief. It was a turnoff. Feeling more in control, Doc flicked his eyes down the prim collar and the small pink buttons....

Buttons—the thought shocked him like ice water— that he could so easily flick open.

He was appalled. What was happening to him? Oh, maybe her body was of the sort a man might call delicate. Not Doc, but another man...

Doc quickly stared down at his clipboard. Sure enough, Francesca Luccetti's personal essay said her greatest ambition in life, next to adopting a baby, was to work at a pet store, since she loved animals so much. Also, she intended to volunteer for the ASPCA and to help the homeless. If she could be reincarnated—which she couldn't, she'd written, because she was Catholic—she would want to be Mother Teresa.

Very definitely not my type.

No, Doc and this woman hadn't a thing in common. And Doc wasn't the kind of man to pursue a woman with whom he had nothing in common.

The strange response of his body had merely been shock, he decided. Secretly, he'd probably been expecting to find a weaker-looking woman, given her medical history. A heart transplant was a life-altering, traumatic operation; Doc had observed the procedure in medical school. He guessed he'd expected to find Francesca Luccetti in bed, not working up a sweat, dancing so breathlessly.

Her fingers tightened on the mop handle, and she now brought the yellow sponge to her lips as if it were a microphone. When she started lip-syncing, he tried to ignore how much real emotion she put into mouthing the words to the love song. Then he watched how her backside swayed while she danced. She was definitely too thin. Not that her lack of curves stopped the room from feeling too warm to Doc, no matter how much he tried to assure himself that she was *not* making his body snap to life, whipping his nerve endings into a frenzy like a lively lasso.

But she was.

There was only one solution—to cut his losses and

run. To heck with his job. To heck with the interview he'd been sent here to perform.

Fortunately, the strange, ethereal feeling of Marta's presence had ebbed and Doc's boot heels had come unglued. Holding his breath, hoping she wouldn't hear him, Doc edged silently backward, moving toe-to-heel toward the hallway.

He almost made it.

But her eyes flew open.

And she emitted a sharp, startled cry. His first thought was for her heart—was she all right? But Doc guessed she was fine because she whirled fully around and gaped at him.

Her eyes—now wide open—were stunningly clear. His breath caught, and for a second, he could merely stare back at her. They were too dark and bright, he thought, taking in those glossy wide-set eyes. Too deep and luminous. Naked. Not the kind of eyes that could ever mask emotions. Though he rarely took off his hat, he instinctively grasped his Stetson by the brim and removed it in deference to her.

Gripping the mop handle, she took an unsteady step backward. Her chest was heaving—either from fear at seeing a stranger in her apartment, or the exertion of dancing. "Who are you?" she exploded. "What do you want? What are you doing in my apartment?"

"I'm Winston Holiday," he shouted over the music. "From Big Apple Babies." For some reason, he found himself adding, "But people call me Doc. I'm primarily a pediatrician for the agency, but I'm filling in as a caseworker today."

"Big Apple Babies?" She gawked at him as if she'd never heard of the place, even though according to the receptionist, she called at least ten times a day to check on the status of her adoption application.

Mustering his most professional demeanor, Doc managed to look squarely into those shining black eyes—as if he wasn't about to hurt her, as if he hadn't caught her in a compromising position, and as if her previously dreamy expression hadn't reminded him of what he most wanted in the world to forget—namely, love. *Cowboy, you've got to get out of here.* "I've come for our interview, Ms. Luccetti." Doc juggled his hat and physician's bag and waved the clipboard. "Remember?"

She was still staring at him, her skin pale. She pressed a nervous, slender-fingered hand to her massive pile of hair, as if to smooth it. "Your name is Doc Holiday? You *are* kidding me, right?"

He offered his usual response—a quick flash of his most engaging good-ole-boy smile. "Well, with a name like Holiday, I figured I had no choice but to become a doctor, ma'am."

Her fist tightened around the mop handle, making her knuckles turn pink, then white. "Oh."

As a doctor, he'd seen every last inch people had to show—and then some. But right about now, he actually felt heat in his cheeks and realized, for the first time in years, he was actually embarrassed. The emotion—like every other one under the sun—wasn't something Doc particularly wanted to feel. Since Marta's death, he'd felt only two things—angry and numb. The anger he came by naturally. Numb was something he worked at.

And now, after only meeting this woman, he was feeling embarrassment and desire, too. Damn. Why did he have to catch her dancing? He jerked his head toward the door. "Look. The door was open. I tried knocking, then I felt concerned. I thought..."

Apparently she was no stranger to anger herself. She was looking more peeved by the second—as if she could only admit by degrees how mortified she felt. If there'd been any doubt before, Doc knew she was definitely Italian now. He hated to stereotype, but her dark eyes possessed the kind of explosive, jealous and thoroughly Italian temperament that could get a man killed. "Uh, Ms. Luccetti, I really was afraid someone had broken in...."

She was obviously torn between berating him for entering her apartment unannounced and wanting to impress him, since this was her adoption interview. Looking stuck between the two responses, she seemed unable to say anything at all.

"Here." He waved the clipboard again. Under the clip were papers printed with the Big Apple Babies logo. "My badge." As if he had to prove he was one of the good guys.

Her sudden curt nod made him feel strangely defensive. He started to say none of this was his fault. *He* hadn't left the door open. *He* wasn't dancing by himself. And *he* very definitely lacked the extremely active fantasy life she apparently enjoyed....

His flash of temper didn't last. Hell, he wasn't exactly relishing the idea of getting down to the business of denying this woman the child she so desperately wanted. He sighed. Why did she have to possess such expressive eyes? Such a crushably slender body?

When she finally spoke, her tone was brisk, businesslike. "All right. Well, I guess...just wait here."

In the kitchen, she lowered the music with an angry flick of a delicate wrist, then she shoved the sponge mop next to the refrigerator. Past her, Doc noticed a small bathroom. And a wall calendar near the fridge with so few activities penned in the empty blocks that Doc guessed her social life was about as lively as his this month.

When she returned, her long slender arms were rigidly at her sides and she was clenching her fists. Her lower lip quivered with so much restrained emotion that he suddenly wished there was something he could say to help.

She tried—and failed—to sound conversational. "Uh…may I ask exactly how long you've been here?"

"Just a second," Doc lied. "I swear. I just came in."

The way she was looking at him—like he was the world's worst Peeping Tom—made him feel oddly exasperated. "You know, we did have an appointment, Ms. Luccetti. And your door *was* open."

"But you were late! I'd given up! Why didn't you call from the bakery, the way you were supposed to?"

Doc wasn't about to explain that he simply couldn't deal with the wedding cakes in the bakery window. It wasn't the kind of thing a cowboy—no matter how urban—admitted to a strange woman. He shrugged. "The door was open."

Her accusing gaze slid suspiciously over the whole length of him, and for reasons Doc wasn't about to contemplate, it suddenly rankled that her gorgeous eyes didn't spark with the faintest hint of female appreciation. Smoothing his ruffled rooster feathers, he reminded himself that a lot of women thought he was good looking. His problem wasn't attracting them; it was battling his own indifference.

She said, "You're not dressed like a caseworker."

He ignored the challenge in her voice, keeping his own calm and professional. "As I explained, I'm also a pediatrician for the agency." That he was a doctor usually impressed women, too.

Francesca Luccetti merely said, "I want a *real* caseworker."

"I am a real caseworker, sug—" He cut himself off before he called her sugar plum. She might think he meant it as a come-on. He never did nowadays. And he definitely didn't right now, not with her. "Look. I know how important this interview is to you, that you want a good caseworker. But don't worry. I'm qualified." *In fact, I'm the best heart-breaker in the business.*

An uncomfortable silence fell.

He found himself remembering how dreamy she'd looked minutes ago, with her head tilted back for a kiss, exposing her slender, creamy throat. In her mind, a romantic man had been embracing her. Maybe they'd been seconds away from making love. Yeah, Francesca Luccetti had been far gone—off to wherever she went in her most private fantasies. Now Doc quickly reminded himself he wasn't the least bit curious about where that was.

She finally said, "Can I get you a Snapple?"

His mouth *was* strangely dry. "Fine, Ms. Luccetti."

She headed for the kitchen again. A moment later, she returned, placing drinks on a card table that had been shoved next to a window. For the first time, he noticed there *were* flowers—fragrant purple flowers in her window boxes, which he could see through white lace curtains as she nodded at two straight-back chairs.

For reasons Doc didn't want to examine too closely, he chose to sit with his back toward the bed. He put his hat on the table and took a sip of his drink. "Thanks," he said. But his voice didn't sound at all like his own. The drawl came out gruff and deep and husky.

Even worse, when she seated herself opposite him, his eyes settled on where her long, slender index finger nervously tapped the closed top button of her blouse. He watched, trying to think if he'd met anyone, besides her, who actually buttoned her top button. *Keep your mind off the buttons, cowboy. Just do your job, then saddle up and bolt for the sunset.* Tonight, he'd feel lousy, of course. Hell, maybe while she was here, crying herself to sleep, he'd sit at home alone in the dark with a good stiff drink. Or more likely, he'd just work late....

He pulled some papers from the clipboard and made a show of arranging them on the card table. They'd both simply have to try to pretend that she hadn't been in the thick of a sensuous fantasy when he arrived. If the truth be told, maybe he *was* wondering what had been going on in her mind.

"Uh...I'm a little nervous," she ventured.

Even her voice touched something inside him he wanted to forget was there. It had an airy, chiming quality, and even though her file said she'd been born here and that English was her first language, her words carried the faintest trace of a rolling Italian cadence. Probably both her parents spoke Italian. Italy was a wonderful country. Doc took vacations there.

"No need to be nervous," he lied.

"But…"

She blushed. "Will, uh, this make a big difference?" She tossed her head toward the kitchen.

Doc couldn't help his lips from curving into a rusty smile. Lord, was the woman even restoring his sense of humor? "No," he assured in a grave drawl, "dancing and lip-syncing will have no bearing on your case. I promise."

"Please don't make fun of me."

The words were so simple, the emotion so direct and nakedly honest, that it was suddenly a strain to breathe. Doc shook his head. "I'm not. Truly."

She swallowed hard. "Oh. It seemed like…"

"I was trying to make you laugh."

She made a sweet attempt to chuckle for his benefit.

He mustered a friendly smile. "This'll only take a few minutes."

The hint of good humor he'd won from her abruptly vanished. Her face fell. "But I'm sure you have a lot to ask me?"

Probably. If only to draw out this interview so I don't have to tell you you're not getting your baby. "Just a few questions."

She quit toying with her top blouse button and began anxiously sliding her cross up and down on its gold chain. "Uh…I'm sorry I yelled at you from the window, too…. Did you hear me yell? From the window?"

Doc nodded.

"If I'd known it was you," she continued apologetically, "I never would have yelled."

"It's really all right, Ms. Luccetti."

"Frankie," she corrected him. "People used to call me Francesca, but I changed it to Frankie."

"Frankie," he repeated. "Like I said before, you can call me Doc."

"Doc."

He nodded again. This was a far tougher case than he'd been led to believe. Oh, Ethel Crumble had warned him that Frankie was sweet. That, in spite of her being twenty-seven, she'd been unusually sheltered because of a childhood illness that had lasted into her twenties. And now he was going to have to be the bad guy. The beast. He was starting to feel edgy and depressed. Dammit, he hadn't felt anything resembling this since Marta...

Marta.

Doc tilted his head. With surprise, he realized there was only silence now. It was as if, when he'd walked inside this room and laid eyes on Francesca Luccetti, a switch had been turned off inside his head. As if the faucet from which came the flood of ranting, raving anger that had plagued him since Marta's death had suddenly, blessedly, been wrenched off. Hell, the next thing Doc knew, he'd probably be smelling the flowers, the way Frankie had told him to....

In fact, he *could* smell them. He realized, with his every breath, he was drawing in the fragrance of the purple flowers in the window box. Frankie's elbows were on the table now; her raised hands were splayed, the fingertips pressed together. He'd watched her glossy, expressive eyes pass from embarrassment to anger. Now they were sizing him up, taking on a faintly manipulative glint that hardly gave him any comfort.

"Since we've already started off on a...somewhat

embarrassing note—'' She paused, nervously casting her eyes downward. "We may as well get this out of the way, too. I'm sure you're aware of the personal details I've divulged to Ms. Ethel Crumble. It's probably right there in my file.''

Doc had no idea what she was talking about. "Your file?''

"Yes—'' Frankie's color heightened, but her voice remained matter-of-fact. "That I want to adopt, in part, because I'm still a virgin.''

The breath left him. Hell, no, Ethel Crumble hadn't put that in the Luccetti file. And what could Frankie's lack of sexual experience possibly have to do with her adopting? Doc failed to see the connection. It took everything he had, but he mustered his most impersonal caseworker smile. Somehow, he even nodded as if this were of extreme significance and murmured, "Very important, very illuminating.'' *Just let her feel she's being helpful, cowboy. It will be of great comfort to her later.*

Unfortunately, something in his manner must have made her feel defensive because she tugged at the blouse button and primly added, "I *have* been to first and second base, of course.''

His heart was hammering, his throat was dry. He couldn't take much more of this. "Of course.''

Lord, she was such a sweetheart, so naive. Not many twenty-seven-year-olds were still sheltered enough to make announcements such as hers. No doubt, the heart troubles she'd suffered had required lots of bed rest at home. Doc could easily imagine the scenario: lots of home tutoring, not many school friends, no dates. Suddenly, remembering her dancing alone made his heart ache. Had any guy ever really held her tight? Held her as if he'd never let her go? She was probably so lonely....

And looking positively stricken. "First base," she said in a strangled voice. "You know, when—"

"Baby doll—" Doc barely registered he'd let the endearment slip. "You don't need to explain a thing to me. I know all about the bases." Hell, he'd hit more than his share of homers.

But never with a virgin.

And you're sure not starting now, cowboy.

Unfortunately, announcements such as Frankie's had a tendency to do very strange things to a man. So, Doc was still busy denying his attraction to this sheltered virgin, whom he swore he wouldn't dare touch, when out of the seeming silence, Neil Diamond had the audacity to start crooning, "Girl, you'll be a woman soon."

Chapter Two

Under the card table, Frankie surreptitiously swiped her perspiring palms down her skirt. Had she really yelled at this man from the window? And had he really caught her dancing like a lovesick teenager? She wasn't really lovelorn, of course. She'd merely been trying to loosen up her tangled nerves before the interview. What a mess. As if this wasn't difficult enough, without having to convince the caseworker she wasn't certifiably crazy. Which she wasn't. She ate right, slept right, worked in Mama's, the Italian restaurant owned by her parents, and went to mass every Sunday with her mother.

Granted, she had a rampant imagination.

But otherwise, no one could lead a more ordinary life.

Which was why she'd be such a wonderful mother. *You've got to think positively, Frankie. Don't worry, the agency will see it your way, no matter how bad an impression you've made today. There's absolutely no danger of this adoption not going through.*

If only she could quit staring at the caseworker.

Which she couldn't.

In her whole life, she'd never yelled at a man in

the street, but when she'd seen his dangerous swagger, and how those long, muscular legs swallowed up the pavement, she'd known he was one serious cowboy. She simply couldn't resist the urge to flirt. He wasn't supposed to wind up inside her apartment, though. Or be her caseworker.

But he was.

And up close, he was a mind-stopping hunk. He could have ridden a horse right off the cover of one of the Western romance novels she loved to read. He was huge and sexy, with such a strapping broad-shouldered body that everything around him looked too small: his white lab coat bunched endearingly across his back. The fraying white seams of faded jeans he could undoubtedly afford to replace strained against his bulging thighs. And three undone pearl snaps at the throat of his soft blue chambray shirt sprung open to reveal mouth-watering, sun-touched tufts of reddish-gold chest hair. Frankie had never seen a man who looked closer to bursting right out of his clothes.

And she could not have felt more delighted.

Or nervous. She stared, trying to concentrate on whatever he was saying, and trying not to notice how his presence made her apartment seem half its size. She tried to ignore how his voice hinted at everything a Southern voice was supposed to—hot, steamy nights, wooded thickets and erotic scents, secret rooms where decent women sneaked off for clandestine trysts with indecent men after sundown.

Fighting back a wistful sigh, Frankie studied his mouth, feeling so enamored she barely heard his words, but just watched his lips move. At first, she'd thought the indentations beside his grimly set lips were from frowning, but when they'd twisted with wry amusement, the lines turned out to be dimples. Between the Stetson hat, and the hint of red-gold stubble on the squarish planes and angles of his jaw, he looked as if he could have spent this morning saddled up on a dusty trail. Yes, he definitely looked dangerous enough to do a little gunslinging. Especially when he angrily thrust his fingers through his hair, to keep it off his broad forehead.

Since he was sitting in a sunbeam, he was squinting—and with the most amazingly clear pale silver-blue eyes Frankie had ever encountered outside her personal imagination. Light seemed to shine from behind powder blue irises that, in turn, were overlaid with a gloss of liquid silver. His eyes reminded Frankie of delicate rice papers she'd seen down in Chinatown that were rich with color and yet nearly transparent.

And he was smart. A doctor—which was what Frankie's mother had always dreamed she would marry.

Still, since this was Frankie's all-important interview, she did wish Big Apple Babies had sent Ethel Crumble. Or…

Anybody but *him.*

A lump lodged in her throat. Gulping it down with a sip of her Snapple, she licked her lips anxiously, wishing they didn't still feel so unaccountably dry. She knew her sexual history wasn't in any agency file, but she'd hoped saying she was a virgin would give her some breathing room. She figured the information might throw him off guard and even up the playing field.

Dr. Winston Holiday, of course, hadn't even reacted. No, his face had remained a grim, impersonal mask of professionalism. Frankie had no idea what he thought.

Which was just as well. After all, she'd been ill most of her life, and during her convalescence, she'd read quite a lot of novels from which she'd gleaned plenty of useful information about men. Obviously, Doc was the angry, brooding type. In fact, the whole man could be summed up in two words: *bad news.* It was a standard equation: Killer Good Looks+ Brooding Anger=Brokenhearted Heroine. Frankie made a sudden mental vow: *If this man should happen to make any inappropriate advances toward me, whatsoever, I'll do everything in my power to defend myself.*

He sighed. ''Uh…Ms. Luccetti?''

She tamped down a blush. With him in the room, she really couldn't concentrate. And she had to. This interview was so terribly important. She pressed her feet together under the table, so she wouldn't accidentally tap them to the music. She'd wanted to turn off the darn CD, to create a more professional atmosphere, but the mere thought of hearing only this man's breath and hers in a small, silent room had made her pulse race too uncomfortably. ''Hmm?''

His lips pursed, as if he'd asked her this a thousand times. ''Full name?''

He didn't have to look so exasperated. After the way she'd yelled at him, and how he'd caught her dancing, she already felt exposed enough. In fact, she felt very defensive. Since Ethel Crumble had said Frankie was practically preapproved by the agency, and she was in no danger of the adoption not going through, maybe she should at least let this man know his good looks hadn't bowled her over, the way they probably did most women.

He sighed again. "Please...Ms. Luccetti?"

She tried to flash him a smile, but she knew it was too quick, too tight. "Would that include my confirmation name?" she ventured politely, as if this, not stargazing, had kept her from promptly answering him.

He squinted back at her with those eyes. Piercing, direct, searing eyes. The kind she'd read about that looked deep inside a woman, revealing a place of longing she'd never even suspected was there until she felt a hard, hot pit in her womb. Frankie ignored how his gaze warmed her personal pit, reminding herself of how many hearts this guy had probably broken. In her mind's eye, she imagined a woman who looked suspiciously like herself, flinging herself across a bed and crying after she'd been loved and left....

"Ms. Luccetti, could we please concentrate on the matter at hand? I'm waiting for your name. Full name," he clarified.

It wasn't her fault that his good looks kept sidetracking her. "Francesca Maria Angelina Sophia Carmella—" She paused. And then, as if he wouldn't guess, she couldn't help but tap his legal pad with a pink-painted fingernail and add, "That would be Luccetti."

His lips twisted into something resembling a smile. Even this paltry attempt transformed his grim visage, deepening his dimples. His silver-blue eyes twinkled faintly now, as if two stars had forgotten to depart at dawn and were left hanging in a morning sky. Even though he was probably a conceited male whom Frankie wasn't the least bit interested in getting to know on a personal level, her lips parted, to tell him he really should smile more. But then, maybe doing so a second time wasn't in her best interest.

He cleared his throat again. "Ms. Luccetti?"

"Sorry," she murmured.

"Address?"

He'd caught her staring again—and she couldn't stop a sudden rush of annoyance at her own behavior. All her future happiness depended on this interview. "You know, you did manage to find my apartment," she began. "So you already know the address and—" She cut herself off. If she wasn't careful, she was going to truly try his patience. Even if he obviously knew her address, he was the caseworker. And the caseworker was always right. She concluded by smiling sweetly and giving her full address, including extended zip code.

"Height."

He's probably over six feet. As her eyes drifted from his face to his broad shoulders, she absently patted her hair, smoothing it. "I'm five-two."

"Weight?"

A woman had to draw the line somewhere. "Is this necessary?"

"Ms. Luccetti, you're the one applying for a baby."

At that, she really had to bite her tongue. She wanted to say that she'd already listed her weight on a previous health questionnaire, and that the orphaned baby she was about to adopt couldn't care less about anybody's waistline. Besides, she'd been filling out a lot of forms lately—for employment, Realtors, and now for this baby—and she was sick and tired of being an applicant. Everybody kept sizing Frankie up, as if expecting her to come up short. Or too thin. Which—as much as she was loathe to admit it—she all too often did.

"Weight?" She couldn't resist shooting him an impish smile. "Would that be before or after my uncle Sal's birthday party?"

He merely squinted those to-die-for eyes.

Great. The brooder really didn't even have a sense of humor. "We had a lot of pasta," she explained, starting to feel marginally more comfortable with his good looks. "And pastries."

His lips curled slightly in what, for him, probably counted as a full-fledged grin. Maybe the interview was getting back on track. "All right," he drawled. "Why don't we just skip that weight question?"

"You know, I did already respond to these questions on the form."

His voice was strangely gruff. "Sorry, I'm just doing my job. Hobbies?"

"None." At least not if he meant sports. "But I have interests," Frankie quickly added. "I love to baby-sit. Nurse sick animals. And I'm a film buff."

A bushy golden red eyebrow arched with genuine interest. "Films?"

Something in his expression made her realize he was thinking of artsy foreign films. She'd been referring to old-fashioned movies, preferably romantic comedies with Tony Curtis and Rock Hudson. "And reading," she added weakly. "I do so love to read."

He nodded, jotted something down.

She swallowed, trying to peek at his legal pad and hoping he hadn't misunderstood. She was hardly an intellectual. Everybody knew Mickey—he was the oldest—had gotten all the brains in the Luccetti family. Other than parenting books, which Frankie was reading now to prepare for the baby, she read mostly romances. "I...had a quiet youth," she said. "Because I had heart trouble, reading was an acceptable activity."

"Of course," he murmured.

"But now everything's different," she added, moving into her prepared spiel. She kept it light and upbeat, not dwelling on the premature contractions of her heart, which had plagued her, or on the surgery, but talking about how grateful she was to have this new heart, her health and a whole new world to explore. She told him about a diary she'd kept since childhood, full of things she wanted to do if she ever regained her health. And about how she spent hours watching scary movies now, just to feel her breath catch and her new heart race. And, of course, how she was now going to adopt this wonderful baby, who'd already made her new heart swell with love.

The only thing she didn't bother mentioning was how she hoped her newfound health might allow her to lose her virginity, preferably with a man who looked like him. It was such a shame he was probably so brooding and conceited. Because he *was* terribly handsome....

"Ms. Luccetti?"

"Hmm?"

He grunted softly, in obvious exasperation. "I said, 'Professional organizations?'"

He'd caught her daydreaming again. Even worse, he didn't seem to like her answers. But she'd been so sick as a kid, so limited in her activities. Her prognosis to reach adulthood hadn't even been that great.

Why couldn't he give her a break? How could she be expected to have professional affiliations if she didn't even have a profession? *C'mon, Frankie. Don't get discouraged.* "No. No professional organizations."

"Volunteer work?"

She sighed in relief. That she did have. "I met Mr. Brazzi in 3C," she began. "He just had hip surgery, so I've been taking in his mail. And Mrs. Delio down on the first floor is blind, so I read to her every afternoon." Frankie left out that the book they were reading was titled *Hottest Renegade on the Range,* and she raced on, adding, "Sylvie in 2C is a single mom, so I said I'd baby-sit. And…" Suddenly realizing he didn't look particularly impressed, she let her voice trail off.

"No formal fund-raising?"

Didn't any of her good deeds count? "No."

"Hospital volunteer, maybe?"

"No." Darn it, she'd seen enough hospitals to last her a lifetime. "Please," she managed to say, wondering why he was giving her a hard time, "do we need to keep going over the same information? I talked to Ethel Crumble at length. She said I'd clearly given this serious thought, which I have. And she all but assured me that my application had been… well—" Even though looking at him unsettled her, she mustered another winning smile. "Basically preapproved."

"Preapproved," he echoed.

Good. At least they were back on the same wavelength. Feeling relieved and encouraged, Frankie continued, "Ethel seemed to think I'm the perfect candidate to get a baby."

Now what had she said wrong? To her, every word

seemed perfectly reasonable, but even though his eyes were kind, he was watching her with reservation.

"You feel you're a perfect candidate?"

She nodded solemnly. "Well, you have to admit I've got a lot on the ball."

"Please don't take this wrong—" his sugary drawl vibrated around that hard, hot pit inside her again "—but, uh, what would those things be?"

"Things?" Frankie echoed stupidly. Had she heard correctly? Was it possible this man actually doubted her ability to mother a child? Was there some problem with her application? Her heart sank. *Don't be upset, Frankie. He's just doing his job. An adoption agency has to be thorough; it's for the protection of the kids. You want the kids to be safe, don't you?*

She felt those beautiful, pale blue eyes slide away from hers. Even worse, he moved the clipboard to the side, as if their interview was over. Although Frankie couldn't believe it, she had a horrible feeling about what was coming.

"Ms. Luccetti—"

Her voice was a croak. "Frankie."

"Frankie—" His gentle drawl lowered a notch. "From our point of view, you must understand that you *aren't* the best candidate for motherhood."

Her lips parted in astonishment. "I'm not?"

He looked as if he would like to be anywhere in the world but here. Tilting his head, he surveyed her for so long that she felt heat creeping into her cheeks. It wasn't fair. She simply wasn't used to having such a seethingly dangerous, good-looking guy watch her this carefully. She became aware of her pulse—strong and steady—at her wrists, her throat. Darn it, after years of possessing a weak, unsteady heart, she'd never get used to the strong, reliable beating of this one.

When she'd first seen this man, the sudden pounding in her chest had actually frightened her. She'd thought no heart on earth could sustain beating that hard without giving out. It had felt…almost unnatural. For the first time since the transplant, she'd actually experienced the sensation of blood whirring in her veins so fast that her ears rang. It was hard to believe, but she guessed this was how a healthy heart responded to a potent, virile male.…

He was fingering the brim of his hat, studying it with his eyes, then he ran those thick fingers through his dark golden hair again, making sparks of burnished red dance on the strands. *Okay. Maybe I would sleep with him,* Frankie suddenly admitted, feeling her insides shake like jelly.

Yes, if she tried really hard, she was almost sure she could overlook his tendency to brood. Except, of course, he was so far out of her league that the playing fields weren't even on the same planet. Even the man she'd imagined while dancing with the mop wasn't this handsome. *Face it, Frankie. Any professed disdain you felt for this guy was merely a defense mechanism. He wouldn't ask you out in a million years.*

Still, it didn't hurt to hope.

And anyway, she was right about one thing. She'd make a great mom. She clasped her hands together, gathering her forces, willing herself to see this man as her caseworker, nothing more. "You said you're a pediatrician. Surely, you must love kids."

He nodded. "I do."

She'd already scanned his fingers for rings, but it

now occurred to her that he could be divorced. Or widowed. "Do you have any?"

"No."

Maybe not, but Frankie could hear the want in his voice. "If you love kids," she pressed, "then you must understand why I want this so much."

"I do, but—"

She hated the plea in her voice. "I want this baby."

His glance, which was like a warm blue summer sky reflected in a silver moon, said he wished things were different. "You only have a part-time job," he reminded her gently, "working for your family."

As if no one else would hire her. It cost her, but Frankie forced herself to say, "I put in applications at three pet stores."

His sexy eyes fixed on a point somewhere over her shoulder, as if he were collecting, sorting and arranging his thoughts—all to better crush her dreams. "Even so, those jobs wouldn't generate enough income to raise a child."

Frankie tried not to panic. "I inherited money from my grandfather, Papa Giovanni." She added, "Grandpa Alberto's still living. Anyway, it enabled me to get this apartment." She didn't mention that the very small inheritance was now all gone.

He glanced around. "It's a very nice apartment."

It wasn't really. It was okay. A junior one bedroom with good plumbing and walls with no cracks. She told herself to try not to resent this man. No doubt, he'd been born healthy and lucky. He probably owned a chichi SoHo loft. He looked like the type.

But she couldn't risk offending him now. "Thank you," she managed to reply. Determined to forge on, she swiftly reached beside her and pulled her prepared folder onto the card table. She showed him some pictures from magazines. "I still haven't decided which material to use in order to partition off the nursery area—glass block or beads. But my little brother, Vinny, has already agreed to do the carpentry."

Not that Vinny knew she was planning a nursery. Oh, she'd mentioned her plans to adopt. But everybody—her four brothers, her parents, her uncles—all exploded in angry Italian while her aunts merely made the sign of the cross over their chests. The changes in Frankie were hard on them. They were used to her being bedridden in a quiet, darkened room, sick and dependent on them. *But the operation was successful. I'm on my own now. Free and independent. Not a clinging vine.*

Across from her, Doc smiled. "These pictures of the nursery *are* nice, but—"

"See, there's plenty of room for both myself and a baby."

He glanced around as if seriously considering.

"I have a large Italian family," she said, rushing on. "So, as you can well imagine, they're all terribly anxious to help." When he didn't respond, she added, "*When* I get the baby."

"So, your family is supportive?"

"Of course," she lied. Actually, her relatives were worried sick, but once they laid eyes on the baby, Frankie knew they'd be thrilled. When he leaned forward, she inadvertently leaned back, as if they were on a seesaw. Her breath caught.

He said, "But you've never even lived on your own before."

"True." Somehow, she managed to muster another

winning smile. "But I've already met a fabulous pediatrician! You!"

He swallowed hard and clasped his huge, broad hands on the card table. "Please, Ms. Luccetti—"

"Frankie," she corrected him.

"Frankie," he continued in that honeyed drawl that made the womanly core of her ache, "believe me, I don't want to upset you. But I'm afraid the prospects just aren't good...."

He meant she didn't have a prayer. Well, she was not going to make this easy. "Good. Then there *are* prospects."

"Well, not really. You see—" He paused, clearing his throat with a low rumble. "You'd need a job that would generate a substantial income. And you don't have a husband."

"No. But I will."

He looked strangely relieved. He shot her another of those grim lip presses that was supposed to be a smile. "Who's the lucky guy?"

There was no lucky guy. "I haven't decided yet."

"Well..." He sighed. "*Right now,* you don't have a husband."

She didn't even have a date. Or prospects.

He continued speaking softly, as if merely trying to help her see reason. "You know, it's difficult. Even when people are married, already homeowners, with stable, high-income jobs..."

He was making her sound so pathetic. She felt as if a whole hive of angry hornets were attacking her where it most hurt—her pride. That he wanted to let her down easy was making her temper flare, too. As hard as her life had been, Frankie had never once expended a second on self-pity. She certainly wasn't about to start now, not with this man.

"To the naked eye—" she bit the words out coolly "—it might look as if my life is going nowhere. But I've been to hell and back. I'm twenty-seven. I've had a heart transplant. And I don't waste my time indulging in fantasies of ambitious careers."

"There *is* the issue of your transplant."

Her eyes stung. That was the real issue, after all. And leave it to him to take the opening she'd offered. She rushed into her rehearsed speech. "I've had no problems. I know—" she raised her hand. "I'll always have to take care because of the organ rejection drugs and possible immunosuppression that could bring on disease. But my operation was an astounding success. *Absolutely astounding,*" she emphasized. That much was true.

The worst thing was the real emotion in his eyes. "I'm sorry," he murmured. "I realize it would be dangerous for you to become pregnant, and so adoption must seem like a viable option...."

Darn it. She'd get herself pregnant in an instant. Her transplant wasn't the problem, her virginity was. Not to mention her strict code of morals. Still, she was very well aware of the brave women who'd had babies after transplant surgery. And they did exist. She knew some of them personally.

Before she'd thought it through, she leaned forward, her eyes now flashing fire. "Someone like you could never understand. But I've lived with danger my entire life. And it's not dying that scares me. It's never having lived."

"I'm so sorry," he repeated.

She fought down a wail. She was grappling with

straws. And she suddenly felt livid. "Were you even really considering me?"

The guilt in those devastating eyes said he wasn't.

Suddenly, she hated him. Hated his handsomeness. Hated him for catching her dancing like a fool. Hated the ease with which he could crush her deepest dreams and desires. She even hated the perfect life she imagined he led—attending swanky parties with countless girlfriends who were all as gorgeous as he.

It was the pity in his eyes that made her snap.

"Look, you can father a baby any time you choose. Why, I bet you could have women lining up, begging you to get them pregnant—"

His light eyes widened, silently asking her to stop. "Please," he murmured.

She shook her head. "Oh, no. You've got my Irish up." Before he pointed out she was Italian, she raced on. "I saw you out there, scowling at everybody, not stopping to smell the flowers. And *you* could be a father? While I—the most positive woman on the planet—have to fight to even be considered for motherhood?" She leaned closer, her strident, argumentative voice rising. "How many women my age stay in contact with doctors? How many have daily exercise programs? How many go to mass on Sunday? Religiously," she added. "No pun intended."

He tilted his head, as if conceding the points.

"Meantime, you—who could be a father—were walking down the street like the Grim Reaper." Her voice rung with the injustice of it. "Well, I've lived with death, so I know how precious life is, how beautiful and fleeting. Unlike you, I don't take it for granted."

He was starting to look positively stunned.

Frankie knew she should never have gone this far. But she still couldn't stop. "For that reason alone, I'd make a better mom than most. And if anything *should* ever happen to me, my family will take good care of this baby. The best."

She took a deep breath. "I'd also add that my touch can calm the most colicky child. Everybody used to say that if there was ever a woman meant to have babies, it was me." Her jaw set. "Now, *that* ought to complete my application, Doctor. Make no mistake. I want the baby. And I'm going to get it."

Her words continued ringing in the following silence.

He lifted a broad index finger. "Baby doll," he drawled, looking at a complete loss, "could you please excuse me? Just for a minute?" He winced. "Sorry, I didn't mean to call you baby doll."

"I don't mind," she snapped, sounding huffier than she'd intended. At least, Frankie didn't think she minded. Before today, no man had ever called her that.

He nodded.

She watched him stand, his broad back straight. For a second, he rested one of his huge sexy hands on the table, as if she'd thoroughly unbalanced him. She hadn't the faintest idea what was going through his head.

She crossed her arms. "Take your time," she offered.

"Thank you," he returned.

And then he strode across the room, through her kitchen and into her bathroom. And he calmly shut the door.

DOC LEANED AGAINST the lip of the sink.

"Just go back out there and lay it on the line," he whispered.

But he couldn't. He felt as powerless as the new-born she wanted. And there was all that damnable romance in the room...the ruffly bed and dainty lace curtains, the heady fragrance of her skin mixing with scents from those purple flowers in the window box.

It had never even occurred to her that she might not get this baby. Hell, he admired her spunk and attitude, and he respected her for trying so hard. When she'd lit into him about being too negative, she'd looked like a woman warrior. The kind of riled-up fighter anyone would want in their corner.

Especially a kid.

It was easy enough to imagine her giving rousing speeches at PTA meetings. Or demanding one more dime for the cookies at school bake sales. She was the type who'd collect hundreds of signatures just so first-graders would get more fruit on a school lunch tray. She was incredibly special; he saw that now. Not girlfriend material for him, of course. The last thing he wanted in his life after Marta was a high-risk fe-male....

He gritted his teeth. "You have to say no."

He just wished she hadn't...unsettled him. He had no idea how she'd managed to do so, while wearing such unstylish clothes and berating him in that righteous voice. No doubt, it was her eyes. He'd never had such a distinct feeling that he was looking straight through someone, right into her soul.

The soul you've got to go out there and destroy, cowboy.

With a sigh, Doc opened the door—and ran right

into her. Instinctively, he grabbed her to steady her, then for reasons better left unexamined, he kept holding on. Oh, he told himself it was pity. That it had nothing to do with how she melted against him.

But the second he stared into those dark, luminous eyes, he was lost. He figured years of convalescence had kept her from socializing much, so she hadn't learned how to use those eyes to lie and hide her feelings. Right now, they held so much heartfelt yearning—for both the baby and him, Doc knew—that he felt positively ill.

Her voice was deep, almost husky with emotion. "You're not going to give me my baby, are you."

Doc shook his head. "No."

He could have released her then, should have. Instead, he leaned against the kitchen counter, pulling her with him. He told himself he simply had no choice, that the hand he nestled under her elbow was merely for her comfort. Since he was crushing her dreams, he was obligated to soften the blow. If you got right down to it, he thought, offering her some physical comfort was probably his duty. His responsibility. Hell, wasn't it really his *job?*

Doc frowned, suspecting his logic was faulty.

"Even if I wanted to," he murmured, "I couldn't give you a baby. Our agency has strict rules." He tilted his head downward, gazing more deeply into those naked, need-filled eyes, willing her to understand.

"But you wouldn't want to?"

His heart wrenched. "Baby doll..." He fought against the gravelly roughness of his own voice, fearing she'd hear it for what it was—gut-level male desire. "Personally, Frankie, I'd love to see you get this baby, but—"

"But you think I'm pathetic!"

His heart hammered. An hour ago, he *had* been thinking that. "No," he said in swift denial. "Not at all! I *never* thought that!"

"But I don't have a job outside my family's restaurant, or hobbies or anything."

Doc shook his head in protest. "Please understand. I'm bound by the agency's rules and regulations—"

"Does the agency tell you to call prospective parents 'baby doll'?"

She had him there. "No, ma'am. But—" The way she suddenly grabbed his shirtfront short-circuited Doc's thoughts. Heaven help him, but after a whole year, he really was responding to her—as a woman.

It was the wrong time. The wrong place. Definitely the wrong female. But the tightening of his groin was undeniable. He tried to edge backward, but he was already pressed against the counter. And she was still gripping him, pleading with those big, black, glossy eyes. Vaguely, he realized Neil Diamond was still crooning. Doc tried to tell himself the way they'd started swaying together didn't mean they were dancing, and that the movements had nothing to do with the wistful dreaminess in her expression when he'd caught her dancing alone.

He imagined her saying, "Oh, Doc. I fully understand now. Thank you for explaining everything so kindly and so clearly. I know I'm never getting this baby, and I swear, I'll never call the agency again."

Then, of course, whatever was left of Doc's heart would break for her. His voice would crack, but he'd repeat the words he'd been sent here to say. "I'm so sorry, but we cannot let you have a baby, Ms. Luccetti.''

And that would be the end of the matter.

A half hour later, Doc would be back in the infirmary. His angry mental harangue would return. His sex drive would vanish. And he'd be far away from this woman with the soulful eyes, who'd remained so positive even when life dealt her a seemingly losing hand.

But Doc didn't have that kind of luck.

''Please,'' she whispered.

Doc realized he'd leaned too close. He could feel her heart now, and he could swear it was familiar, as if he'd felt it beat against his chest before. He was so close, she had to feel the powerful strength of his awakening arousal.

''Please,'' she said again, the soft, humble yearning of her tremulous voice heating his whole body. ''Please give me a baby.''

And then, driven by something so undeniable he could no longer fight, Doc made the most unconscionable, unprofessional move of his life.

He swept his head downward and closed his lips over Frankie's.

Chapter Three

Killer Good Looks + Brooding Anger = Brokenhearted Heroine.

Frankie tried to remember the equation. But she'd simply prayed too long that something like this would happen to her. Besides, with this man's mouth scorching hers, only a fraction of her brain was working, so reciting even the simplest mathematics was impossible. Fortunately, she'd hugged enough hunks in her fantasies that this real-life embrace came easily enough and she was able to quickly wreathe her arms around his neck.

As she reveled in the firm, pressured nibbling that nuzzled apart her lips, her heart raced, making her dizzy. And when his tongue plunged, teasing her teeth with a practiced, all-knowing dexterity that made her knees weak and her throat constrict with emotion, she decided this was already far better than anything she'd ever read about.

He was towering over her, six full feet of hard male body curling around her and infusing her with heat that had her swooning. Every blessed thing he was doing made her sigh—how he splayed his well-muscled hands on her back. How his palms felt so damp and warm through her blouse that she thought she'd burn. And when his fingertips roved down her spine, urging her chest to his, her breasts ached so badly they hurt. Her nipples strained against her cotton stretch bra, and each slow thrust of Doc's kissing tongue only served to further irritate them. When his insistent knee nudged hers, silently suggesting she spread her thighs, she quickly complied, and the blood in the whole lower half of her body seemed to drain right out of her.

She'd never felt so oddly distracted and unexpectedly frustrated. He seemed to know it, too. He pushed himself off the counter with his hip, firmly sliding those big strong killer hands farther down her back, until he'd curved them right around her bottom. While he squeezed, his tongue turned as slow and lazy as the drawling voice that, in the next instant, courted her with murmured endearments.

It was more than a woman could take. Especially a woman with a highly active imagination. Disconcerting, too, because he was in such complete control. Already, Frankie knew she was mere putty in his grasping hands.

Somehow, it didn't seem fair. Doc didn't have to wrestle with a whole lifetime of lonely, frustrated passion. He had the edge of real-life experience. *She* hadn't even been kissed once since junior high school, when boys began to fully understand the implications of her illness and started going with other, healthier girls.

Besides, those boys she'd traipsed to first and second base with had been just that—*boys.*

Doc was a hot-blooded, fully aroused man. There was no mistaking it when he caressed her backside, urging her to press herself against his groin. Frankie arched instinctively, and through the thin cotton of her skirt, she could feel the long, hard metal track of his zipper, not to mention just how eagerly the insistent bulge behind it was pressuring the threadbare denim of his fly.

Her new healthy heart went wild then—pumping and pounding until Frankie's breath rattled, and her blood started racing far too many places at once; it flooded her head and rushed into her fingertips, making them tingle as if she were hanging upside down. Lower still, searing heat coiled around her womanly core, wrapping it like string around a finger, making her remember every blessed, blistering-hot fantasy she'd ever had about men who looked like Doc.

He groaned.

She'd read about this in her novels. And when a man groaned as deeply as that, from low down in his belly, he was far, far gone. In such a state, even the most cautious, rational, pragmatic man would very quickly lose the last vestiges of his remaining control. There was simply no help for it. He'd become like the worst kind of cavemen—his eyes taking on a feral glint, his movements becoming predatory.

That's when he'd growl something like, "Lady, you're really asking for it."

"For what?" Frankie might say coyly.

"The best and worst of me," he'd grate out. Then he'd fling her down without apology on the nearest bed, and he'd take her in a frenzy right then and there.

Frankie *was* a woman. Still, the longer Doc kissed her, the more she was personally beginning to understand that primal, predatory, supposedly *male* impulse.

Which was why she heaved a loud, annoyed sigh when Doc leaned away, his breath ragged against her mouth, his lips wet. His low-voiced drawl was nearly a growl, just as she'd expected, so Frankie waited with breathless impatience for him to say he was hellbent on having her.

But he said, "We've got to stop this right now!"

Frankie couldn't believe it! He'd set her whole body on fire! Was he crazy? "What?" she gasped, her chest rapidly rising and falling with her uneven breath.

"Please—" Doc's ragged voice lowered to a seductive, breathless drawl that skittered along her bare neck. "Baby doll, we really can't—"

Of course they could! What kind of caveman was he? What kind of caveman would say this? *Darn it,* Frankie suddenly fumed, the physical frustration he'd built inside her having driven her to complete madness. *If you're not going to give me my baby, Mr. Doc Holiday, then I think this is the very least you can do for me!* Vaguely, Frankie sensed her logic was faulty, that the near proximity of this man was making her lose all perspective. She wanted him. Desperately. "What?" she chided, flashing him a tight, coy smile. "Can't finish what you started?"

The bait had been dangled low. But Doc had enough male pride and ego to take it. "Oh, believe me," he assured her, his arms tightening roughly around her back. "I'm more than capable."

She merely rolled her eyes. She was panting, not sounding nearly as bored as she wished she did. "Prove it."

His raspy breath warmed her lips, and his firm arousal was undeniable, pressuring the juncture of her thighs. He shook his head as if he couldn't believe this was happening. "C'mon, Ms. Lu—Frankie," he growled, "I'm not going to pretend I don't want you right now, but—"

Her strangled voice sounded like someone else's. "Who's asking you to *pretend,* cowboy?" Without letting him answer, Frankie simply grabbed his lab coat, pulled herself on tiptoe and slammed her lips on his again.

The kiss sizzled. It burned.

And then it blew out like a fuse because the fool man had the nerve to drag away his wet, kiss-swollen mouth a second time. He simply was not cooperating.

"Baby doll—" he tried to say, his syrupy drawl fast becoming a dry, hoarse whisper. "We've *really* gotta stop—"

"But you want..."

Me. And badly. Every blessed inch of bold evidence was painfully obvious to Frankie.

His voice was a soft pant. "We've got to stop right now," he clarified. "I mean, *right now.* Or else—"

One more word, Frankie thought, and she'd kill him. She really would. "Or else what?"

Doc jerked his tousled curls toward her sleeping alcove. "Or else we'll be rolling around on that ruffly bed of yours, baby doll."

Her head bobbed up and down, her flushed cheeks hot. "Exactly."

His lips parted in astonishment. "But, Ms. Lu—I mean, Frankie" he said, correcting himself again. "You've never even *been* with a man."

"Then don't you think I ought to start?" she swiftly countered, berating herself for divulging she was a virgin. Obviously it was the biggest mistake of her life. Still, she'd gotten Doc this far. And she wasn't letting him get away. More determined than ever, she rose on tiptoe and locked her lips on his.

Surely this would bring him to his knees. He was only a man. And Frankie knew if you could just get a man to what was called "the point of no return," the beast inside would take over. She just wished Doc didn't seem to have such a painfully high threshold.

Finally, his voice cracked. "Baby doll, I swear—" He dragged a gravelly groan across her lips again. "I'm now beggin' you with my very last breath. *Please...*"

She was too hot and bothered herself to do anything other than ignore him completely. Moving her hips against him, she shivered and slipped her tongue between his lips again.

"Oh, Frankie," he said brokenly.

Hearing the raw need in his voice, Frankie was sorely tempted to show him some mercy. But then she reminded herself that he obviously thought her life was going nowhere fast. Something she did must have worked. Finally, his blessed hands were in her hair, those strong fingers massaging her scalp. He leaned back a fraction. "You know," he said, panting hard. "You are seriously trying my patience, woman."

"I know," she returned sweetly.

He merely shook his head. And then he cried uncle with a soft sigh, hauled Frankie right off her feet and carried her to the bed. As his body covered hers on the mattress, he delivered thorough kisses, his lips pressing harder, his tongue diving deeper, and his hands seeking every inch of her. For years, Frankie had been making a long list of things she wanted to do if she ever got a man naked in her bed, and now she vowed to fulfill every one of her fantasies, in case this turned out to be her only chance.

She started with unsnapping Doc's shirt and stroking his chest hair, barely aware that her own blouse was now untucked and that Doc was unzipping the side zipper of her skirt, which now rose, bunching around her waist. Suddenly, she froze. He was unbuttoning her blouse! All at once, she remembered the scars on her chest. "Not my shirt," she murmured breathlessly. *Not in the daylight.* She hazarded a glance into his eyes, and her breath caught. Because this was real, so real. Doc wasn't a hero from a novel, or a caveman. He was just a man.

Now emotion flooded her. He was watching her with such undisguised tenderness. Tilting his head, he drew a gentle finger down her cheek, until his palm cupped her chin. She heard, really heard, the softly playing music she loved, and smelled the sweet scent of flowers, and saw, over Doc's shoulder, how gently the breeze lifted the lace curtains. "If we're gonna do this, honey bunch," he whispered hoarsely, the faint stir of his breath feeling warm on her cheek, "I want to see all of you. Every inch."

She considered. He was a doctor. And she was actually proud of her scars, since they were from battles she'd fought and won, proof she'd survived and been blessed with a new life. And yet, somehow, her scars seemed even more private than the other things she and Doc might be about to share.

"No," she whispered, shaking her head.

He surveyed her a long, tender moment. And then, with a barely perceptible nod, he let her have her way. Leaning forward, he closed his warm lips over hers for what could have been minutes or hours. Every-thing got hazy. She let him touch her through the blouse and bra, moaning as her small breasts swelled. The unbearable frustration he was giving her as he rubbed circles with his flattened palms, then gently pinching the already stiff tips of her tortured nipples, reduced her to whimpering laments as she struggled with his clothes.

When his lab coat and shirt were gone, she went for his belt, then raked her fingernail slowly down his zipper. The metal track was like a flint against which she struck the match of her nail, and it set Doc on fire. With a soft grunt, he reached down, unzipping himself. A second later, she was pushing down his jeans, her hands smoothing the silken, golden hair on his thighs.

If Frankie relived this a thousand times, she'd never believe it was happening. Not Doc's whispered words of encouragement or how sweetly he held her, since she was shaking so badly when he slipped off her skirt, panty hose and panties. Or how they wound up side by side—with both her bare legs trailing around one of his and her face half hidden against his neck.

She wouldn't believe the transformation that came over him as he urged her to pleasure him, guiding her fingers around where she most yearned to touch him. His eyes grew paler still as she stroked him, and as he stroked her back. With every mutual touch, she felt more broken. His silver-blue eyes drifted, the lids getting thicker and heavier, the dreamy irises becom-ing more silver than blue, as if the heat she was stok-ing inside him was more than a touch, making what-ever was between them burn bright, like a hot sun on a silver afternoon.

Finally his strong hand closed over hers and he brought her hand to his heart, cradling it. And then he concentrated on her completely. His touch, like his kiss, became gentler. In her mouth, the brush of his tongue painted a soft seascape, while lower, the brush of his palm against her moist curls made her gasp, especially when he began strumming a finger back and forth against the bud of her desire.

Oblivion, she thought. This was it. While Doc held her there, she suddenly wanted to say she'd never expected this. That she wasn't really ready for this level of emotional surrender. That she didn't even know him.

But it was too late. She'd crossed the line.

She exploded while he wrapped his warm body protectively around hers. Then, and for a long time after, Doc's comforting palm stayed curled and molded over her glistening mound, catching the small contractions that had shaken her.

She finally swallowed hard. It had been so wonderful. But she couldn't help but say, "I...I wanted..." *You inside me. I wanted you to make me a woman.*

"Don't you worry, baby doll—" Even though his voice was deeply husky and hoarse with need, he flashed her a lazy, faintly bemused smile, his heavily lidded pale eyes smoldering with arousal. "You're in capable hands here. And you don't need to explain a thing."

When he found his wallet and drew out some condoms, Frankie couldn't believe it. She hadn't even thought of protection! That's how far gone she was. Watching him, she tried to remember that long list of things she was supposed to do if she was ever lucky enough to wrestle a naked man into her bed.

But now she couldn't remember even one maneuver.

And anyway, Doc was in complete control. Covering her body with his, he took her lips in a kiss that was pure possession. She gasped and clung to him—feeling fearful and exhilarated, as unsure as she was needy. As he settled his elbows beside her head, something watchful came over his eyes, a recognition of the seriousness of this act. He was reminding her that what he was about to take couldn't ever be replaced.

His voice, now stretched to breaking by his own restrained need, cracked. "Are you sure?"

She wanted him more than life. But she couldn't find her voice, so she simply nodded.

Sighing against her lips, he murmured kisses and sweet nothings on her cheeks as his thigh parted hers; her once crisp blouse, now damp and bunched, was the only barrier between them. Gasping, she suddenly felt him...*there*. Heavy and hot and pressuring. A high whinny escaped her lips, then a cry as he started pushing inside.

Not even the soft salve of his drawling voice could soothe. He pushed a fraction deeper. Then deeper. Each slow inch was a melting burn for which there were no words. He'd entered her like the night sky—coming slow and then plunging her into total darkness until he was moonlight and stars inside her. With her eyes shut tight and the whole world in seeming darkness, Frankie saw glittering stars against her closed eyelids, and she silently wished this man would never leave her.

It was a crazy wish.

She couldn't help but wish it as their slow joining turned her inside out. His patience alone destroyed her. Mindlessly, she opened all the way for him as he lifted her knee and curled her leg around the rolling, rippling flesh of his back. Surely he could feel the heat of her womb. Sweet heaven, she was coming apart. And as he drove himself in all the way, she shattered, sobbing out his name, arching to accept him, knowing she'd never felt so strong. Beautiful. Or wonderfully alive.

Doc's answering cry said his body could take no more. With a last pleasuring thrust, he drove into the hot pit of her, his fingers dragging down her hair, pulling her to him by the silken strands as he clamped his lips over hers and the deep, sweet pulse of him throbbed inside her.

For a long time they lay in silence, still joined. The world came back slowly. She noticed the romance of the afternoon again—the scents of flowers, how the white lace curtains lifted in the breeze, the soft music. She knew you were supposed to say something now, but she wasn't sure what. "Uh...Doc?"

There was a long pause. "Yeah?"

Tucking a damp wayward lock of hair behind her ear, Frankie ventured, "Uh, it was really good for me."

The slow, lazy chuckle that licked around her ears warmed her to her soul, making her feel terribly pleased with herself. So did the flash of his glistening white teeth when he shot her an irresistibly broad grin. "Believe me," he whispered huskily, "it was just as good for me as it was for you."

"Somehow, cowboy," Frankie couldn't help but

whisper back, a soft smile stealing over her lips, "I sincerely doubt it."

But she was sure glad he'd stopped to smell the flowers.

OBVIOUSLY, HE'D LOST his mind. Oh, yes, Doc had really done it this time, and he should be committed. Granted, a man could only take so much, especially after a year of celibacy, and she *had* come on awful strong, but that was still absolutely no excuse. Hell, it had been hours since the afternoon surrendered to twilight, more hours still since midnight.

The bewitching hour.

Time for you to turn into a pumpkin, cowboy. Doc shifted his weight in the straight-back chair at the card table, and stared between the blank legal paper on his clipboard and the sleeping woman in the bed. She was nude, except for the crumpled blouse she'd refused to take off, and even though the garment was restricting her, Doc knew she didn't want him to see her scars, so he left it as she wished and simply covered her bare legs.

Now he stared out the window. Past the fragrant purple flowers and lazily blowing lace curtains, high above the graffiti-painted rooftops and Woo Long's wedding cakes, a perfect full moon was gleaming over Manhattan in the liquid night sky. Like the lining of a precious round shell, its color served as a sore reminder to Doc of the pearl he'd just taken from Frankie Luccetti today.

And this evening.

And tonight.

He blasted himself once more. He'd had no right. No cause. It was shamefully, mindlessly unprofessional. In fact, he hoped she sued. What had he been thinking? Where was his self-control? Uttering a soft grunt of self-disgust, Doc shook his head. Even now, he couldn't believe how badly he still wanted her, how she'd stripped him of all his reason.

Just looking at her, he felt his chest squeeze tight. Under her blouse, he could make out the curves of the small breasts. And her hair… There wasn't a knot in it, as he'd first imagined. When he'd finally removed all the pins and ribbons, the dark mass did hang nearly to her knees. Touching it, Doc had felt he was holding his splayed hands under a faucet, feeling nothing more than the silken resistance of water rushing though his fingertips.

And he'd never forget the emotion in her dark eyes when he'd loved her in the twilight. She wasn't sophisticated enough to hide her fear. Or her need that surpassed the fear. No woman had ever looked at Doc like that.

He swallowed hard, hating himself. Well, not a damn thing had gone right since he'd gotten here. First, she'd yelled at him from the street, then he'd caught her dancing. And even now, he was haunted by the impression Marta had been in the apartment, standing next to him at the threshold, like an angel.

Or demon—if, by chance, the ghost of Marta *had* been here, somehow playing matchmaker.

Which she wasn't. Doc was a man of science; he didn't believe in ghosts. Oh, he sorely wished he had some otherworldly excuse for his bad behavior. Or for a sign that there was a life beyond this one, especially since he'd lost his parents at a young age, and then Marta had died. But he only believed in things a man could see and touch.

Like Frankie Luccetti.

He'd touched her, all right. Even if he hadn't seen all of her. He eyed her blouse. That bothered him more than he wanted to admit; even though she'd let him take her virginity, she hadn't trusted him enough to take off her blouse. Dammit, he knew she'd had serious surgery. He could easily guess what her scars looked like. And in so many ways, she *had* trusted him....

He felt suddenly breathless. If he'd been plagued with anger this past year, he now couldn't get Frankie out of his system: Her dark, luminous eyes as she'd crouched over him, exploring his body. How she'd touched a man intimately—*him*—for the very first time today. How as she'd done so, the long black strands of her hair caught the light like dark prisms, making a rainbow of colors gleam in the sleek, shiny mass. He could still feel her, curling on his chest to sleep, her Rapunzel hair feeling like a thousand filaments of silk.

He never believed such an attraction possible. He'd grown to know Marta slowly. It was nothing like this. And this was crazy, he reminded himself. He and this woman had nothing in common. He'd come here for the sole purpose of explaining to her that she wasn't a candidate for motherhood.

Which meant there was only one thing to do.

Doc told himself it was the best thing. The honorable thing. And then he lowered his head, poised the pen over the paper, and he started to write.

SLOW DOWN! SHE THOUGHT. But in the dream the speed of the apple red convertible felt too good. The wind was so strong, like fingers combing Frankie's hair, and it tempered the heat of the hot sun on her cheeks. Beneath her, the car vibrated, sending a thrill right into her bones.

Like chalk on a newly washed blackboard, a white line bisected the long, straight stretch of black asphalt. On either side of the road, buttery yellow wildflowers melted into tall green grasses, but she didn't have time to stop and smell the flowers.

The triangular median had popped into sharp focus! Just ahead, a tall, whitewashed fork pointed both ways. Should she go right or left?

She pressed the gas. *Forget about making a decision. Just live for the moment—for the thrusting fingers of wind in your hair, for the rush of cool, moist air reddening your cheeks.*

The fork in the road was closer. She was bearing right down on it. She had to decide. But it was so confusing. There were so many roads. So many options in life...

The fork in the road was right in front of her.

What should she do?

"What should I do?" Frankie murmured, coming awake slowly, as she usually did, with bits of dreams still sliding through her mind. She'd had this one before, many times since her transplant operation, and she wasn't sure, but now she thought she might have been wearing a wedding gown. Hazily, she realized that the shiny red convertible represented freedom, since she was now free of the bondage of her illness. Maybe that's what the dream meant. Since she had a new life, she was in the driver's seat—independent, free and in control of her destiny. Because she had so many decisions to make, there was a fork in the road. Now, of course, she sensed the dream had something to do with a special man....

She became slowly aware of the warm, soft ache of her body, the sweet soreness of muscles she'd never used. Her cheeks felt flushed. She'd lost her virginity. Finally, it had really happened. She opened her eyes.

But he was gone. She knew it immediately, instinctively, before she even glanced around, and she felt the hurt of his absence in a bone-deep way, as if she'd just discovered a part of herself was missing.

She tried to tell herself she hadn't really expected him to stay. Gingerly pulling the sheet around herself, she got out of bed and headed for the folded sheet of legal paper that was anchored to the card table by Doc's empty Snapple bottle.

Between the street lights on Mott and the light of the full moon, she could make out the note.

Dear Francesca,
First, I want to thank you for the night. I hadn't been with anyone for a long time. I want you to know it meant something very special to me.

Although that is the case, I'm not ready for a relationship right now, certainly not one such as you deserve. I know a woman like you will settle for nothing less than to be loved completely. I know you'll find the right man. I also wish the best for you, even though it didn't work out for you to start a family by adopting at Big Apple Babies.

I hope you'll forgive me for leaving without waking you. Maybe it would help if I tell you that my fiancée died a while back, and that's why

I really don't want to get involved. Please take care of yourself, and know that this night meant something very special to me.

Yours,
Doc

Frankie tried to tell herself it was perfunctory, but not unkind. That Doc was just being honest. But her eyes settled on the phrase "a woman like you," and her throat constricted with painful emotion. When she read the signature again, a lump lodged, not going up or down. *Yours, Doc.* Well, he wasn't hers, was he?

"I hope you'll try to understand," Frankie muttered, mimicking the phrase. *As if I might not!* she fumed. *As if I don't have a life of my own!* "Although that is the case..." she mocked, trying to push away the devastation she felt. Why, this letter didn't even sound like a love letter, it sounded like an assignment for a business writing class.

She heaved a sigh.

Anger was making her feel better. She told herself suddenly, righteously, she wished he'd stuck around so that they could get clear on a few things. First, she hadn't had many opportunities to explore her life and find herself. So if he'd thought she meant to date exclusively, he was wrong....

"But, Frankie," she imagined him protesting, "I'm the first man you've ever been with."

"And you won't be the last," she'd say calmly. "Our time together doesn't give you any exclusive rights."

"But, Frankie—"

"Sure," she'd continue. "I saved myself for a long time. But now I want the chance to be on my own.

Certainly, the night meant something special to me, too. After all, I was a virgin. But let's face it, Doc," she'd say. "It *was* just a night."

But it wasn't.

She was in love with him. Hopelessly, painfully, completely in love. Frankie knew people didn't really fall in love in a few short hours. But she had.

And he hadn't stayed. Now tears pressed her eyelids. After making love, it felt so wrong to be reading this letter by the light of the moon. She'd felt such a strange pull to him—it was so much more than his sun-kissed good looks. Deep in her heart, she knew he was meant to be her man.

But nothing was hers right now. She hadn't gotten the baby. Even the heart that carried her life blood wasn't her own. A soft, sighing sob escaped her. Why couldn't he just stay? Lie and say he loved her?

Suddenly, she hurt with the ache of a lifetime. Hurt deep down in her soul for the physical love she'd glimpsed today, but would live without. And for the baby she'd so desperately wanted to raise.

Somehow, she pulled herself together. She was a positive person. She'd go on doing the next right thing. She'd apply to other adoption agencies. Yes, she'd just chalk this up to a two-word lesson about healthy hearts: they broke. Staring at the moon, she murmured, "Guess bad luck in love came with this heart, cowboy."

After all, Frankie had overheard only one fact about the nameless, faceless donor whose heart now beat inside her—the young woman had died tragically on her wedding day.

Chapter Four

Nearly nine months later, the present

"Now, you listen here, honey bunch," Doc drawled as he reopened a curtain he'd previously closed out of deference to his pint-size patient's privacy and the busy corridor outside. "Green peas are victuals. Not only are they jam-packed with protein, fiber and vitamin A, they're low in cholesterol, too. So, from here on out, I advise you to use them strictly for eatin'. Not for shovin' up that cute nose of yours, okey dokey, Shirley Q.?"

Tucking a frizzy lock of red hair behind her ear with a shaking hand, the mortified five-year-old named Shirley Quincy trembled with relief. "Okey dokey, Dr. Holiday," she squeaked, still sounding nasal.

Doc smiled kindly. Where most little kids got confused and called him Dr. Holly-day, or Hollandaise, Shirley had got it right. She was brighter than most, more articulate, and probably destined for trouble because of it. "For now," Doc drawled ruefully, "I guess you'll just have to tell all your girlfriends you came in for your first nose job."

Shirley actually got the joke, and if her lower lip hadn't still been trembling so badly, she'd have giggled. She was seated on the edge of the stainless steel table in the emergency room of Saint Vincent's hospital with her plaid skirt tucked neatly beneath her. Her skinned knees hung over the table's edge, and her dangling loafers swung perilously far above the floor.

"Now, believe me, I do admire your more experimental approach to life, Shirley," Doc continued reassuringly, rising from his stool and patting a small sweater-clad shoulder that seemed smaller still beneath his broad hand. "But next time you get a great new idea, as you did with those peas, you should confer with an adult first. Confer," he added. "That means ask."

Shirley's eyes stayed glued on Doc's mouth; her own quivering lips silently echoing the movements of his as if she were committing every word of this life-and-death diagnosis to memory.

"Now, if your mom's not here by the time I clean up, Shirl, then I'll shanghai you back to preschool in a jiffy-split and she can meet you there. Okay?"

Shirley nodded. Looking determined to be good, not only now but for the rest of her life, she clasped her hands in her lap and didn't move a muscle.

Doc started tidying the examination area. What a day, Doc thought. He'd volunteered his lunch hour to give free exams to some school kids, who were around the corner from Big Apple Babies. He was almost done when reports surfaced that a seven-year-old hellion had stolen his black bag and that a preschooler—it was Shirley—had been discovered with a noseful of frozen peas. Even now, Doc had to bite his tongue to keep from suggesting to Shirley that, next time, she at least thaw the peas first.

The trouble kids could get themselves into truly boggled the mind, Doc thought as he put the lid more snugly on a Biohazard waste can. Because Doc's black bag had been stolen, Doc had to bring Shirley all the way to Saint Vincent's ER, and now, before he could head back to Big Apple Babies, he still needed to track down the bag. Doc just hoped the shady seven-year-old thief who'd stolen it wasn't extracting his classmate's teeth.

He heard a tremulous sigh behind him. "Doctor?"

He turned. "Yes, Ms. Quincy?" That made her giggle. "Hasn't anybody ever called you 'Ms.' before?"

"No, *Mr.* Doctor," Shirley returned with a coy smile. Then, trying to sound conversational, she said, "How many little girls do you have?"

On his job, it was the question little girls most asked of Doc. "Not a one," he admitted.

"Not a one!" Shirley's eyes bugged in disbelief.

"Nope."

"But you'd be such a great daddy." She blushed and raced on. "'Specially if somebody gets hurt and needs a doctor at home. They could get all cut up and bloody and—"

"I'll take that under advisement," Doc swiftly assured her. That was the other thing he could never believe about kids: how downright gory they liked to get.

"Do you have a wife?"

"No, ma'am."

"Girlfriend?"

"No ma'am."

"But don't you *want* kids? Maybe girls?"

Doc adjusted his cowboy hat more snugly on his head and looped his stethoscope around his neck. "Why, sure I do."

"Then why don't you get some?"

Doc only wished having a family was that easy. "I might, someday." How could a grown man explain the failures of his love life to a kid? As he turned to fill in Shirley's chart, he tried not to think of the missed chances and broken promises, the pain he'd lived with, never knowing if Marta was really going to marry him or not since she'd wrecked her car on the way to their wedding. *And what if, last year, you'd actually picked up the phone and called Frankie Luccetti? Huh, cowboy?*

Nowadays, it was hard to convince himself that making love to her had been wrong. It had felt too right. She'd made him smile for the first time in so long, even if he felt guilty about how often she'd crept inside his mind since.

Oh, he'd almost called her. Even now, he recalled the shock of need he'd felt for her. The intensity of their lovemaking had been unprecedented.

And the emotions hadn't ever gone away. Autumn had slid into a stark, cold winter, and on lonely, snowy nights when the whole city was locked down tight, Doc would get out of bed and stare at the endless avenue of darkened storefronts, and at the moonlight glistening in the snowdrifts, just thinking of her, his mind traversing the distance between his SoHo loft and her ruffly, frilly bed. By the time he'd finally slip back under the covers, the sheets were always glacially cold. It was as if Frankie Luccetti had folded the map of his emotional world in half, stapling the

North and South Poles together and making everything feel doubly raw and frigid.

Lately, since spring had rolled around, early evenings seemed worse. Doc often found himself setting
the table with a hand-woven placemat, fancy plate
and candle, even though he was only eating by himself. Again. Once, he'd simply sat there with his hand
on the phone for an hour while his supper got good
and cold.

But then he'd imagine meeting Frankie. How
they'd eat out, then maybe head to her place. Later—
maybe weeks, maybe months, but definitely sometime—they'd wind up having the usual long, awk-
ward talk, where they regretfully admitted their mistake, saying the affair was leading nowhere because
they had nothing in common.

It all seemed so useless.

But Doc hadn't forgotten her. And he wondered if
she'd slept with a man since him. He doubted it. She
wasn't the type. Still, the thought of her lying with
another man goaded him. No matter how many times
Doc reminded himself he had no claim on her—even
if he *had* been her first lover—biting jealousy gnawed
at him when he so much as entertained the notion of
her having a boyfriend.

The next thing Doc knew, he'd be imagining that
faceless, shadowy boyfriend: sliding a guiding hand
beneath Frankie's elbow as they walked—it was always in Central Park. Or paying for her movie—it
was always at the Sony Cineplex. Or kissing her
hard—nine times out of ten, at the corner of West
Fourth Street and Seventh Avenue, but sometimes
also on top of the World Trade Center at night, when
the lights were bright.

Those kisses really fired up Doc's temper. Until he imagined them a little longer...and the faceless, shadowy imaginary boyfriend who was plunging his warm tongue deep between Frankie Luccetti's lips became none other than *him.*

Now he could only shake his head. All those imaginary dates had been far more vivid than Doc wanted to admit.

Oh, Doc had gone on other dates—*real* dates. Mostly because everybody at Big Apple Babies—especially his boss, Jake Lucas, and Jake's wife, Dani, who worked right here in the hospital—kept playing matchmaker. They'd whittle Doc down, just like the wood Doc's brother, Shane, used to sculpt on the porch when they were kids in Texas. They'd say, sure, Doc was hurting, but that he had to move on, that his life couldn't end with Marta. And then Doc would take some female friend-of-a-friend to dinner because he was so plumb tired of saying no.

'Course, nothing lit a candle to that moonlit night with Frankie. Sometimes, Doc would feel a sharp tug at his heart—and realize he was remembering those soft, dark, luminous eyes that were so vulnerable and without guile. Or how Frankie's black silken hair had swept across his body, feeling like streamers of wind-blown sand crossing his bare skin as they returned to the dunes.

Nowadays, even the way he'd caught her dancing with that damnable mop only served to amuse him. And he didn't feel the least bit angry anymore, just lonely.

"Are you okay, Dr. Holiday?" Shirley suddenly squeaked. "You sure got awful quiet."

And you're awful perceptive, kid. Doc quickly finished his work. Shaking off the shroud of the past, he drawled, "Shirley, if you must know, it's 'cause every time I meet a nice young lady, such as yourself, I go into deep, ponderous thought, wondering if I *will* get to have a daughter like you someday."

Shirley giggled, flushing bright pink with pleasure.

Smiling back, Doc realized the truth in the words. He loved kids. And the way they hung on to him, he guessed the feeling was mutual. *Forget it, Doc,* he thought with a sigh. *That time's behind you. Your ship's come and gone.* Somewhere over the past couple of years, he'd settled down into the Adirondack chair of his bachelorhood, trying to tell himself he didn't mind in the least.

But it was a damn fool's lie.

Doc minded a lot. At least that murderous anger he used to feel had vanished the day he'd bedded down with Frankie. It wasn't much of a consolation prize, but hell, it was something.

So were the kids he got to treat. He shot Shirley a grin. "C'mon, Shirley-girly," he said, "whaddaya say we split this here banana stand?"

"*Popsicle* stand," she corrected him, looking faintly embarrassed for him, as he knew she would.

"But we're gonna split," he countered. "And I've never heard of a Popsicle split, now, have you?"

"A Popsicle *split!*" she exclaimed, pursing her lips and tilting her head, as if to say he was simply impossible. She wouldn't be the first female to think so.

When little Shirley giggled, Doc felt another twinge of longing for kids of his own. He thought of Frankie Luccetti, too—of the baby she'd always wanted and didn't get. She probably would have made a good mother. It was just too damn bad that life didn't deal out desire and opportunity in equal measure. Too bad for both him and Frankie. Doc sighed. He was just about to lift Shirley off the examining table when he noticed Dani Lucas through the windowed wall.

"Mommy!" exclaimed Shirley, pointing at the stranger who was on Dani's heels.

Good. This took care of Shirley. Now all Doc needed was to ferret out the second-grader who'd stolen his black bag, then Doc could get back to work. As Dani strode purposefully toward them, Doc couldn't help but think that his boss, Jake, was lucky. Oh, his wife was naturally beautiful, with a heart-shaped face and mouth, round chocolate eyes and high, proud cheekbones. Even her nurse's uniform couldn't hide the fact that she was gorgeous. But it was more than that. Marriage and motherhood suited her so well. It was hard to believe that Jake and Dani's son, Ty, was finishing second grade now, and that their baby, a little girl named Annie, who was Doc's godchild, was now nearly a year old. At her job in the ER, Dani had just gotten a promotion, too....

And she was about to exert her newfound authority.

Doc should have known. Once an extra doctor showed up in a busy Manhattan emergency room, he might never make it out again. That Doc was a pediatrician didn't matter. Dani would shanghai a family dentist into surgical scrubs if she could. The hospital was desperate for able bodies.

Sure enough, Dani burst breathlessly into the examining room, saying, "Good to see you, Doc. But there's no time for small talk. I need you out front. And don't worry—" she paused long enough to flash him a brilliant smile, even as she took a death grip on his arm. "I'll put in a good word with my husband if he harasses you about your long lunch hour."

Safely depositing Shirley into her mother's arms and feeling another lightning-swift twinge of regret over the fact he'd never have a little girl such as Shirley to call his own, Doc followed Dani into a busy hospital corridor where all hell seemed to be breaking loose. "What's the trouble?"

"A cabbie just pulled up with a pregnant woman."

Dani was already jogging down the immense corridor, and Doc's long-legged leisurely strides kept pace. "Aw, Dani, I won't make it back to Big Apple Babies infirmary until midafternoon," he protested, even though both of them already knew he'd help her out. "And then I'll have to work until midnight."

"You always work until midnight."

"But tonight I had plans."

"What? Another romantic, candlelit night with the Mets?"

"Close. The Dodgers."

Dani merely tightened her grip around his biceps. Over her shoulder, she called, "Johnson's patient's coding in four. Get Levine in there. And this doctor needs a gurney on Greenwich Avenue."

"Now, Dani—" Doc playfully shook off her grasp. "To anyone other than a health care professional, my refusal might seem callous. But you and I both know that life goes on without us. Babies get born, cuts get stitched, medicines get administered. Even on our days off. Besides, doll face, a stressed, overworked doctor, such as myself, is the single—"

"You're definitely single—" Dani cut in. "Despite

all my efforts to find a woman who can improve you to the contrary.''

''I was saying, the single most dangerous thing to have on a hospital ward ain't the patient, but the tired doctor.''

''Which is why I'm putting you out to pasture, Doc,'' Dani shot back. ''On the sidewalk,'' she clarified. ''Not a ward.''

''Aw, doll face, have a heart.''

She counted off on her fingers. ''One—for a physician, you have appalling grammar, Doc. And two—I hate it when you call me doll face. And three—could you please take off that cowboy hat? I mean, this *is* a hospital.''

He merely grinned. ''That's what I love about you, Dani. You're the only woman I know who refuses to put up with me.''

Her lips twitched. ''Good. Since you love me so much, go get the expectant mother out of that cab and inside this hospital.''

''I'm wavering,'' Doc conceded as they rounded a corner and the electronic double doors leading to Greenwich Avenue came into sight.

She laughed. ''Maybe you'll even wind up delivering the baby. And maybe the woman'll name it after you—her savior.''

''What? She'll name it Baby Doc?''

Dani hooted. ''I guess that'd make you Papa Doc. But wasn't he a dictator?''

''Of Haiti.'' Doc shot her a grin. ''Okay, look. You've convinced me. I'll watch the mama. But only if you promise not to fix me up on any more dates. Deal?''

Dani considered. ''Deal.''

Doc didn't believe a word of it. He glanced at his watch and blew out a sigh. No doubt this meant he really would be working until midnight tonight.

"I owe you," Dani said.

Doc sighed, leaned over and ruffled the light honey hair of the wife of his best friend. "No problem, sugar britches."

Dani tossed her head. "And quit calling me that!"

His look was all innocence. "I thought it was *doll face* you hated."

Dani shook her head ruefully. "Doc, somewhere on this planet is the one woman who can lasso you. Since she's your other half, she's probably as tricky as you, so you'd better watch out."

"When she catches me, will you throw the bachelor party? You know, the one with blond dancers wearing spangle pants?"

"No!" Dani exploded. "I might never see my husband again!"

"Afraid I'll drag him to a harem, huh?"

"Oh, I wish you'd get that close to a woman, Doc, 'cause heaven knows you need one." She flashed him a saucy smile. "But you can leave my husband home. I can take care of him."

"I'll just bet you can, darlin'."

As Dani veered off toward her work station, Doc flung his head back and laughed at the banter, a deep belly laugh that did his heart good. Yeah, since that day with Frankie Luccetti nearly nine months ago, his good humor had actually returned. "Oh, get out of here," he called in a teasing drawl, though Dani was nearly gone and he was already striding through the electronic double doors. "I've got a baby to deliver."

"I owe you, Doc," Dani shouted, blowing him kisses over her shoulder. "Really."

"Like I said, no problem."

But a minute later, Doc half wished he'd run. He found the pregnant woman lying flat on her back on a cab seat that was less than hygienic. Her water had broken, soaking her dress, and she was fully dilated.

As he crouched, trying to angle his broad shoulders inside the open door of the cab, Doc could barely see her. One hand covered her forehead—he glimpsed only the hint of a mouth contorted by labor pains—and the other was molded over her very pregnant, swollen belly. Her chin was tucked in, exposing the mess of very short, shiny black curls that covered the crown of her head. Fortunately, she was bare-legged and wearing a long, loose dress, which would make things easier, if it came down to an actual delivery. Which it well might, judging from her cries of pain.

Not that they were stopping the impatient cabbie from trying to collect his fare. "This meter's running," he reminded Doc, revving the motor.

"You'll just have to wait, partner," Doc drawled calmly.

But the driver was resolute. "No babies in my cab." He mustered the same enthusiasm he might for warnings such as "no smoking" or "no cigars." No babies. As if babies had the audacity to be born in his cab every five minutes, and the cabbie was getting darn sick and tired of it.

Under other circumstances, Doc might haul the driver out and give him a lesson in how to treat a lady. But from the second he'd hit the doors, Doc had become a pure professional again. His senses were honed, and he was doing numerous tasks at once:

Thrusting out his hands and letting a nurse slip on latex gloves. Explaining to the patient that he had no choice but to examine her right here. Memorizing the cabbie's licensing information on the dashboard, in case he decided to report him later for being a jerk.

"We do need that gurney out here, if you can get it," Doc said to the nurse. "Otherwise, get what you can—blankets, water, instrument table, suctions, clamps, a stool...." He rattled on.

"Aw, man," groaned the cabbie. "This is a *cab*. A *vehicle*. By definition that means it's supposed to *move* somewhere. So, c'mon. Let's move it, people."

The nurse shook her head in disgust. "Only in New York."

Doc had always heard he had a lethal stare, and the rumor was probably true. When he crouched in the cab's door again, he shot the cabbie a long sideways glance. A second later, the cabbie swallowed hard, as if he'd just escaped within an inch of his life. Then, after a beat of hesitation—one Doc allowed for the man's pride—the cabbie also reached over and flicked off the running meter. "I guess I can wait here a minute," he conceded.

By the time that battle was over, Doc's mind was already fixed on the war. He asked a nurse to open the opposite cab door and station herself behind the woman's head, and he mentally blocked out the busy street sounds—the angry, persistent car horns, the jackhammers and shouting. He ignored people who were starting to drift near the cab, craning their curious necks, and he concentrated on his own practiced patter, the endless stream of comfort and encouragement designed to relax the patient as he examined her.

"Breathe real steady," he drawled in a voice as

thick and smooth as honey, now thankfully feeling someone slide a stool beneath his behind at the curb. Not that it made the examination any easier; Doc needed to get farther inside the cab, but at this angle his broad shoulders couldn't negotiate the small enclosure.

"How do you feel? Can you talk to me?"

No answer. But her pulse was strong and steady; her breathing too fast, but rhythmic. She'd probably been to birthing classes, which was good. And she'd quit shrieking.

"This is positively medieval," Doc muttered, so low she couldn't hear. Her contractions were following one right after the other. This baby was coming any second. The instant blankets were thrust into his hands, he slid them beneath her and over her knees, though he knew she'd be thinking more about the baby than her modesty.

Lowering his voice another notch, he said to whomever had just rolled an instrument table next to him, "I need her medical history. Conditions we should know about. Allergies to medications? And the obstetrician's name. Husband. Can somebody contact the family?"

Doc sensed more than saw one of the suits from the front desk dart outside with a clipboard. Grimacing with disgust, he bit back his temper; still, the low, lazy singsong of his warning drawl was far more chilling than a shout would have been. "Get those insurance forms out of here."

"But, Doctor—"

"Blue Cross can wait."

"United Health," the nurse at her head called. "She says she does have insurance. With United

Health. And her doctor is a guy named Krill at NYU Med.''

Doc frowned. That made no sense. The only Krill he knew over at NYU Medical Center was a heart specialist who headed up a team of highly trained transplant surgeons. "Krill?"

"I know. But that's what she said, Doctor."

Before Doc could inquire further, the patient released a loud, sharp cry. The sound—one long high note—slit the air like a knife.

"Just breathe." She was doing well. "Now push." He waited. "And push. The baby's positioned just fine. I can see the top of the head. Push again. Bear down real hard, honey."

A female voice murderously growled, "Why don't you shut up?"

Her fury didn't faze Doc. He was glad she was a tigress because they had a spot of trouble. "Whoa," he said. Something didn't look right. Damn. Raising his voice—enough to be heard but not so much he'd frighten her—Doc yelled over his shoulder, "I really need that gurney, if I can get it."

A hospital volunteer ran between the double doors and the curb. "There's no gurney!" she cried. "Can we get her in a wheelchair?"

Doc shook his head. "No. Can you get those people away from us?" He felt the curious onlookers gathering behind him. Poor woman. Glancing up, he tried to see her face again, to gauge how she was doing, but the roof was low and the cab seemed full of nothing more than her swollen belly.

"Push again," he said. "Bear down hard."

She heaved a pain-racked sob.

Hell. It was coming. And now he could see the

problem. The cord was wrapped around the baby's neck.

"Baby doll," Doc drawled calmly. "I want you to listen to me very carefully. You *cannot* push anymore. Not yet. You're gonna feel a lot of pressure, a lot of pain. But no matter how bad it gets, you'll just have to curse and scream. I need to untangle the cord."

She sounded terrified. "The cord?"

"It's a problem," he said, even as his hands worked to release it from its knot around the baby's neck. "But it'll be fine if you don't push until I tell you." He just wished the woman wasn't out here like this.

Doc felt the woman's next howl rip right into his own heart. That health care professionals always kept a polite distance was the world's worst lie. The pain and terror in her agonized, wrenching sob made every ounce of fresh spring air squeeze right out of Doc's broad chest. He fought it. He couldn't afford to react emotionally. Slowly, carefully, he kept doing what had to be done. "Good girl," he said smoothly. And she was. Doc had often heard that flesh-tearing pain like this couldn't even be borne. But whoever she was, this woman was a New Yorker to the core. Probably born and bred. The type who happily coexisted with stress, crime, noise, hostility and crowds. Like the cabbie who, in spite of the high drama in the back seat, was actually yawning and reading a magazine.

The poor woman's body was tucked. She was propped up by a nurse in back; her knees in front were raised and bowed with the power of the cramps. Her toes curled, and now her slip-on shoes fell off. One landed on the curb, the other on the floor of the cab. She was unleashing strangled, deep-throated cries. And she was screaming, too. Cursing Doc, as if he'd personally brought her to this fate.

But she still didn't push.

She really was a fighter. He'd never seen anything like it. ''Almost there,'' he said. And then relief flooded him as he moved the cord. Doc's palm slid beneath the head. ''Now you can push. It's gonna come fast, doll. It's gonna—''

But nature had already taken its course. The mother doubled, loosing a blood-curdling high cry. And even though Doc was a pragmatic man of science who only wished he could believe in the world of the spirit, he thought, *Please, let it be a healthy one.*

And then the baby slipped out, right into his gloved, waiting hands. Doc was so ecstatic that a wide, lopsided grin instantly split his face. ''Welcome to the world, baby doll! How was that for your very first slicky-slide ride?'' And then he very gingerly shimmied his massive shoulders farther into the cab, snuggling the tiny wiggling newborn into a blanket and nestling her on the woman's belly. To the mother, he said, ''I'm so proud of you! Looks like you've went and got yourself a gorgeous healthy baby girl! She sure is a beauty! I mean, a *beauty!*''

Doc simply couldn't contain himself at moments such as this. Unable to keep his eyes off the sweet little baby girl he'd just delivered, he quickly clamped and cut the cord and started suctioning her mouth and nose. A beauty, hell, Doc thought, his grin getting broader still. She was anything but. She was wrinkled and messy and looked like a cute little alien from a sci-fi movie. But that hardly stopped him from sigh-ing and saying, ''Nope. I couldn't feel more satisfied

if I'd just helped deliver my very own daughter.''
Yes, he had Frankie Luccetti to thank for moments
like this. After all, it was she who'd restored his ability to feel life's joy.

Doc blew out another relieved sigh. "Phew! Well,
both you girls just made some man a proud papa."
That said, Doc was finally able to remove his gaze
from his handiwork. He glanced up, prepared to see
all the light, joy and gratitude in the mother's eyes.

Mortified dark eyes stared back. And then Frankie
Luccetti's hands started moving swiftly over the baby,
checking fingers and toes.

Doc couldn't breathe. All the air was sucked clear
out of him. His first thought was that she'd cut all
that long, glorious hair, so he hadn't recognized her.

And then he realized he'd just delivered his own
daughter.

At least he thought he had. "I'm a notoriously
quick study," he managed to say in a slow, shocked
drawl, his eyes riveting on the baby. "I mean, I was
top of my class. And while it wouldn't take a brain
surgeon to figure this one out—a mere pediatrician
might do—I have to ask…" His throat went bone dry.
"Frankie, is this my baby girl?"

Ignoring him, she continued checking the newborn.

It had to be his. Shameless tears stung Doc's eyes.
Could this really be his very own baby? Not knowing
what in the world to do, Doc did the only thing a man
would—if he was Texas born and bred and found
himself in the presence of his newborn daughter. He
sucked in a deep breath, and for the first time since
that day he'd made love to Frankie, Winston "Doc"
Holiday reverently removed his hat out of deference
to a female presence.

Doc was smart. Well educated. But underneath it all, he was an extremely simple man. His voice was raw. "Please, Frankie—" He held his hat over his heart, his chest feeling tight. "Is she?"

Frankie's voice was so even. Later—when it was really clear that she wanted no part of him—that's what Doc would remember most. Even after all her cursing and screaming, after all the physical pain she'd endured, even after he'd delivered a baby they both wanted more than life safely into her arms—her tone, when she finally spoke to him, was as even as a level. It was the kind of thing that could humble a cowboy—no matter how citified—into throwing up his hands and admitting he'd finally met his match.

"We have never asked you for anything," Frankie stated regally, holding the baby protectively. "Nor will we."

Implied in her words was the information Doc sought—that he was, indeed, the father of this baby. But he couldn't believe Frankie's tone. Especially not when she then turned from him to the cabbie—and with all the chutzpah that was every native New Yorker's birthright—said, "Excuse me. But I was occupied and did not hear. How much did you say that fare was?"

"I CAN'T BELIEVE THIS," Doc muttered moments later.

He needed to be a daddy right now, not a doctor. His heart ached with the need. He had to talk this out with Frankie. And to sit down alone with his sweet little newborn baby girl for a moment and savor the quiet and look deeply, really deeply, into her eyes.

"I'm your daddy, baby doll," he'd whisper.

Even though his teeny-weeny sweet slice of sugar pie was just a newborn, Doc expected, however illogically, to see some light of recognition in her gaze. Oh, yes, he wanted to cradle this crying, blanketed bundle against his chest, to clean her up, then kiss the licking wisps of jet hair that were now snuggled under her white skullcap. He wanted to make sure this baby girl understood that he was the able-bodied strapping Texas man who was blood-sworn to protect her.

Instead, Doc said, "Try calling again. Get Krill and his team from NYU Med, as well as her obstetrician. And make sure the monitors are set up—heart, vitals, everything. There was some ripping, so we need to stitch her." Doc strode alongside the fast-moving gurney with long, rangy strides, his hat shoved snugly back on his head, one hand on Frankie's shoulder and the other steadying the baby.

"And we're taking them up to the new wing, where the rooms are nicer and there's more security—" Even years of practiced calm in medical situations couldn't entirely conceal that Doc was feeling like a bouncing rubber ball; he was a new father, spurned lover and busy doctor—all rolled into one. That was two more roles than he wanted to juggle right now. When would he get to hold his baby girl? "I want the baby in the room. And can we get a corner room for them? Something large? With lots of light?"

There was a pause. "Lots of light, Doctor?"

Vaguely, he realized that sounded as strange as if he was asking for lace curtains and purple flowers, of the sort Frankie was used to at home. The nearby medical personnel weren't cognizant of Doc's relationship to Frankie and the baby, of course. But dammit, it was Frankie. And it was his daughter.

"Yeah," Doc said. "Light. Lots of it." He didn't want Frankie or his little girl in the darker rooms of the old wing.

"Yes, Doctor," came the reply.

"And flowers. Maybe we could get some purple flowers." It *would* make the room homier for Frankie.

"Doctor?"

"You heard me."

"Uh...get some flowers," someone shouted. "The doctor said purple. Try the gift shop, I guess."

Frankie had already given him the whole story in a clipped tone that Doc had tried his best to ignore. She'd simply breezed over the fact that she hadn't bothered to tell him about the baby, and she said she'd been scheduled to enter the hospital early, to be monitored by her obstetrician and Krill's team of specialists, in case there were complications. Her labor had come unexpectedly, as fast as lightning, so she'd left one quick phone message for her family and fled into a cab, stopping at Saint Vincent's, since she'd never make it all the way to the medical center on East Thirty-fourth Street.

Only when the medical aspects were dispensed with, did the spurned lover in Doc return. "How much was the fare?" he drawled with a soft sigh. "I still can't believe you said that."

Clutching their baby in an unnervingly proprietorial fashion, Frankie spoke in an annoyingly steady voice. "It was a reasonable question, Dr. Holiday."

And now she was calling him Dr. Holiday? Tamping down his confusion and lovingly rubbing the sweet, tiny shoulder of his little daughter, Doc leaned low over the gurney. In a hushed tone, he said,

"Please. We seem to be on such different wave-lengths here, Frankie—"

"Let's make that Ms. Luccetti."

Was she crazy? His eyes roved over her as if seeking physical signs of disturbance. It was the wrong time to notice, but he could see she'd gained weight during the pregnancy, and he liked the way it filled her out, putting needed flesh on bones that had been too gaunt. Even under the circumstances, her new haircut was flattering; perspiration-dampened curls artfully licked her wide forehead and fuller cheeks and tapered to points that, like slick black arrows, drew attention right to her best feature, her expressive dark eyes. Wistfully, his gaze lingered on her hair, and Doc remembered how those once-long silken strands had felt on his bare chest, his naked thighs. On his aroused sex.

At the recollection, pinpricks of awareness attacked his lower spine. In a situation like this, Doc suddenly decided, he couldn't afford to indulge any masculine pride. "How can you be so cold to me right now, baby doll?" he whispered. "In these last minutes, my heart's swelled so big that I can't believe my lab coat'll close over my chest. Why, my whole being's concentrated on your health and the baby's. She's cute as a button, she really is. And we're going to make sure you're both fine now."

"I see you're the same old smooth talker."

"Smooth talker? What are you talking about?"

"Take a look," she snapped. "We're fine."

Better than fine. Damn. His little Italian firecracker had just given birth in a cab. Now she was flat on her back, and still, somehow, getting the best of him. Again. She sure had a way of manipulating him that

Doc could live a million years and still not figure out. Sure, on the day they met, he'd thought he was taking pity on her and comforting her, by kissing her like that. But now he remembered how she'd come on so strong—rising on her tiptoes, nuzzling against his shirt, rolling her hips against his groin—until no man could have said no to her.

And thank heaven he hadn't, Doc thought, his gaze turning liquid again as he stared at the baby. She was simply adorable, all cuddled in the soft white blanket on Frankie's chest. His gut turned to mush. "Oh, please, Frankie—"

"Ms. Luccetti."

He wasn't even angry at her tone. How could he be angry when they'd just had a baby? He murmured, "You didn't mind me calling you Frankie nine months ago."

"That was before I got my 'Dear Frankie' letter—" After a moment, she added, "On a legal pad, no less. Not even decent stationery."

His lips parted in silent protest. It truly hadn't occurred to him to go to a Hallmark store at 3:00 a.m. "How can you talk this way?" He tried to keep his voice hushed. As he helped slide the gurney into an elevator, he realized nurses and orderlies were exchanging quizzical glances behind his back. He forged on. "Frankie, we brought a life into the world just now. A *life*. A child. I just don't understand you."

"I don't understand you, either."

Doc thought he was being clear. "Hmm?"

"Your accent."

As usual, the higher his emotions, the thicker his drawl, and right about now, his words had all the muddy consistency of year-old, refrigerated molasses. When he got really upset, no one on the East Coast could understand him—at least not north of Tampa. "You didn't tell me about this," he said, adjusting his hat on his head and trying his best to tamp down the drawl. "You were pregnant for nine months—"

"Eight and a half," Frankie countered. "Astrid is premature."

Something wasn't quite right with what she'd said. "I know the baby's immature."

"All babies are immature, Dr. Holiday," Frankie corrected him smoothly. "I said *pre*mature."

Damn if she wasn't making fun of him. "Technically," he drawled, his lips compressing, "she's not at all premature, just early." Suddenly, he was a doctor again. "We do have everything ready upstairs, right? Can they both be cleaned up immediately?"

"Yes, Doctor."

"Good. If we could just take care of weight, footprints, ankle tag…"

"Yes, Doctor."

After that exchange, he felt more in control. Had he really said "immature" instead of "premature"? He couldn't believe it. He was still so stunned he couldn't even talk right. And he was usually so calm. Both in medical situations and with women.

At least until he'd met Frankie.

And their daughter.

"Astrid?" he suddenly questioned. That was what was wrong with what she'd said.

"A name of Teutonic origins, it means 'impulsive in love.'"

"Astrid Holiday?" He immediately imagined some teenage boy saying things such as, "Astrid, you really

send me. You're out of this world." And that his
feelings were a case of Astrid projection. Oh, Doc
knew firsthand what horrible teases men could be.
She's our daughter, Doc thought in mute protest, not
a comet. He was starting to feel as helpless as his
own little girl. Didn't Frankie even think he should
have a say in naming her?

"Astrid *Luccetti,*" Frankie corrected him.

Staring down at Frankie and the baby, Doc suddenly felt something cold twist in his gut. Hell, if
Frankie hadn't given birth in the back seat of the cab
today, he'd never even have known. Confused and
feeling deeply betrayed, he cupped Frankie's face,
gently placing a thumb on her cheekbone and drawing
down the skin beneath her eyes. The lover in him
stared into the dark depths, wondering why she hadn't
called, while the doctor in him checked the dilation
of her pupils.

"Any word from Krill yet?" he asked.

"He's on his way, Doctor."

Doc's heart suddenly wrenched. Frankie looked as
reserved as a saint; the baby in desperate need of a
cleanup. A lump lodged in his throat, sticking in the
proximity of his Adam's apple. When his eyes drifted
over Frankie again, he felt downright powerless. Not
a day went by that he hadn't thought about their lovemaking. Suddenly he was remembering all the love
that helped them make this beautiful, precious baby.

He couldn't tell her how he felt; instead he settled
on something innocuous. "You cut your hair."
Something in her eyes softened. He could see her
throat work when she swallowed hard. Keeping one
hand molded gently over the baby's soft head, Doc
found Frankie's hand and squeezed. "Look here,

Frankie," he began, "so we've got a little water under the bridge—"

"A trickle."

He was thinking big—floods. Rivers. Oceans.

She merely stared up at him with those devastating dark eyes and waited.

"I want to talk, Frankie. I know we'll work something out."

Her breath caught, with what might have been hope or even anticipation. But what she said was "It's *been* worked out."

Nearby, someone grabbed Doc. Real anger welled in him. Someone was asking him to be a doctor again. And he wasn't Frankie's doctor. He never would be. He'd been her lover, and they'd made this baby. Let someone else check monitors and administer medicine. Right now, he was just a simple man who had a heartfelt need to talk to this woman. Because the message was starting to sink in—Frankie hadn't called him. She hadn't let him know about the pregnancy. She didn't want him in her life.

"Doctor?"

Not even the sight of his darling child could completely temper his sudden spurt of emotion. "What?"

"Dr. Krill and his team are here now."

Krill? For a second, Doc's mind didn't catch up. Just as he became aware of newcomers eddying around him, he realized Frankie's bravado was starting to give way. Her lower lip trembled. Tears pooled in the glossy black eyes that always made him feel too much. And then, in spite of the fact that she professed not to need his help, she looked at him for support. "The baby's really okay?"

The sudden trust in her eyes filled Doc. He knew

he made her feel safe. He squeezed her hand again. "Oh, yes, baby doll," he said, relief flooding him. Maybe she was just scared, he decided. She could be moody, even sling accusations if she wanted to. Doc sure wouldn't contradict her. Not after she'd given birth.

Her voice trembled. "I've had a very hard day."

It was the greatest understatement he'd ever heard. His chest ached. Two minutes around this woman, and he was tangled in knots. "Of course you have," he soothed. "Why, doll, I should have my head examined for even thinking of my own feelings at a time like this. Yes, we don't need me—a mere pediatrician—we need a psychiatrist. I'm so sorry. I'm just surprised. And the baby—" He forced himself to say it for Frankie's sake. "Astrid. It's a great name. And she's…" There were no words. "Beautiful," he said, for what had to be the umpteenth time.

A little smile lifted Frankie's lips.

"She really is." He could only hope he was warming whatever chilly waters had been eddying around Frankie's heart. "Already a mover and a shaker, too. Just look at the way she squirms." He bent even farther over the side rail of the moving gurney, closer to Frankie. "But why didn't you call?"

"I couldn't."

Was there another man in the picture? Maybe so, because Frankie's eyes said things between the two— make that three—of them weren't going to be simple.

Suddenly, someone edged Doc aside. The swinging double doors to the new wing opened—the gurney slid through, and then a young member of Krill's team grabbed Doc by the upper arm. "I know you're the doctor who delivered," he said. "Nevertheless, this is a very special case and we absolutely cannot bring you farther.''

Damn right it was a special case. "That's my baby.''

The doctor—a fortyish blond man in a lab coat—was firm. "We know you delivered Ms. Luccetti's baby.''

"No, it's *my* baby.''

Krill's assistant merely looked confused. "You're her husband? She got married?''

No, he hadn't married her. Shoot, he hadn't even called her.

Guilt rushed in on Doc. He hardly felt proud of getting Frankie pregnant, given her medical history. Oh, he'd been careful, but not nearly as careful as he should have been. He remembered the sinful way he'd covered her body with his, staying so deep inside her for so long while his erection slowly softened, how he'd breathed the natural, heady fragrant oils of her skin and the musk of her hair. Wild horses couldn't have dragged him away from Frankie. He swallowed hard.

"I'm the father of the baby,'' Doc explained, considering simply pushing past the man. "I need to make sure Frankie remains stable. That the baby's—''

"Unless you're immediate family, you have to wait out here.''

With that, the assistant nodded meaningfully at a security guard to keep an eye on Doc. And then he shut the door. As the swinging door flapped on its hinges, Doc felt as if he'd become a patient, not a doctor, that he was being shut out of his own domain. He wondered if he'd entered the Twilight Zone.

When he glanced back down the long corridor, he

decided he probably had. Because a mob of what looked to be hysterical, gesticulating Italians were charging toward him, which could mean only one thing—he was about to meet Astrid's extended family.

Chapter Five

Only seventeen people showed up, which was hardly a crowd if you were Italian, and everybody squeezed inside the hospital room feeling as comfortable as sardines. Widowed Grandma Benedetta had come. And Papa Giovanni, but only in spirit, God rest his soul. Then Grandpa Alberto and Grandma Arabella—Frankie's father's side. And four uncles—Big Sal, Giuseppe, Mario and Happy Paulie, as well as aunts Sophia, Christina, Andrea and Carlotta—Frankie's mother's side. Frankie's four brothers were there, exuding seething, dark-eyed machismo, and, last but not least, came their father and mother, Primo and Mama Carmella.

"The first grandchild!" Aunt Sophia kept exclaiming, rolling her huge dark eyes heavenward and shaking her hands in the air. "And only seventeen people are here to welcome her into this world!"

This low turnout was the biggest Luccetti family tragedy since Uncle Big Sal lost all his money on the horse races. However, all was not lost. The remaining Luccettis had rescheduled their flights and were now on their way, posthaste, from Sicily.

As a knock sounded at the door, Aunt Sophia shook

her head ruefully for the umpteenth time. "Who could have predicted this baby would come early and that the Sicilian relatives wouldn't be here yet?"

Frankie stiffened at the sound of the knock. *Please don't let it be Doc. Not now.* She had no more experience with men than she'd had eight and a half months ago, so Frankie had no clue about how to deal with him, since he'd rejected her. Outside, she'd still felt numb and in shock. On one level, she was secretly glad Doc had materialized. She'd been so terrified in the cab, and she'd needed his touch and voice to make her feel safe, especially when he'd said the cord was around Astrid's neck. It was the scariest moment of Frankie's life, even worse than her transplant surgery.

After the delivery, it was all Frankie could do to harden her heart and brace herself against that deep, thick rumbling drawl and constant patter of love talk that, in spite of her tired, wrung-out and yet elated maternal state, had only served to remind her of the crushing love she felt for him.

She was just lucky he hadn't come to the room. At least not yet. The woman at the door was a nurse. "Ten more minutes, Ms. Luccetti. I'm sorry, but then I'll have to come back for the baby. We need to run some tests and administer shots."

Frankie nodded, the lace collar of her full-length, high-necked white gown scratching her chin. While Aunt Sophia had exclaimed the gown looked "sinfully expensive," which it was, everybody knew it was the only suitable attire for a new Luccetti mother. Astrid was also now cleaned up and dressed for show, in a hand-stitched pink gown that was twice her length. As Frankie looked at her, all her aches and pains vanished. She was barely aware of her cramps and stitches, or of how tired she felt. No, her plans to adopt hadn't gone through, but Frankie had gotten a beautiful daughter all the same. Other people had cared for Frankie her entire life, but now she could give that nurturing back. More than anything, that desire to love and mother filled her as she held Astrid.

She and the baby cuddled deeper into countless pillows—some gifts from her relatives, some compliments of the women from Saint Anthony's Church, where Frankie attended mass and where Astrid would soon be baptized. Frankie sent her daughter a soft smile. "I'm your mama," she whispered, barely aware of the crowded room, long accustomed, through her illness, to having chattering people mill around her bedside. She didn't notice the white tabs on her chest, either, or the lines leading to various monitors, all of which attested to her stable condition.

She felt so swollen with love—sore and tired, relieved and well. She trailed kisses on Astrid's head, her lips brushing the skullcap. Astrid had been born with a stork bite, a tiny pink strawberry-shaped mark on her forehead that turned redder when she cried, and which Frankie had been told would go away in a few days. Now Frankie's fingers gently traced it, then crept beneath the cap to touch Astrid's soft black strands of hair. While she said a prayer for her own health and the baby's, she watched Astrid's tiny chest rise and fall with each breath.

"We made it, Astrid," Frankie whispered softly on a rush of relief. She'd given birth prematurely in a cab, and yet there had been no complications so far. Surely God was on their side. He'd never take Frankie this far, never give her a new heart, a healthy baby and so much hope—only to let her drop.

Fortunately, Winston "Doc" Holiday wasn't fitting into the divine scheme of things. Dr. Krill's assistant shut him out; that was a positive sign, wasn't it? Frankie was glad, too. And now, with her family here, she and the baby were completely protected. When Doc showed up, her family would toss him out on his ear when they figured out he was Astrid's daddy.

In fact, her highly protective brothers might even kill Doc while defending her honor. She tried to tell herself it was a pleasing thought. No, Frankie decided. There was no way an overgrown cowboy could pass muster with the New York branch of the Luccettis. With the Sicilians, he didn't have a prayer.

Frankie's frown deepened into a scowl. But why was Doc working at the hospital when he was supposed to be at Big Apple Babies? The second she'd seen him crouch beside the cab, she'd ducked and hidden her face. Childbirth was painful and scary enough without the delivering doctor being the same one to whom you'd given your virginity, who'd gotten you pregnant and then rejected you.

Helping Astrid sprawl more comfortably on her chest, Frankie whispered, "Yes, that cowboy's got some nerve, doesn't he?" He would hardly be supportive of Frankie having Astrid. Not when the last time Frankie saw him, he'd declared her unfit for motherhood. Not when, on the very day of Astrid's conception, he'd rejected Frankie's application to adopt a baby.

"C'mon, Astrid," she whispered, "let's work up a good head of steam, so we can defend ourselves." After all, given his intrusive personality, it was only a matter of time until the man arrived. Frankie didn't know what was taking him so long. "But don't worry, I won't give into his charms." Not this time. Oh, no. Not after the way he'd seduced her, instead of doing the job Big Apple Babies had sent him to do. How unprofessional of him! Frankie suddenly fumed. How crass! How *male!* Outside, had he really asked why she hadn't called him? As if she actually would, after what happened.

In spite of her righteous mental ruminations, Frankie suddenly swallowed hard. Because, in reality, she would have called.

In her life, opportunities for love had simply been too far and few between. Even now, as much as she'd prefer to deny it, she knew *she'd* really seduced *him.* She was still dreaming of being with him, too. Oh, she'd probably never make love again, not to him or anyone else, no matter how much she craved a man's vital flesh when he held her naked, covering her body with the power and weight of all those shared emotions. But Frankie could—and did—fantasize.

Frequently, she'd visualized the taut skin of Doc's muscular torso, the great power in his legs. As her body filled out during her pregnancy, she'd shut her eyes, imagining Doc's huge hands gently cupping the undersides of her breasts while his tongue soothed the hurting nipples. His hands would stroke her, playing a lullaby on her skin, strumming her to sleep. She'd often dream in a haze of half wake, half sleep, until the sensations were so real that she could swear Doc was really beside her. Yes, since their coupling, Frankie had thought of doing things with Winston "Doc" Holiday that she'd very definitely never read about in her romance novels, things that didn't exist anywhere but in her own, very fertile imagination.

Of course, her imagination hadn't been all that was

fertile, she thought, dropping another string of kisses onto Astrid. And heaven, if Father Gianetti at Saint Anthony's had guessed at Frankie's thoughts, he wouldn't recommend any more Hail Marys and Our Fathers. He'd simply send Frankie overseas, to become a full-time missionary. So, she reasoned, it was a very good thing she'd gotten pregnant.

Otherwise, she would have broken down and called Doc. She would have humiliated herself, forgetting both her pride and the note Doc left. If the truth be told, she'd probably risk such a sin again, just to feel the way she had in Doc's arms.

But she wasn't about to be led into temptation after she found out she was pregnant. Not after Doc had left that awful letter, rejecting her. Not when there was nothing—nor could there ever be—real between them. No, she'd have to content herself with the fantasy of Doc. Besides, there were already plenty of tough, overly protective male Luccettis ready to dote on Astrid, so the baby hardly needed a daddy.

And Frankie knew the score. Sex with Doc had been just that—sex. It was dumb luck, a fluke. Doc was movie-star handsome. Successful, healthy, experienced with women. He was out of her league. To him, she'd been a loser. With no career, no boyfriend. No hopes of a husband. Just a woman who'd desperately wanted a child.

He'd given her one, too. "Oh, Astrid," Frankie murmured, feeling panicky, nuzzling her daughter's cheek. "What are we going to do?"

"Frankie?"

She glanced up—and right into those pale silver-blue eyes that always made her blood rush faster. Doc's lips—cool, firm lips that Frankie well remembered warming to her own—were curled in what wasn't really a smile, and he tapped the brim of his bone white Stetson hat, staring at Astrid in a proprietary way. Darn it, the cowboy's gaze was so searing and hot on Astrid that it could have been a brand.

"Ah!" Mama Luccetti cried, swiftly pulling Doc into the center of the room. "A doctor!"

Now, this was the last thing Frankie expected. But seeing his lab coat and the stethoscope around his neck, her mother naturally assumed he was a physician on Doctor Krill's team. *And if he has any sense,* she thought, *he'll leave before I announce he's Astrid's father.*

Awareness crossed Mama Luccetti's features. "Ah! Are you the one who delivered the baby? Our very first grandchild? In the cab?"

"Yes, ma'am, but that's not why—"

Before he could finish, Doc was swallowed up by the sea of dark suits and dresses her family favored. A pastry box appeared, and Mama Luccetti withdrew a hot-dog-size *cannoli.* Thrusting it toward Doc, she cried, "Here, *mangia! Mangia!*" Eat, eat!

Doc's drawl was so sugary-thick that all Frankie truly understood was its ability to still send a slow shiver of arousal through her. She thought he said, "No, thank you, ma'am, I've eaten."

It was his first mistake.

Frankie guessed it could have been worse; the sweet-talking cowboy could have called her mother "baby doll." She nestled farther back in the bed with Astrid to watch the goings-on, since at this rate, Doc would dig his own grave soon enough. Frankie wouldn't have to utter a word. If she'd been trying to help him out—which she definitely was not—she would have advised him to swallow the pastry whole, then demand a second. Among Luccettis, refusing Mama's food was a capital offense; it was even worse than breaking some commandments.

"He didn't eat," Mama Luccetti said, sounding thoroughly unnerved.

"Papa Giovanni," said Aunt Sophia. "God rest his soul. *He* would have eaten it, Carmella. And he loved your *ravioli*."

"Papa loved to eat," came Uncle Big Sal's support.

"Ah," sighed the four aunts, crossing themselves. "Papa Giovanni. Such a man!"

Frankie had to fight not to smirk as Doc's features dawned with awareness. Oh, it was terrible, but Frankie was taking real pleasure in this. Before, Doc was so cocksure. But now he was completely out of his element—a huge, strapping cowboy dressed in a white lab coat and plunked down in a sea of short, dark Italians dressed in black. The lab coat made him look like a white whale among minnows. A tall white birch among plump round blackberry bushes.

It was a sight to behold.

If Frankie hadn't been cradling Astrid, she would have clapped with delight. Oh, she sure bet Doc wished he'd eaten that *cannoli* now.

Unfortunately, as he edged toward her bed, her confidence slipped away. So did her eyes. She just couldn't bear to look at him. She reached up with her free hand and toyed with the cross she wore around her neck. Maybe it was only wishful thinking, but she could swear his gaze lingered on her hair, and she wondered if he was remembering how he'd once smoothed the strands, brushing them across his naked thighs. She fought the urge to lift a vain hand and fiddle with her new short, curly hairdo. Did he like it? The back of her throat went painfully dry.

"Frankie," he said softly, pressing the bedside button without asking her permission and moving the mattress so her feet were raised. "We really need to talk."

Shifting Astrid in her arms, Frankie pressed the button, lowering her legs again.

He put them back up. "You should be elevated."

She knew that, but she could see better with her legs down and she was peeved by how he took charge of her and the baby, as if she needed him—or anyone—to take care of her. Between her prone position and his breathtakingly broad frame, Doc was towering over her, so she blew out a sigh and left her legs where they were. He looked like a giant as she stared up at him. Her hold on Astrid tightened and she stared protectively at the baby. She was so small, her wrinkled face splotchy, her tiny eyes shut.

"Aren't you going to say anything, doll?"

Doc was a good foot away, but the low huskiness of his voice seemed to whisper on Frankie's neck. She tried fixing her gaze at a point over his shoulder, but it wound up drifting over the golden licks of silk curls that glinted with red and spilled from beneath Doc's western hat. *Say something, Frankie,* she thought nervously. *Take the upper hand or you're doomed.*

"Please—" He glanced around at her relatives. "Can we have some time alone? It's personal."

"Alone?" Mama Luccetti echoed. "Personal?"

Even when Uncle Big Sal lost all his money on the horse races, no one had ever asked to be alone. To a

Luccetti, asking to be alone was even worse than refusing Mama's cooking. Wanting to be alone could mean only one thing—that a man had things he couldn't share with the family on his mind. And that meant sin.

Mistake number two, Frankie thought.

Sensing he'd said something wrong, Doc glanced cautiously around, sizing up the group—and Frankie's mood improved another fraction. Yes, as soon as they found out who he was, Doc was in big trouble. Still, she wished her family wasn't getting so quiet, clearly sensing the unmistakably fiery energy coursing between her and Doc. That was another rule: Quiet Luccettis were dangerous Luccettis.

"I think you'd better go," Frankie warned.

"I'm not leaving until we talk."

Well, she thought, glancing around the room. She was only trying to save his life. Apparently, she had no choice: she'd have to turn Doc over to her family—and let them rip him apart. Because, if the truth be told, she couldn't do it herself. These lonely months had nearly killed her. Every day, as much as she was loathe to admit it, she'd hoped and prayed this fantasy man would call. She'd dreamed that they were married, a family with a new baby. She didn't even know him, really, but she'd started loving him the day they'd met. And then, like a fool, she'd never stopped.

"Doc..." she began.

"Doc!" Mama Luccetti gasped. "This is *Doc?*"

"Not Doc-damn-his-soul-to-hell?" whispered Aunt Sophia in shock. "Not *that* Doc."

"Yes," said Frankie. "*That* Doc."

Aunt Sophia continued, "The Doc who..."

Took our sweet angel Francesca's virginity?

The words hung in the air. The brothers stepped forward, looking murderous. The aunts crossed themselves. And Frankie sighed with relief, nestling back with Astrid again as the room exploded in angry Italian.

Doc, of course, had no idea what anyone was saying.

Thrusting her hands into the pockets of her roomy black cardigan, Mama Luccetti withdrew Doc's note. She always carried it. The yellow legal sheet had been opened and refolded so many times it was limp. Everybody in the neighborhood had read and analyzed its contents. Frankie's youngest brother, Vinny, had even faxed a translation to Sicily.

Doc squinted at the paper, taking in his own signature. Then he stared at Frankie. "That lady read my note?"

This was too good to be true. "That 'lady' is my mother—" Frankie was pleased her tone sounded regal "—Carmella Luccetti."

Doc looked faintly exasperated. "Pleased to meet you, Carmella."

The room went dead silent again. Mistake number three, thought Frankie with satisfaction.

"Mrs. Luccetti," Doc swiftly corrected himself.

But, of course, it was too late. Her family already thought Doc was disrespectful of his elders. Frankie continued, "Of course my mother read the note. I share everything with my family."

Doc had no chance to respond because Mama Luccetti began cursing him in Italian. She cursed his family, his family's family, and then, forgetting he was Astrid's daddy—if only technically—she even cursed his children. Long used to passionately volatile Luccetti tirades, Frankie merely dipped another loving kiss onto Astrid's wispy dark eyebrow. Astrid, a born Luccetti, ignored all the yelling and slept on peacefully.

Frankie sighed. Actually, she hadn't shared Doc's note with her family. As happy as they were about the baby now, they'd been devastated by the pregnancy. When Frankie refused to name the father, this entire group of relatives had arrived en masse at her apartment to search. The DEA looking for illegal drugs could not have been more thorough than the Luccettis while they snooped for clues leading to the man who had made Frankie pregnant.

Uncle Guiseppe had even emptied a box of laundry detergent. While Frankie's brothers had searched drawers, vowing swift and bloody vengeance, Aunt Sophia had wrung her hands, exclaiming, "No man— no *real* man—would do this to our sweet angel, Francesca. That man has to be a dog! A *dog!*"

Mama Luccetti, in her infinite wisdom, had found Doc's note neatly folded under Frankie's pillow.

"Mama," Frankie said now.

But Mama Luccetti wasn't anywhere near finished cursing Doc. In her tightly closed fist, which she now shook in his face, she still held the crumpled legal paper. Suddenly, as if only now noticing Doc's seemingly stupefied expression, she gasped. "Isn't he even Italian?" she asked in English, staring around the room. "I curse him for ten minutes and he doesn't even understand!"

"Not Italian?" Aunt Sophia dropped into a seat, her olive skin turning starchy white.

Uncle Big Sal clapped a hand to his forehead. "Our

sweet Francesca sleeps with a man and he's not even Italian?" He stared at Frankie in disbelief, for confirmation.

Frankie winced. "He's from Texas, I think."

"You're sure he's not just northern Italian?" asked her father, Primo. "Up north, they're blond."

"Papa Giovanni, God rest his soul," interjected Aunt Sophia hopefully. "He was blond."

Doc's face had taken on a murderously calm expression. When his eyes met Frankie's, they carried a warning: she was going to pay for putting him through the ringer with her family.

Doc glanced around the room. "I am from Texas. Anybody here got a problem with Texas?"

Apparently, all four of Frankie's brothers did. Vinny, Mickey, Eddie and Chris stepped forward—their strong white teeth flashing against olive skin, their jet black curls falling rakishly on their foreheads. Frankie felt a small rush of pleasure at having her and Astrid's honor so admirably defended.

At least until Doc stepped forward, too.

Then Frankie's eyes widened. Was Doc crazy? Didn't he know he could get himself killed? And how could he look so self-contained at a time like this? Wasn't he at all cowed?

Her eyes fell over him. How his strong shoulders strained the lab coat and how his thighs bulged beneath his jeans was enough to send a shudder through her. The taut, gold-stubbled skin that stretched over his determined jaw quivered once with an angry tick, and his eyes flashed out danger. Just looking at him made Frankie's hands start to sweat beneath Astrid's blanket. Maybe, Frankie thought, it was her four brothers she should be worrying about.

So many tears of rage now clung to Mama Luccetti's eyelashes that Frankie started to feel guilty. "Why did you try to kill my little girl?" Mama Luccetti demanded.

"Kill her?" Doc's sigh said he hadn't wanted to kill her in the past, but that, right about now, he could wring Frankie's slender neck.

"Kill her," Mama Luccetti confirmed. "All her life, my Francesca was a sick girl with a weak heart. She couldn't play with the other kids. Couldn't run. Couldn't…"

Frankie blocked out the tirade, cuddling Astrid and dipping her head again to kiss the baby. The last thing Frankie wanted reiterated was the saga of her illness. By the time her mother was done telling Doc every detail, even his skin had taken on an ashen pallor.

"And this is the sick little girl you get pregnant?" Mama finished, staring at Doc as if he were lower than an earthworm. "How could you?"

Yes, how could he? Frankie thought, momentarily swept away by the vehemence of her mother's speech. For a second, Frankie, too, damned Doc for what he'd done to her. At least until, heaven help her, she remembered she was desperately wishing he'd do it again.

"How could I?" Doc echoed softly.

"Yes, how could you?" Frankie piped in.

"It was rather easy," Doc shot back, his eyes fixed on her. To her mother, he said, "I didn't seduce anybody. In fact, if memory serves me correctly, it was quite the opposite. From what I—"

Frankie gasped. "Oh, no, you don't! Not in front of my family. You're not going to talk about—"

He merely flashed her a bemused smile that said

two could play at this game, and that he didn't much appreciate her putting him on the hot seat. "Oh, I thought you share *everything* with your family." With a lithe turn of his powerful body, he addressed her mother again. "Why, from what I remember, Mrs. Luccetti, this sick daughter of yours did not exactly feel taken advantage of."

There was a stunned, horrified silence.

Clutching Astrid, Frankie reached for the call button, in case she needed to ring for help. Her oldest brother cupped his hand around his ear. "What did you just say about my sister?"

"You heard me." Doc came forward another pace. "Come on. I'll take you on. All four of you. But I'm not leaving here without talking to Frankie. Alone."

"No man ever touched my Francesca before," warned her father, Primo.

One of Frankie's brothers spat an Italian expression.

"Oh, Astrid," Frankie murmured, waiting expectantly. She'd read about scenes like this. She wasn't proud of it, but she'd had countless fantasies where men fought over her. Usually they had a gun duel outside a dusty Western saloon. Or a sword fight near a French villa. Once, she'd even imagined a paddle fight from rafts in a castle moat. In reality, she guessed these guys were simply going to punch out one another's lights with their fists.

"Well, *I* touched her—" A slight smile played on Doc's lips. "But I sure don't—and won't—apologize for it."

Doc was taking yet *another* step forward!

Frankie clutched Astrid even closer. Then something went wrong! Frankie's brothers stepped back!

But it was Doc who was supposed to run! To feel cowed and terrified by her killer brothers!

Instead, he said, "Now, you good old boys can go ahead and kill me...." Absently touching the brim of his hat, Doc holstered a thumb through a belt loop, looking like some hired-gun renegade. "But whaddaya say, we get one thing straight?"

Frankie's whole family strained forward.

"Now, with all due respect..." Doc began.

This time, something *really* went wrong. So horribly wrong that it took Frankie a full second to figure out what it was: Doc had spoken that sentence in perfect, fluent Italian. Even worse, he casually swept his hat from his head, held it over his heart and sent a cursory nod toward her and the baby. Then he turned back to address her family, not her. Darn it. This was just the kind of respectful, gentlemanly gesture that Mama Luccetti loved. It was another family rule: court the family, not the girl.

One of Frankie's killer brothers actually sat down. Great.

Now Doc was looking at everyone *but* her. "With all due respect," he continued in that irritatingly perfect, formal Italian, "I am not sorry for the day I spent with your daughter. It was a wonderful, special day. I'm a pediatrician. A doctor. And I've always wanted children of my own. I want to know you all...to know Frankie more. To know the baby..."

Frankie had to stop him! Didn't this man understand what he was saying? Apparently, his grip on the Italian language wasn't nearly as good as it sounded. Because in the old country, this was tantamount to a marriage proposal!

Sure enough, a palpable sigh of relief sounded in the room.

Mama shrugged. "So, we call Father Gianetti. And then they get married next week."

Doc didn't seem the least bit perturbed.

"He's not going to marry me!" Frankie burst out, wondering where the fool cowboy had learned Italian and hating him for it. The only consolation was that he *had* understood Mama's curses. "He doesn't even know what he wants! He never even called me! He ran into me again by accident!" Her eyes searched the room. Didn't they know about men like him who were too sexy for their own good? Didn't they know he was completely insincere? Didn't they know he didn't want a baby? That he'd only made love to her out of pity? "Can't you all see through this man? What about that awful letter he left me?"

No one seemed to care anymore.

Wonderful. All Frankie and Astrid needed was these seventeen people wrestling Doc to the altar. The Sicilian relatives would probably threaten his life if he didn't marry her. Frankie suddenly wished she'd grown up far away from Little Italy.

Mama Luccetti sighed. "Young man, where is your family?"

"I don't have much of one. My parents died when I was young. I've got one brother here in New York, but we were raised by separate aunts who live out of state."

"Not much family?" Uncle Guiseppe leaned forward, his black bushy eyebrows furrowed in concentration. "Well, if you're not Italian, what are you?"

"American."

Everybody nodded approvingly. It was the next best thing to Italian.

"But I've traveled all over Italy," Doc assured them. "Even learned Italian."

The family nodded their approval with even more enthusiasm.

Frankie tried again. "We're not getting married! I don't even know him! He doesn't even *like* me! He never called me!"

Mama ignored her. "Young man, do you go to mass?"

Doc shook his head.

Everyone in the room gasped and made the sign of the cross on their chests, except Frankie. Right about now, she wasn't about to pray for Doc's mortal soul. No, she didn't care if Winston Holiday did happen to go to hell. Not that even his lack of faith mattered now. Frankie knew that her gullible, soft-hearted mother was still stuck back on Doc's damnable plea that he had no family. That had been the end.

"He has a family, Mama." Frankie hated the pleading tone that crept into her voice. "He told us he has a brother and two aunts."

"One brother," her mother returned curtly, throwing up her hands. "Two aunts. What kind of family is that? No wonder he won't eat!"

Frankie's father sadly shook his head. "No family. No wonder he was afraid to call our Francesca."

Frankie groaned. Doc wasn't afraid of anything. She watched as her mother now pulled Doc aside, as she did every doctor she got her hands on. She only half listened as her mother discussed the changes in Frankie. Explaining how docile Frankie had been before her transplant operation, what a good girl, how quiet. But now Frankie needed space. She'd cut off her hair, moved into her own apartment, changed her name to Frankie, and now she had a baby without a father....

"Strictly speaking," Doc drawled, kindly patting Mama's arm in assurance, "that baby does have a fa—"

"No, she doesn't! And I'm not docile anymore," Frankie quickly interjected, her voice coming out more forcibly than she intended. "I don't want any part of this man! I'm on my own now. Independent. I make my own decisions! I'm raising Astrid by myself! I don't need a man!"

Looking scandalized, the aunts crossed themselves again. Aunt Sophia murmured, "Every woman needs a man, dear."

Guiltily holding Astrid, Frankie sighed. "I love you all, but I've lived my whole life with you hovering around me, protecting me, making decisions for me. Sorry, but this is my baby. My life, my—"

"Whoa," Doc said. "Hold your horses. That's my baby, too."

And then the worst possible thing happened.

Mama Luccetti said, "He's right, Frankie." And in the Luccetti family, Mama's word was the law.

Not a moment later, Astrid was in Doc's arms. Pure panic seized Frankie. The nurse was coming soon, and she'd wanted to hold Astrid every possible second. Didn't they understand? Astrid needed to be held by her mother.

But Doc was cradling her now. Astrid settled easily on his chest, waking up and making small sighs. "I've got a way with kids," he explained to Mama Luccetti. "That's why I became a pediatrician."

"A doctor for babies," echoed Mama, as if she couldn't have planned this better herself. "My Francesca has a way with babies, too." Not about to stop there, she added, "Francesca cooks, too. Anything you like to eat, she can make."

"What?" Frankie couldn't help but mutter under her breath. "Rocky Mountain oysters with Red Dog beer?"

Frankie hated to break the news. A way with kids was probably the only thing she and Doc would ever have in common. "He's doing this on purpose," she said, sighing. He was playing her family, making her mother and aunts like him.

And what woman could resist the picture he was making now? His hat was off, the baby was in his arms, and afternoon sunlight danced in his golden hair. His lips lingered on Astrid's head, right on the stork bite, where Frankie's lips had previously been. Everything turned quiet, except for his lulling endless banter that drove Frankie crazy, making her want to hate him. And love him. That soft croon was hard to describe—holding an underlying trace of mockery, as if to say Doc knew he sounded like a darn fool, but that he couldn't care less what you thought about it.

"There now, li'l slice of sugar pie," he whispered as he smoothed Astrid's long pink dress. "Anybody ever tell you you're the prettiest girl in the world? Well, it's true. Hands down, no contest. And you've made me the proudest man...."

Frankie could only shake her head. The way he crooned was simply not to be believed. And just the sight of him tore at her. She felt as if she'd lost her child. As if the only time Astrid had really been hers alone was while she'd been in the safe haven of the womb. And now Doc looked so protectively big and Astrid so defenselessly little. The whole scene made Frankie want to cry. Her mother and all the aunts merely sighed, clasping their hands over their hearts and smiling benevolently.

"I'm your daddy, baby doll," Doc murmured now. "Yeah, I'm the Texas man who's blood-sworn to protect you."

It was really too much. Even Primo probably liked him now. Frankie's brothers and father just loved anything that had to do with being blood-sworn and protecting women.

Suddenly, Doc nodded, as if he'd finally found in Astrid's silvery blue eyes just the thing he was looking for. "That's right, little darlin'," he murmured. "I knew you'd know I was your daddy."

Frankie had never felt so betrayed. When the nurse came, Frankie barely even got to kiss Astrid goodbye.

Then Mama said, "Everybody, these two need to talk."

Frankie simply couldn't believe it. Feeling positively trapped, she watched her family file from the room. First went her brothers who had sworn bloody death and vengeance to the man who'd made her pregnant. They casually kissed Frankie's forehead and shook Doc's hand on their way out.

One by one, the aunts wished her luck, as if Frankie was actually going to use this time to make Doc agree to marry her. Aunt Sophia leaned close and whispered, "Next time, Frankie, wrap the rascal, eh?"

Frankie had absolutely no idea what she meant.

Only when she realized it was her aunt's way of telling her to use a condom in the future did Frankie turn beet red to the roots of her hair. It was the first piece of sexual advice she'd ever received from her family. And she could only hope she never got any more. Besides, she and Doc had used condoms. They just hadn't worked.

Her father, at least, shot Doc a parting, warning glare that meant no hanky-panky.

Doc was looming larger by the second. Frankie could feel those broad shoulders as surely as if they were around her, and feel the bemused tilt of his mouth, as surely as if it covered her own. She could see the suppressed passion in those eyes. Eyes that she knew grew transparent with intimacy, as if her touch pulled back the curtains on the windows to his soul.

Everything suddenly seemed to slide off kilter. She tried not to look at him, knowing he'd see her memories. Her fantasies. How every full moon since their night together had left her aching for him. She could never let him guess how much she'd dreamed about what could never be between them—marriage. A family. "Mama, you can't leave," Frankie said shakily. "I just had the baby. I'm really tired, and I'm having some pain. I've still got a line to the heart monitor—" Faintly, she realized her voice was becoming a wail. "Mama, he's a manipulator!"

Mama Luccetti merely shook her head. "I know." She threw up her hands, as if to say, But what can I possibly do? "Frankie, you're independent now. On your own. Tired of help from your family."

Frankie's lips parted in protest. How could her mother use her own words against her?

Just as Mama turned on her heel, Doc's eyes met Frankie's—and she silently damned him for looking so cool. "Mrs. Luccetti," he said, "could you please leave me that scrumptious-looking *cannoli?* Why, I do believe you misunderstood me, ma'am. I just wasn't hungry when I came in.''

Her mother was nowhere near that pastry box.

"Mangia," said her mother with a final wave of her hand. "Eat and enjoy, son.''

Son! Frankie fumed. Had her mother really called Doc son?

Those devastating silver-blue eyes had never left Frankie's. "Eat?'' Doc returned softly. "I most certainly will.''

And then Frankie was the very last place on earth she wanted to be. Alone with—and about to be gobbled up by—Winston "Doc" Holiday.

Chapter Six

"Get out," Frankie warned.

"No way, baby doll." Doc stared down at her in the bed, resettling his hat snugly on his head and feeling more relieved than he intended to let on. Not only had he gotten to hold his sweet baby girl, but he'd escaped the Luccetti clan with his life intact.

There were some things in life an honorable Texas man simply had to accept—strange names such as Astrid and in-laws being two of them.

In-laws?

Where had that come from? Oh, Doc knew her relatives thought he'd all but proposed to Frankie, but he assured himself he was just buying time. Which he had. If Mama Luccetti had a say, Doc guessed he'd have all the time in the world to talk about the baby with Frankie—even though marriage was out of the question.

Not that the mother of his child didn't look good enough to marry. Now that Doc wasn't busy keeping Frankie's brothers from killing him, he could give her all his attention. After all the discomfort she'd caused him with her family, he hardly cared that his gaze was unsettling her and making her squirm.

"What *are* you looking at?" she fumed.

"You."

He fought not to add some yummy sounds—mmm, mmm, mmm. Oh, he knew she was a real pistol—naive and more than a little prickly—and he had to treat her with kid gloves. Especially since, before he left this room, he intended to reach some understanding about their child. But how had he ever remembered this lovely woman, the mother of his darling little daughter, as plain?

In her high-necked white lace gown, with the tiny gold cross at her throat, she looked so demurely maternal that it brought out the protective male in him. Her face, fuller since her pregnancy, was framed by short dark curls that rested on a peaches-and-cream complexion. Oh, Doc missed her long hair, but then, a man could still have his fantasies. Besides, this style made her look more mature. And she had breasts now. Through the lace, he could glimpse the tops of sweet full mounds. His gaze dropped over the sloping curve of her belly, her rounded hips. And Doc suppressed a rumbling, chesty moan. Suddenly, it seemed an eternity since he and Frankie had shared her white ruffly bed on Mott Street.

He remembered how his libido had deserted him after Marta's death, how last year, a woman could have danced naked on his bare chest and he simply would have dozed. Then Frankie changed all that, making him feel like a man again. A healthy, hot-blooded man who'd desperately wanted a woman to hold. Who'd wanted *her*.

And who wanted her right now.

"What?" She sighed. "Are you going to stand there all day, just staring at me?"

"I could," Doc shot back, tipping his hat. "'Cause I can't tell a lie. You look really good to me, Frankie."

She tried—and failed—to look nonchalant, Doc was pleased to note. Then she sized him up, as if he was her sworn enemy, instead of her one-and-only ex-lover with whom she'd cuddled, spoon-fashion. From the wary look in her eyes, Frankie hadn't forgotten the sweet lovin' that had made their baby any more than he had.

She arched an eyebrow. "So, I look good, huh?" she said, as if the very idea bored her to tears.

"Yeah."

Doc was sorely tempted to tell Frankie just how good. She was glowing. Her skin's delicate scent was arousing him even now, and his fingers held memories, as surely as his mind—of touching her silk hair under the light of the moon. He imagined molding his palm around her head and smoothing the short dark curls, then guiding her sweet lips to his chest....

He realized his heart was hammering. His mouth was dry. Months had passed, but she still had a powerful hold on Doc. No, the baby wasn't the only reason he felt so tangled-up. Frankie Luccetti confused him plenty, all by her sweet, naive little lonesome.

Right about now, she was making him feel like a Texas bronco rider. Or the riled bull to her red flag. Now that they'd met again, there was no turning back. Maybe he didn't want marriage, but there was no denying he wanted her as badly as he had the day they'd met. And he wanted his baby girl. Turning abruptly on his heel, Doc headed to the door, closed it, then returned.

"Doc," she warned, "you'd better open that door."

She had some nerve, telling him what to do after all he'd been through. After delivering his own child, he'd had to fight through Krill's team of egotistical surgeons and then her family—and all so he could simply hold his own daughter. His voice was soft, like water flowing over smooth rocks. "I don't want any interruptions."

"What are you doing at the hospital, anyway? I thought you worked for Big Apple Babies."

Doc shrugged. "It's a long story, doll." Not that he was going to explain.

"Well then, exactly what do you want?"

Where should he begin? If Frankie guessed even half of the wants Doc had conjured in his fantasies over these last months, she'd flee into the hospital hallway. "You know I came here to talk about Astrid. But—" he shot her a quick smile "—if you want to talk about our relationship, that's fine."

"We have no relationship."

"That so?" Without another word, Doc lay down on the bed, casually stretching out his big body right next to hers, crossing his cowboy boots so they hung off the edge. Rolling to his elbow, he faced her. He had to fight not to lay a soothing hand on her belly, knowing how much she must hurt. "Since there's no you and me," he began, feeling powerless but to come another careful inch closer, "we'd better start talking about Astrid. Now, if I read your mama correctly, darlin', I'll be welcome to visit that sweet baby girl of mine any time I want."

"You might win over my family," she shot back,

"but you're sure digging yourself into a foxhole with me—"

"Foxhole? Is this some kind of war?"

"It most certainly is. I mean to fight, since I don't want you in this room or in my and Astrid's lives."

He reached for her wrist, and ignored the shock when his fingers felt her creamy skin and rapid pulse. "From a strictly professional point of view, I'd say that, given the wild way your pulse is racing, you're not telling me the truth." The comment angered her, and her eyes turned so furiously brilliant they dazzled him. He dropped her wrist, as if the contact hadn't sent his own heart rate skyrocketing.

"I never wanted to see you again, Doc."

"That's a little harsh. Can't we compromise, doll?"

"And I'm not your doll." She crossed her arms over her chest, the tempo and pitch of her voice rising. "Just so you know, I hate how you fling around words such as that. You don't mean them."

Maybe not. But Frankie only pretended not to like it. Her flushed cheeks told him so. "Nine months ago, I distinctly remember your saying you didn't mind."

"You've got quite a memory."

He flashed her a quick smile that would have been flirtatious in other circumstances. "It's photographic—and I meant every word," Doc defended smoothly. "At least when it comes to you and our beautiful baby girl."

Frankie's lower lip looked pouty. Decidedly kissable. "I'm trapped in this bed, Doc. Need I remind you, I just gave birth? And I don't want to talk. So, why can't you simply be a gentleman and leave me alone?"

He couldn't help the lazy huskiness that tinged his words. "No gentleman would leave a woman who looked like you alone."

"As if you are a gentleman." No, he was capable of stripping away both his and her civility, right along with their clothes. As if remembering that well, Frankie drew in a quavering breath.

"Am I making you nervous, sugar plum?"

"Of course not," she said mildly.

But he was.

"You know, Frankie…" His voice lowered, as did the gaze he licked down her body, and when his silver-blue eyes returned to hers, the look was candidly frank. "You liked my way of talking before. I seem to remember an afternoon, the very afternoon our daughter was conceived, in fact. I remember the sunlight on your lips and eyes, and your hair spillin' over the pillow. And later when the moon rose…"

Doc's voice trailed off; he simply couldn't talk anymore. What kind of craziness was he saying? Drawing in a sharp breath, he remembered this exasperating, impossible woman embracing him, while he nuzzled love words in the midnight strands of her hair. She'd been so soft and sweet, clinging to his arms, that he'd been swept away by the sheer beauty of her. It might have been right at that moment that Astrid was conceived…. Maybe the baby was named right, after all. Because it was as if some strange convergence of the stars had brought Doc and Frankie together that day.

She'd turned bright red. "Don't remind me of that day."

Right about now, Doc could think of little else. "Don't remind you?" His drawl had thickened, not only with memories now, but with anger over the way she was shutting him out.

"It's just something that happened, Doc." She sounded faint. "Please. Let's forget about it."

Why? So you can raise our baby alone, forgetting all about me? Are you crazy, woman? Doc inched a breath closer and Frankie sank farther back into the pillows. "I'm beginning to think you're seriously deranged," he murmured. "And don't you dare turn into a shrinking violet," he added in warning. "'Cause we both know you're anything but."

"I'm a lady," Frankie announced coolly.

"Yeah. And I had your teeth marks on my left shoulder for days, just to prove it."

She primly clutched the collar of her gown. "You most certainly did not!"

"Sorry, baby doll. But your dentist could have taken a cast from my bare back and fitted you for dentures."

There was a very long, very strained silence.

She pursed her lips, glancing longingly at the monitors to which she was attached. But she was trapped—and obviously none too happy about it. "Look, Doc—" her voice became suspiciously even "—because of my long illness, I haven't had many opportunities to explore my life and find myself. But things are very different now. Oh, I know you were the first man I ever slept with. And you certainly won't be the last. However, I do want you to know that day we spent together meant something very special to me. I simply cannot stress that point enough. After all, I *was* a virgin. But let's face it, Doc," she concluded, "it *was* just a night."

Judging from her practiced tone, she'd rehearsed

that sweet speech a million times, in case she ever saw him again. He didn't know why he was torturing himself, letting her rile him like this, but he prodded, "Just a night?"

She nodded, pleased he was getting the picture. "That and nothing more."

Maybe he'd have let it go. But while she was parroting those well-rehearsed lines in that prim tone that was driving him to distraction, she'd somehow forgotten to mention their daughter. "Oh?" He was unable to keep the irony from stitching through his words, lacing them tight. "Would you really like to forget?"

"Yes, indeed I would."

"Hmm. *Indeed.* And I had you pegged for an honest woman, Frankie."

"I said I want you out of my life!" she exploded. "That's as honest as it gets!"

"But you're not telling me why. Most women I've ever met would be happy to find that the father of their baby is willing to negotiate support. Especially if he made a doctor's wages. And especially if she herself isn't even employed."

"Who said I'm not employed?"

"Are you?"

Frankie tossed her head of dark curls, inhaled deeply and stared studiously at the ceiling, as if enduring Doc's insufferable presence only because she'd exhausted all other possible options. "I think it's more appropriate for me to stay home with the baby, don't you?"

"You know—" He squinted at her, coming close enough that he could feel her breath. "I was glad to see you, Frankie. But now I'm gonna lay it on the line. You have no right to shut me out. Keeping a man from his flesh and blood may not be a capital offense, but in my book, it sure comes close." She turned slowly toward him, her darker eyes fixing on his paler ones, like two dark, glossy flies alighting on honey.

"Oh," she said dryly, with a hint of a smile. "I heard. You're a Texas man, blood-sworn to protect your women." Doc watched in fascination as she actually feigned a yawn by tapping her palm over her lips. "Why, Doc," she said, with a slight hint of a drawl he felt sure was meant to mimic his own, "for a minute, you sounded just like my father."

"Texas and Italy might be worlds apart. But when it comes to a man's responsibilities toward women and children, I daresay your papa and I probably *do* see eye to eye."

At that, she dropped all pretenses and merely looked appalled. "I can't believe somebody actually gave you a medical degree."

"I'm sure Columbia University knew what they were doing."

Ignoring him, she plowed on. "Don't they educate chauvinism out of men in medical school? Didn't you at least get sensitivity training?"

"Must have missed class that day."

Actually, Doc was starting to feel quite sensitive. Especially when he adjusted her monitor's line; he caught a whiff of her sweetly scented hair and considered kissing her, even though he was sore at her. Maybe *because* he was sore—and he knew a kiss would knock her off balance. He wasn't proud of wanting to pull the rug out from under a new mama. But he'd about had it; doctors were people, too. So were new daddies. "C'mon, Frankie. You owe me an explanation about why you're shutting me out."

"For one, I can't forgive you."

"What did I do?"

Her eyes widened. "You broke up with me!"

He wanted to say that breaking up was something else—it was screaming, throwing pots, smashing glass objects. Breaking up implied a previously stable relationship. It wasn't two neatly penned paragraphs on a sheet of legal paper left on a card table after a one-night stand. Instead, he wisely said, "That was before the baby."

"You came here to see the baby, not me. So, go look at her!"

Instead, Doc reached and threaded his fingers through Frankie's. "I knew the note might hurt you a little," he admitted, squeezing her hand. "But I thought it was best, Frankie. I didn't think we..."

Her expression was distant. "Were a suitable couple?"

No, he hadn't. But he didn't want to say it now. This woman sure got under his skin like a chigger and gnawed. He felt annoyed. Exasperated beyond reason. Not to mention seriously misunderstood. "I told you. I didn't want to get involved because my fiancée died."

She didn't give an inch. She merely glared at him, their eyes a fraction apart, her breath warming his lips. "How am I supposed to take that? That you're disinclined to date a woman who's had health problems? Afraid another woman might up and die on you, Doc?"

He couldn't believe she'd said it. "Frankie, you are cruel."

She shot him a saccharine smile. "Believe me, right now I'm certainly trying."

"I'm starting to notice just exactly how you operate, Frankie Luccetti."

Unfortunately, with Frankie's hand in his, Doc was noticing some sinfully wicked stirrings, too. Or maybe it was just as well, since they were helping him block out what she'd just said to him. He knew it was true. He never wanted to lose another woman he loved. He heard Dani Lucas's voice in his mind. *Join the living, Doc. Marta's gone. It's time to find yourself a woman.* "My fiancée died," he said again. "Have a heart."

"I've already had two hearts in my lifetime." Frankie shot him a droll glance. "I don't need a third, thank you very much."

Something inside his own hardened. "As unreasonable as you're being right now, I think maybe you *could* use a third heart. A softer, kinder one."

He watched her swallow that down. "No doubt your family tiptoes around you," he continued, against his better judgment. "But don't you forget, I'm a smart man, Frankie Luccetti. I watched how you sat back, tossing me to the wolves. Apparently, when it suits you, you play poor, sick Frankie. When it doesn't, you're independent and on your own."

Her wary expression said she knew he had her number, and something inside him flickered in response, unsettling him on an even deeper level. Hell, Doc had known people for years without so honestly pointing out their character flaws. But somehow, he couldn't let this woman go—not physically, or now, it seemed, emotionally. He didn't know why. Maybe it was pride. But he wasn't about to let her play her standard games with him.

She eyed him warily. "Were you trying to make a point?"

"Yeah, when we argue, don't throw your illness in my face. I'm a doctor, so it doesn't work on me." The next words came almost against Doc's will. "Besides, the way I know you is as a *woman,* not as a sick little girl. With me, you can't have it both ways."

"Good. Because I don't want it at all."

The feigned indifference in her tone sent him to his limit. "One thing's for certain. You're definitely not a simple woman to deal with."

Her luminous eyes were dark as coals now. She knew she was getting to him, and he could swear she was loving every minute of it. Her voice suddenly became a soft taunt. "So, is that the kind of women you like, Doc? Simpletons?"

It was too much for him. The next thing he knew his hands were thrust deep into her hair; the jet black strands felt fluid, like ink gushing through his fingers, and with that ink, Doc swore he could write out every other blessed thing he wanted to do with the rest of her body.

There was a breath. Just a moment when he stayed a fraction away, with his hungry, aching lips nearly touching hers. Staring into her eyes. Hers staring back. Both of them suddenly panting softly in the silence, breath mingling.

"Baby doll," Doc whispered, "I'm warning you. You were always a woman to me, no little girl. And I play a grown man's game."

"I hope you're prepared to lose."

Her shining eyes didn't hold half the confidence of

her words. His throaty answering chuckle was swift. "Rest assured, I play to win." And then his warm, plundering mouth simply descended. Already, as his tongue dipped, he knew she wouldn't fight, that she was rendered as powerless by their attraction as he. And when her tongue struck against his, like match to flint, his mind sparked with images, and he knew he'd starred in some of her wilder dreams.

His hat tumbled off, and when her fingers threaded through his hair, Doc figured she'd suffered the way he had, fending off restless nights when the sheets stayed damp and hot, no matter how she tossed and turned. Maybe she'd even lain in bed, the phone resting on a belly ripe with his child, her hand on the receiver, unable to swallow her pride, unable to forget his letter.

As if in proof, she emitted a soft sigh.

Right before his lips captured hers again, he whispered, "I've thought about kissing you for months, Fran—" He almost managed to speak her name, but it was lost in another deep kiss of lovers coming home to nest. He inhaled—a breath meant to lasso in her scent—and he suddenly felt his head spin, his heart hammer.

The door flung open. "Doctor! Doctor!"

Doc wrenched around, feeling stunned and dazed.

The nurse looked uncertain. "The call button?"

Doc's eyes shot to Frankie's hand. She'd hugged him so hard that she'd pressed the button. It brought a bemused smile to his lips. So did the graph on Frankie's heart monitor, which indicated she was every bit as excited as he.

Chuckling softly, Doc calmly explained, "I dropped my pen on Ms. Luccetti's bed, nurse. Unfortunately, when I leaned to get it, I slipped and fell. Oh, how clumsy of me. But Ms. Luccetti, well, she had the call button in her hand...."

"Right," the nurse murmured, blushing furiously and not believing a word.

The second she ducked out, Doc turned to Frankie again. "Are you all right? I didn't hurt you, did I?" He pressed his hand very lightly on her belly, imparting warmth and comfort.

"Of course not." In spite of a smile she couldn't quite hide, she brushed two slender fingers over her glistening mouth, as if his kiss were something to be quickly wiped away. Her gaze grew solemn. "Look," she said, sighing guiltily, "I *am* really sorry about your fiancée. I mean it."

His eyes softened as he lifted his hand from her belly and gently brushed a strand of hair from her forehead. "I know," he found himself saying. Realizing she was trying to foster a distance, he reached and grasped her fingers again. Smoothing the back of her hand with his palm, he continued, "Honestly, I don't know what we're going to do here, Frankie. But I want to see my daughter. And about us...about what's between us—"

"I'm not interested, Doc!"

So much for gaining ground. She was looking panicked again. But he'd already told her he didn't play games, and that included lying. Her kiss said she'd missed him. "Well, I'm interested." He became conscious of the warmth of her hand in his, pulsing with energy that made his own skin warm, vibrating to the touch. "C'mon—" He didn't even know how they wound up like this, breathless with his thigh stretched over hers. "Frankie, both times we've met, we've wound up in a bed. Seems to me we should get to know each other.''

''My, don't you make it sound appealing.''

He merely shrugged, leaning over and grazing his lips over her cheek. Above the white collar of her delicate white gown, her skin was flushed a sweet pink with desire. Pressed against her side, Doc could see and feel the way her body had filled out—her wider hips, the slope of her belly, her swollen breasts. Ah…ten minutes together and it had come to this again. He desperately wanted to kiss her.

''There's one thing you need to understand,'' she said.

''What?''

''Astrid and I are making a life together.''

''Of course you are. You're her mother.''

''That's right.''

''Frankie, I know this is difficult. But I'm her father. I know you don't have much experience with men, and I was the first guy you were ever with—''

''I knew you'd say that someday!'' She'd obviously waited months to recite the rehearsed line. ''Sure, I saved myself for many years,'' she continued, ''but now I intend to look around and examine my options.''

''Are you done yet, darlin'?'' When she shot him a faintly peeved glance, he sighed. The last thing he wanted to hear right now was rehearsed speeches. ''C'mon, Frankie, I don't want you angry. In fact, I want you the way you were a second ago—kissing me like crazy. I want you, me and the baby to start spending a little time together.''

''You think I would agree to that? Don't flatter yourself.''

He'd never felt so exasperated. "Why wouldn't you? I said I'm sorry I didn't call. Especially now, since it's making a discussion about our child impossible."

Frankie stared at him. "You think that's what this is about?"

He raised an eyebrow. "Isn't it?"

"The last time we met, you rejected my application to become an adoptive mother," she said, her dark eyes flashing. "Have you completely forgotten you didn't exactly come to my apartment for a date?"

Doc winced. "What I did was unprofessional. It's part of the reason I left the way I did. But it's the one—the only—aspect of this I'd like to forget."

"Well, let me tie a string around your finger, Doc." She poked at his lab coat. "You came into my home, you pointed out that I had nothing to offer a child, you threw my medical history into my face. All to show I'd be a bad mother."

He shook his head. "Well, I didn't mean—"

"And it gets worse! You slept with me out of pity. You thought I was a loser with a life going nowhere fast. Admit it, you felt sorry for me."

He shook his head again in swift denial.

Her glance was withering. "Now who's being dishonest, Doc?"

She had him there. How did this woman manage to keep getting the best of him? "Fine, Frankie. But I'm doing the best I can. I didn't ask for this."

"This?"

Why couldn't she understand? "I didn't expect to see you again. To meet your family. And I definitely didn't expect to find out I was a father."

"There we have it."

"Frankie, it's not that I don't want the baby," he reminded her. "I do. But I didn't ask. So now I've got to adjust. And that I didn't call you wasn't personal—"

"Not *personal?*"

"No. I didn't call because I'm not ready for a relationship. Can't you understand that I don't want to be ripped apart again? You're damn right, after losing my fiancée, the fact that you could still have complications from your surgery scares me. I'm not ashamed of that." Why then did he damn himself for opening his heart? He'd never wanted to talk about his emotions with any woman, especially not this woman.

Her voice was almost a whisper. "Maybe I don't want to get hurt, either."

Her sudden honesty brought him all the way to his knees. Emotion blindsided him. Everything in her eyes reminded him that he'd been her first man—the *only* man whose lips had touched hers and whose hands had supported her lithe body while she took her release. He'd watched her, giving herself for the first time, surrendering the most precious part of herself with desperate abandon. Oh, no, he thought. What have I gotten myself into?

Staring into Frankie's eyes, he realized this woman had the kind of power over him that could only come from the stars. From the mysterious convergence of planets when they met. Or from mystical, romantic, pale late-summer moons.

All things Doc didn't even believe in.

"I can't make any promises about the relationship that could evolve between us," he said, his chest feeling tight. "All I know right now is that I want to see my daughter." He wanted a family. This baby girl who would call him Daddy. "If you don't want to see me—" his breath caught, but he forced himself to say it "—that's your choice. But I'm in Astrid's life. And nothing's taking me out of it."

The dead calm that had descended on Frankie gave him pause.

She said, "Not even the fact that you made love to me in my home on the day you came to deny my application for a baby?"

"You'd try and use that against me?"

She nodded slowly.

"You sorely underestimate me, baby doll," came his warning drawl. "You can strip me of everything I have. Profession. Money. Home. Even the shirt off my back. But there's no way you'll keep me from my daughter." He stared at her. "What I don't understand is why you'd even try, Frankie."

The answer, Doc realized with sudden shock, was in those deep, luminous eyes that couldn't mask her feelings. Frankie Luccetti was completely, head-over-heels in love with him. And she was scared to death he'd reject her again.

"Doc, I'm sorry," she said. "But I'm taking you to court."

Chapter Seven

Staring down from the witness box, Doc surveyed
Frankie coolly. In the front row, Astrid was squirming
against the front of Frankie's simple pink dress, bun-
dled in a bright green cotton blanket. Yes, his sweet
little slice of sugar pie was wiggling like a worm on
a hook, crying as if she was about to actually become
fish fodder. Poor thing. Doc desperately wanted to
hold and comfort her.

Instead, he answered the question posed to him.
"Yes. I visited Ms. Luccetti on the day you mentioned."

"And even though you're actually a trained physician, you entered Ms. Luccetti's home in the capac-
ity of a caseworker?" asked the Honorable Judge T.
Winslow. "Is that correct, Doctor?"

Doc was seething. Listening to Astrid's inconsol-
able crying was bad enough. But answering these
questions was simply beneath him. Sure, weeks ago,
Doc had been willing to talk. But now Frankie had
actually filed complaints of ethical misconduct and
harassment. He couldn't believe she'd done it.

"Doctor?"

Doc merely stared at the judge. Enveloped in his

huge black robe, Judge Winslow looked like Justice Incarnate. He was corpulent and red-faced, with long wisps of gray hair that raked over his massive balding head. Doc's lips twisted with irony. No wonder the man had reached his eighties in spite of having a heart condition; he looked ornery enough to live forever.

The judge cleared his rheumy throat. "It's a simple question. Did you—or did you not—enter the home as a caseworker?"

Doc blocked out Astrid's wails. "Yes, I did."

"And you then proceeded to have sexual relations with Ms. Luccetti?"

This was too much. Doc couldn't abide having his and Frankie's private moments made public. How could *she* stand this? Her family was in the courtroom, listening. What was going through her mind? "With all due respect, sir. Is this really necessary?"

The judge's voice roared like thunder. "This is my court! Family court. And although your lawyer wrangled for this more informal hearing, I am still the law here! My questions are quite necessary, I assure you!" When the judge's furious eyes landed on Astrid, the gavel came crashing down. "And silence that baby!"

Doc rose halfway from the chair, prepared to defend his own, but Astrid fell abruptly silent. Doc frowned. For all the judge's bombast, he was rumored to have a way with kids—and a bark that was far louder than his bite.

Judge Winslow glared down from the bench at Doc. "Now, could you please answer with a simple yes or no."

"Yes," said Doc.

"And after said sexual relations, you made no move to contact Ms. Luccetti. Correct?"

Said sexual relations? It sounded so…inhuman. Clinical. "Correct."

"Did you *think* about contacting Ms. Luccetti?"

"Yes, sir. I did.…"

Doc continued answering the questions, feeling betrayed. The judge was supposed to be on their side! Jake Lucas, Doc's lawyer and his boss, and executive head of Big Apple Babies adoption agency, had specifically asked that wily Judge Winslow review this case in an informal hearing. Now Jake smiled encouragement at Doc. Jake was seated across the aisle from the Luccettis, sandwiched between his wife, Dani, and Doc's brother, Shane.

At least Jake was trying to help. He'd been mad at Doc, of course. Inclined to go hard on him, too, since Jake was also his friend and he didn't want to show favoritism. Jake had promptly removed Doc from casework, but things could have been far worse. Doc could have lost his job. Secretly, Jake and Dani were still hoping Doc and Frankie would wind up dating. When the Lucases had learned about her and the baby, they'd known something magical must have happened to Doc. Something unprecedented, unexpected and wonderful.

But it wasn't wonderful, Doc thought now.

Frankie wouldn't so much as look at him.

And Judge Winslow wasn't helping in the least. Doc had been so sure he would. After all, the judge and Jake went way back. Years ago, when Jake was a burnt-out prosecutor, he'd received a mysterious, anonymous check for the start-up capital for the agency. Recently, it had come to light that this old cantankerous judge was one of Big Apple Babies private backers. There were apparently others—all secretive Manhattan philanthropists.

Judge Winslow had a reputation for being as highly unconventional as he was confrontational. He'd also been known to play matchmaker in his courtroom. Doc had been hoping this judge would fix things so Doc, Frankie and the baby would have to spend some time together.

But the old man's piercing gaze showed no mercy. He was glaring at Doc as if Doc were less than a man. "Was there any romance involved in this unethical scene of seduction?"

Doc simply couldn't believe this.

The judge heaved a ponderous sigh. "Yes or no, Doctor?"

"Yes."

"Would you kindly mind elaborating?"

"Flowers," Doc found himself saying, feeling utterly ridiculous and yet feeling his gut clench with the power of the recollections. "Purple flowers and lace curtains. It was…a breezy late summer day." In spite of Doc's temper, all the afternoon's romance came rushing back. Once again, he felt the strange sensation that had pulled him over the threshold of Frankie's apartment, the feeling that Marta's ghost was in the room. "Neil Diamond music," he added. "She was playing Neil Diamond." The words sounded in his mind, *You'll be a woman soon.* Boy, hadn't that turned out to be the truth?

"And did you feel affected by this romantic environment, Doctor?"

So affected he'd lost sight of every business ethic he'd ever possessed. Remembering how the pale, pearl-silver moon rose at twilight over the skyline of Manhattan, Doc suppressed another wave of helpless fury. Either at himself or the judge's bizarre line of questioning, he wasn't sure which. "Yes, I felt deeply affected." His eyes sought out Frankie's, willing her to remember. She glanced away, but not before those shared memories coursed between them.

"So you proceeded to have sexual relations?"

The judge made it sound so callous. "Yes."

As he continued answering, Doc took in the somber oil painting behind Judge Winslow. It depicted three women in angelic white dresses—the three Fates, he realized now. One spun the thread of fate, the second gathered, the third clipped. Doc figured they weren't on his side, any more than the judge. Or Frankie. At the hospital, he could swear he'd seen love in her eyes. And her naked honesty when she'd said she didn't want to be hurt had floored him. But was Doc right? Had he really touched her so deeply that she feared him this much? That she'd bring him to court, and go to such extreme lengths to keep him away from her and Astrid? But people didn't fall in love in just one night, no matter how special it was. Still, he could swear he'd read that love in her eyes. And ever since, her every stolen, veiled glance that communicated anything but love had seemed like nothing more than smoke and mirrors.

He concentrated on the judge. "Doctor, are you now sorry about what occurred between you and Ms. Luccetti?"

Doc's eyes settled on Astrid. "I want to know my child." And Frankie. But the way she was treating him now, he wasn't about to admit it.

"That wasn't the question."

Doc sighed. Was he sorry he'd slept with Frankie? Sorry he'd held her naked in his arms and awakened her body while she'd touched him so tenderly, cracking open his shut-down emotions? "No," he finally said. "I'm not the least bit sorry."

"You may step down. Ms. Luccetti?" continued the judge. "Once Dr. Holiday is seated, please come forward."

As he stepped down, Mama Luccetti sent Doc a supportive smile from the front row, which made Doc wish he remembered his own mother better. The Luccettis weren't exactly breaking ranks. But even the Sicilian relatives who'd visited had respected Doc's willingness to care for the baby. If Frankie's charges stuck, they knew Doc's professional life could be ruined, and they admired him for not backing down to Frankie's threats.

Whenever she could, Mama arranged to watch Astrid at Frankie's alone, and she'd bring in Doc to see the baby. Doc always left the apartment with food, usually packed in containers from the family's restaurant—tomato sauce, veal and meatballs. Tarts and *cannoli*. Doc and his brother, Shane, had never eaten so well. The only time he'd been near Frankie was at Astrid's baptism. Even then, Mama had apologized for Frankie. Nervously wringing her strong hands against her black dress, she'd said, "Francesca's uncontrollable!"

Not that Frankie was.

Doc had seen this scenario countless times before. Patients with lifetime illnesses were given a reprieve, and relatives who'd been necessarily protective for years were suddenly pushed away. Frankie was just trying her best to make up for lost time.

Under other circumstances, Doc would have helped. Under these, he'd sided with her folks, visiting his daughter behind Frankie's back, devouring Mama Luccetti's meals, and taking Frankie's father small gifts—boxes of cigars, Italian newspapers. Now Doc squeezed in between Jake and Shane, whose black Stetson was tossed on the seat out of deference to their surroundings, exposing a mass of jet hair, so like Frankie's and Astrid's. Shane's formidable eyes shifted from the baby he had a right to call his niece.

"You did good, bro," Shane whispered.

Doc nodded in thanks for the support as he watched Frankie take the stand. Her simple, classy pink sweater dress was just tight enough not to hide the sway of her filled-out hips, and the bright blue-and-pink silk scarf that wrapped around her slender neck made her black curls look as dark as night. That she took Astrid with her made Doc's heart ache. Astrid was too young to be in such a real-world place as a witness box.

"State your name and address."

"Francesca Maria Angelina Sophia Carmella Luccetti," she said. "And this is Astrid."

Astrid seemed calm enough. But Frankie was starting to bristle as Judge Winslow leaned his ponderous body forward and glared at her. "This man wants unlimited access to his child. Your family wants him to have access." His voice rose as he spoke. "So what is the difficulty, young lady?"

The flash of Frankie's eyes made Doc wary. He'd seen her mad. And it looked as if she and Winslow were oil and water. Even though the judge was the last enemy she should want to make, her chin jutted out defensively. In spite of himself, Doc admired her usual fighting spirit. At least, until she started talking.

"I was taken advantage of!" she began right-eously. All Doc's temper returned as Frankie explained things from her point of view: how he'd declared her unfit as an adoptive mother, then used her vulnerable state to seduce her, making her into a mother, after all. "And I was a *virgin*," she stressed in a low, wounded tone. "How was I supposed to know what to do?"

She'd known very well what to do. To Doc's left, Jake was scribbling notes, in case this ever came to a juried court. One look at the legal pad reminded Doc of his note to Frankie. He winced. Shane reached over and squeezed his elbow supportively.

Judge Winslow said, "So, the seduction was all on his side?"

Frankie's tone was nearly inaudible. "Yes."

"Talk about perjury," Doc muttered.

The judge roared, "Are you sure? Pardon me, miss, but in my day, as I have said many times in this family courtroom, it took two to tango. So, let me rephrase this, Ms. Luccetti. Did you mind Dr. Holiday's actions?"

"I most certainly did."

"Well, let me rephrase this again, Ms. Luccetti. Did the good doctor restrain you in any way? Did he threaten you?"

"Of course not!"

"I really can't believe this," Doc whispered.

Shane shot him a glance of censure. "Sorry, brother. But you should have thought about that months ago, when you did the deed."

Doc's jaw set. Shane was in agreement with the

Luccettis, and felt Doc should marry Frankie. Somehow, everyone seemed to be overlooking the fact that the woman had dragged him into a court of law.

Doc suddenly snapped to attention.

Judge Winslow was glaring at him. "Could you take the stand again, Dr. Holiday?"

Wasn't this out of order? Well, Doc guessed having a crazy judge was symptomatic of this whole strange situation. Once Frankie was in the front row again and Doc was reseated, the judge said, "Well, Doctor, having heard all the facts, I'm at a loss. You've acted in a manner that this court cannot condone. Your ethics are beyond abominable. You seduced a very sheltered young woman to whom your relationship should have remained professional. A woman with delicate health."

Doc's heart sank. Was he going to lose contact with the baby? "But—"

"No buts!" roared the judge.

Guilt washed over Doc. His eyes drifted from Frankie to the adorable bundle in her arms. "Sure, I did something wrong," he ventured. "But Frankie and the baby are fine…healthy. And you—" his eyes returned to Frankie "—are not going to make me feel guilty. Because if you were honest—"

The judge interrupted. "You'd be advised to address the court, Dr. Holiday, not Ms. Luccetti. And confine your remarks to the facts!"

Doc understood the need for objectively viewing facts. But didn't the judge understand the emotions involved here? "I was trying to say that, if Frankie was honest, she'd admit she's not sorry, either. She desperately wanted a baby. That's why she was applying to adopt. She didn't have a chance in—"

"In hell!" The judge banged his gavel furiously. "Was that what you were going to say, Doctor? Were you actually going to curse in my courtroom?"

"I was going to say a chance in a million," Doc murmured.

Not that his denial mattered. The judge was obviously angry—and from the look of his red face had worked himself into a state. "My pills!" he muttered distractedly. With shaking hands he fumbled under his robe, withdrew a pill from a vial, then shoved it under his tongue.

Doc raced on. "I'm sorry, judge. But she didn't have a chance of adopting a baby. And she wanted one so much. My heart went out to her, and I wanted to comfort her. And then...something came over me." Doc thought of how unusually compelled he'd felt to be with Frankie. "When I saw her, something strange happened. I've never believed in a spiritual life...."

In the front row, Frankie's aunts all crossed themselves.

Doc forged on. "But I felt some...almost supernatural pull to her...."

"As if he's not even responsible for his own actions!" Frankie burst out. "Isn't this the devil-made-me-do-it defense, Your Honor?"

"Order!" Judge Winslow banged down his gavel like an angry child until his blue eyes bugged and his face turned as dark as an eggplant. Doc went on alert, in case the man needed professional help. "Take it easy, there, judge," he drawled in warning.

"Easy?" Judge Winslow roared. "You behaved horribly, Doctor!"

"I know. But when I saw our baby, I wasn't sorry.

Are you really going to deny a little girl her father, just because of how she was conceived?''

"I haven't decided," the judge stated. "Though I am hard-pressed, given the letter of the law and your lack of professional ethics, to rule otherwise. Legally, you've given this woman everything she needs to limit your access to your child...."

With the thunderous voice still ringing in his ears, Doc's heart broke. How could he convince the judge to let him see Astrid?

Suddenly, the most unexpected thing happened.

The gavel tumbled to the floor. Gasping, the heavy judge clutched his chest near his heart, his black robe bunching in fistfuls. And then he whirled around and fell flat on his back.

Or he would have if Doc hadn't caught him. It took all Doc's own considerable bulk to bring the judge down to rest on the floor behind the podium. Lying on his back, clad in the long black robe with his corpulent belly protruding, the Honorable Judge T. Winslow looked like a great beached whale.

"Get an ambulance!" Doc yelled, beginning standard CPR. Strangely, the judge's heartbeat felt strong, even if his breath seemed to have ceased. As Doc swiftly leaned to perform mouth-to-mouth, a beefy fist grabbed Doc's lapel.

"Before you get too personal with me, Doctor," whispered the judge, with a wily, blue-eyed wink, "I'll be under cardiac arrest for two weeks, probably down in the Bahamas. When I get back, I'll turn down the case for health reasons, then it'll take Jake Lucas months to file papers and get a new judge." The judge's fleshy lips twitched. "Meantime, good luck with the girl. From what I've seen of her fiery Italian temper, you'll need it.''

With nothing further, the old man's blue eyes rolled back in his head and his body stiffened, as if rigor mortis were already setting in.

"Leave it to Jake," Doc whispered, feeling vindicated. The Honorable Judge T. Winslow—matchmaker extraordinaire—had been the perfect judge, after all.

Chapter Eight

"I've grown very accustomed to your pushiness, so I'm not even going to react to this most recent invasion," Frankie warned some weeks later when she entered her apartment and found Doc already in it.

"Good. Pleased to hear it, doll."

She sent him a suspicious sideways glance. "How did you get in, anyway, cowboy?"

As Doc rose from the couch, he tipped his Stetson at the ladies, then he took a yawning Astrid from Frankie's arms. Splaying a huge supportive hand under the baby's behind, he sprawled her across his chest and bounced her, crooning, "Now, come to papa, you itsy-bitsy, teeny-weeny bikini of a baby girl. Whaddaya say? Want to smooch, sugar dumplin'?" Doc dropped a loud kiss on Astrid's forehead, where her stork bite had been. "Now, when you grow up, and fellows start talkin' to you about Astrid projection, darlin', we're gonna punch out their lights, right?" Doc raised one of Astrid's tiny fists and made punching motions, presumably for practice.

Frankie groaned. "I can't believe you're her father. And I can only hope that whatever gene makes you talk like that is recessive and can't be transmitted."

Doc merely smiled. He, of course, was crooning for the sole purpose of annoying Frankie, though Astrid seemed to like it. "I can't tell a lie, darlin'," he said, pulling Astrid's stroller across the threshold and closing the apartment door. "I confess, I broke and entered your home."

"Why, you low-down burglar." She headed straight for the telephone. "Obviously, since you're a self-confessed burglar, I should call the police."

Leaning lithely, Doc caught the tail of the white silk blouse she'd worn to dinner at her mother's and pulled her to him. "No, really—" Resettling Astrid on his hip, Doc fished in the pocket of jeans that could not have fit more snugly and held up a key. "I used this."

Frankie made a vain swipe, but Doc repocketed the key with a playfully frank smirk that said, If you want it, come and get it. Taking in how his jeans shaped the contours of his lower body, Frankie was very sorely tempted. "For having been so mad at me during court," she managed to say, "I can certainly see you've changed your tune."

"Oh, you haven't even heard this new tune yet. I came over here to sing you and Astrid a lullaby."

The mere idea of him singing to her in bed made Frankie's pulse stutter. "More smooth talk," she murmured. *That's all this is.* Frowning, she watched Doc's big shoulders fill the doorway as he entered her kitchen with Astrid in his arms. He opened and shut the refrigerator door, then checked her cabinets.

"While you root around, shouldn't you let me hold Astrid?"

"Root around? Does that mean you think I'm a wild man, Frankie?"

Frankie couldn't help it. Her imagination took flight, envisioning Doc as a mountain man in a lonely rustic cabin, dressed in furs that would warm her skin after they made love....

Frankie suddenly gulped. Nervously, she fiddled with her cross, zipping it up and down its gold chain, listening to the familiar, reassuring grating sound it made. Things had been so much simpler right after the court date, when she was still ignoring Doc. But it had been only a matter of time until he'd managed to coax her into talking to him again.

"Frankie?"

"Hmm?" She had to wipe the look of fear off her face.

"Don't you worry. Astrid's safe with me."

Well, I'm not. Doc certainly had a way of insinuating himself. Now he was peering beside her refrigerator, where she stored her folded grocery bags and the mop he'd caught her dancing with all those months ago. She flushed at the memory. "You know, you should take off your hat when you're inside," she suddenly said. "Men are supposed to. According to etiquette books, I mean."

"I couldn't agree more." Casually, Doc tossed his cowboy hat to the counter.

Her frown deepened. She had to admit that gesture made him look heroic, like Glenn Ford or John Wayne. Or the other Doc Holiday—the legendary one from the shoot-out at Tombstone. Yes, it was easy enough to imagine Doc, after a hard day rounding up buffalo, dismounting his horse with flair, trail dust puffing around his boots. He'd toss his hat near a bonfire, quickly make himself a soft bed of pine needles, then whip out a harmonica. While he played

"Home on the Range," she—dark-haired Francesca Two-Heart, the sweet, innocent young squaw he made love to frequently in the wilderness—emerged from the forest and came to him by the fire wearing only moccasins. She knelt before Doc, a soft pleading in her midnight eyes....

Frankie blinked. She really had to quit indulging these fantasies. They were not at all harmless. If she kept this up, she was going to get into big trouble. Or into bed with him.

"I'm sorry," she suddenly continued, her breath catching. "But Doc, I'm simply going to have to ask you to leave."

He merely smiled. "Nope."

"Well then, could you at least stay out of those cookies I just baked?" She was truly starting to panic now, and feared the man's take-charge attitude was bringing out the control freak in her. "Uh, they're for that poor judge's family."

Doc turned slowly around. "Frankie, I...uh, wouldn't worry about Judge Winslow overly much. It's been a few weeks now...and I have a suspicion he's doing just fine."

"He is. Being a good citizen, I called. Which means soon we'll be back in court." Not that she was sure how she felt about that. She'd desperately wanted Doc out of her life, but he was making himself indispensable now. Oh, maybe she wouldn't pursue it. After all, she couldn't help but be excited by Doc's obvious flirtation.

He opened the refrigerator door again.

"You're not hungry, are you?" Her guilt deepening, she added, "If you are, Mama packed some left-over tortellini in garlic and basil sauce."

Doc lifted his face and grinned like the Cheshire cat. "See, Astrid?" he crooned. "I knew if I stuck around, dropping these liberal hints, your mama would start offering to feed me, the way a good woman should."

Suddenly wondering what on earth she'd been thinking, Frankie spun on her heel and made a beeline toward the telephone again. "Forget the word *tortellini* passed my lips. I take it back. I'm calling my brothers right this min—"

"I thought you were calling the cops."

"I would, but I don't want my daughter to have a father with a criminal record. I'll call Vinny and Mickey instead. They'll throw you out."

"Hate to break it to you, but it was Vinny who gave me the key to your apartment."

"That traitor!" Frankie emitted a quick, peeved sigh. "Well, he probably had even less choice than I do. You must have told him some inventive tale about why you had to come over here. In fact, you probably went so far as to tell him I had actually invited you." She arched an eyebrow in Doc's direction. "I've finally figured out what kind of doctor you are, you know."

"Oh?"

"A *spin* doctor.

A low, sexy chuckle sounded. "Sugar plum," he said, his exaggerated drawl making her insides feel unaccountably shaky. "I just told Vinny the God's honest truth. That I wanted to see you and Astrid."

And of course Frankie's useless brother had handed Doc a key. Men. "I guess birds of a feather flock together."

"Chirp, chirp," said Doc.

She rolled her eyes. Her matchmaking relatives were simply not to be borne. They were always making sure Doc and she bathed, fed and shopped for Astrid together. This week, Doc, not Vinny or Mickey, had shown up to take her grocery shopping, while her mother baby-sat. Doc had also taken Frankie and Astrid to visit cousin Gina, who did hair in Queens, then to Astrid's doctor, where Doc and the other pediatrician wound up making an appointment to further discuss Astrid's development over a game of golf next week.

After that, Doc and his brother had attended Uncle Big Sal's fiftieth birthday party, and Aunt Sophia had invited Doc and Shane to Mama and Papa Luccetti's upcoming anniversary party. Tonight Frankie and Astrid had eaten their first Doc-free meal in an entire week.

It had been such a relief.

But now, it seemed, they were only granted this brief reprieve because Frankie's family was busy scheming behind her back. While she and Astrid innocently ate their tortellini and a warm bottle, respectively, all the relatives were imagining Doc getting cozy in Frankie's apartment. Her family naturally assumed that if a man took a woman's virginity and gave her a child, he'd eventually come around and decide to marry her. Not that Frankie faulted her relatives. She used to think in that exact same archaic way.

Now, of course, she was much more enlightened. Accusation tinged her voice. "Just how long have you been here, anyway? I suppose you searched through all my drawers?"

"Don't worry. I only looked for the black lace stuff."

"I don't have any black lace stuff."

His eyes twinkled with amusement. "I know that now. When would you like me to take you shopping?"

Not *if*, she noticed, but *when*. "Never." She'd grown so accustomed to the casual way he talked about sexy subjects that she rarely even blushed anymore. Still, he hadn't managed to weasel in here to visit since the day they'd made love. Usually he met her at Mama's or saw Astrid here, when Mama was baby-sitting. Frankie's mouth went dry, and her voice sounded rusty. "Hmm. Well, make yourself at home."

"Already did. Hours ago. Thanks."

He continued pacing, now in the living room, ducking his head and cooing at Astrid. "Oh, admit it, Frankie..." he drawled over his shoulder.

She slipped past him, heading for the kitchen to slide Mama's leftovers into the fridge. After some debate, she'd decided Doc could heat them himself. Yes, if he was wily enough to crack open the sacred safe of her apartment, the man could surely figure out how to operate a mere oven. "Admit what?" she said absently.

"You kind of like me. Aunt Sophia says you do."

Not "your" Aunt Sophia, she noticed. Just Aunt Sophia. As if he were related to her. "Well, I can't cry over spilled milk," she conceded. "You are Astrid's father. And...well, as you say, you're a doctor, making good wages. And you said you wanted to help support her financially...."

Doc shot her a droll glance. "Right, Frankie. I knew all along you were the gold-digger type."

She kept the tone light. "Exactly. Just remember you're never any bigger to me than your wallet, Doc." Raising an eyebrow, she glanced around, noticing his lab coat, stethoscope and physician's bag. They were next to a large navy blue L. L. Bean duffel. In spite of her best efforts, her voice sounded strangled. "Excuse me—" Her index finger shot into the air. "Far be it from me to intrude on the pleasant, relaxed evening you seem to be having here. But what's that?" She pointed the raised index finger.

"My suitcase."

"Uh…you certainly don't intend to move in here?"

"Don't I?"

Just stay calm. She inhaled sharply. She could handle this. Most heroes in the books she read were also overly sexed men whose veins swam with undiluted testosterone. Searching her mental archives, she tried to remember how heroines in her favorite novels had handled them.

In one of Frankie's favorites, *The Most Arrogant Count,* the heroine had tied the hero to cliffs above the rocky English coastline. While shadowy, subterranean creatures slid along the dark, dank stone walls of the nearby castle, Frankie could just imagine Doc, spread-eagled and tied to the cliffs. He would be bloody, of course. His torn lab coat ripped to shreds by the merciless elements and exposing a bare, brawny, golden-haired chest streaked with mud.

Helpless, Doc would shout her name in the darkness, begging for her mercy as the tide rushed in. Waves crashed below, and inch by inch, the water lapped upward on his lower body, soaking his old-fashioned britches that clung so tightly. And then she—Francesca, lowly castle scullery maid—would brave the spider-ridden secret passageway, carrying only one flickering candle. She would creep down the damp stone dungeon steps, and out into the wind-swept stormy night, clutching the neck of her thin muslin robe to her throat, drawn to the sea...drawn by her lord's voice as he cried out for his release....

Frankie blinked. No, that certainly wouldn't do.

Darn. She hadn't had the good fortune to be kid-napped and brought aboard Doc's pirate ship, either, like the heroine, Prissy, in *Prissy's Pirate*. If she had, Frankie would simply draw Doc's own sword on him, then make him walk the plank into dark, deep churning waters. Or banish him to the galley to row the ship. Or anchor him to the mast with thick, chafing ropes, so that later, she—Francesca Nightingale, nurse extraordinaire—would be forced to rip the hem of her white uniform and expose her bare thighs while she made bandages and soothed those hideous wounds for him, administering a balm of sensual-smelling ointment....

Frankie blinked again, still zipping her cross up and down on its chain. Well, she guessed there were infinite possibilities. If only she weren't stuck in a New York City apartment. "Really, Doc," she finally ventured in a suggestive tone, angry at herself for not coming up with anything better than this, "What do you say? Isn't it about time we put Astrid in her crib, so you can head on home?" It didn't work. Doc kept pacing with Astrid, and Frankie watched glumly, barely able to keep her eyes off him.

"C'mon," he chided in a teasing drawl. "You're

not being your usual sunny-side-up self. Over the past week or so, your positive attitude seems to have deserted you. I just don't understand it. Can't you see the benefits of my staying here with you and our daughter?''

"Not really. You expect me to feel optimistic?"

"You might as well."

Because she had absolutely no other choice, Frankie supposed. Briefly she wondered why exactly he and her family were torturing her. She surveyed him for a long moment. Taking the high ground never worked. Like water, maybe she should seek his level and pretend, however temporarily, that what he was proposing was reasonable. She mustered her most practical tone. "But there's only one bed."

"We've shared the bed before."

She felt a little faint. "Once was enough."

"Come on, be honest." Doc flashed her another perfect grin. "I know you're still a little mad right now. But admit it, you kind of like me, too."

Like him? He was funny, sexy and absolutely irresistible. But he was out of her league. Even worse, he rarely tried to hide the fact that he wanted her sexually. He'd come back into her and Astrid's life like a whirlwind. Railroading. Steamrollering. Taking charge of the situation. But he didn't want any committed relationships.

He was the proverbial Peter Pan, she suddenly thought. He was too good-looking for his own good, wounded badly in love before, and yet a constant flirt and tease. He'd conned her into sharing the diary she'd kept from childhood, where she'd written down all the things she'd wanted to do if she were ever healthy, and he'd promised to help her fulfill every one. He'd told her about dates he'd imagined having with her during the months they were apart…. But she couldn't get confused. He wanted to have his cake and eat it, too. And she was the cake, while Astrid was the dollop of ice cream on top.

"See, I knew it," he drawled with a wicked grin. "The mere thought of cohabitation left you pleasantly speechless. You like me."

"I carried your child to term without calling you. Then I took you to court to have you legally removed from our lives." Frankie shot him a meaningful glance. "Does that sound like true love to you, Doc?"

"Who said anything about true love?"

That gave her pause. "Look, I *do* like you, Doc, but…" She glanced around helplessly, wondering how she was going to make him leave.

Doc merely laughed, then sat on the bed. With a start, she strode swiftly across the room, grabbed his sleeve and tugged, careful not to upset Astrid, who was now sleeping. "Oh, no, you don't, Doc."

He reached out, cupping her face, his thumb grazing her cheekbone. All of a sudden, those gorgeous eyes were dead serious. "Why can't we live for the moment, Frankie? Take our relationship for what it's worth and see where it goes?"

Her whole body felt strangely frozen. Her arms were stiff, her hands now clenched in nervous fists. "I can think of a lot of reasons. *Good* reasons," she stressed.

"But isn't that what you told me you wanted? The freedom to explore yourself?"

He was twisting her words around. Using her very own speeches against her. She was really starting to worry. "Doc, this is my apartment."

"I know. I've been here with you before. Remember?"

Her cheeks felt hot. "Of course I do." Her eyes trailed over Astrid. Why was it so difficult to think with this man touching her? Maybe he should stay here. Maybe he was simply being reasonable.... Her heart pounded. And taking in how small her sleeping alcove seemed with his huge body in it, she knew she desperately wanted him to stay.

His gaze followed as hers darted around the apartment again, while she tried to decide how to handle this. "You've done a lot with the place, Frankie," he said with approval.

Her throat felt raw as she glanced over at the nursery area, which was set off from the living room with glass block. She'd made new white, filmy tie-back curtains for the alcove. Only now did she realize how romantic they were. She ached to simply sit beside him on the bed and watch the baby sleep. Or, of course, she could carefully lift Astrid into the crib, then wedge herself between Doc's thighs and push his chest gently, so he'd lie back on the mattress....

He was watching her in a careful way that made her feel as if she were wearing all her inner thoughts on her sleeve. She suddenly realized he hadn't tried to kiss her since she'd come home. That, in itself, was highly suspicious. Doc was always trying to kiss her. Not that she let him. She put her fists on her hips. "This is *my* apartment," she repeated, trying a different intonation. "I'm letting you come over and see the baby." What more did he want?

Doc grabbed Frankie's hand and threaded his fingers through hers. "Don't you remember telling me that you were afraid of only one thing?"

Here goes. Another past conversation coming back to haunt me. At least Doc didn't make her nearly as nervous as he used to. In fact, nowadays he was sometimes merely exasperating. "Enlighten me. What did I say I was afraid of?"

"You said you weren't afraid of dying, but of never having lived." Her breath caught. It amazed her that he'd remembered that. Doc's gentle grip on her fingers tightened even as his lulling drawl gentled. "There's so much I like about you, Frankie. Your positive attitude. How you're taking charge of your life. I like watching you be a new mama." His hand trailed up, touching her curls. He smiled with approval, his eyes sparkling. "I like the trim."

That pricked her vanity. "You do?" Nobody in her family liked her short hair.

Doc tilted his head, surveying her a good long while. "I like it a lot."

Frankie thought her cousin Gina had done a good job. There was a long silence, then her eyes slid from his to the mattress. "I hope you know I would never, *ever* have sex with you again," she said. "If that's what you were thinking when you packed that duffel bag."

His lips twisted in a bemused smile. "Never?"

She refused to be teased. "Maybe a woman with more experience could handle something like that," she said honestly. "But I can't."

"I wouldn't, anyway. Not tonight," Doc said. "Not without at least two forms of protection." His expression was suddenly veiled, his eyes hooded, and his voice lowered another notch. "Frankie, I never told you, but it hurt me that this pregnancy could have caused you serious problems. Your mama was right.

I'm glad she yelled at me like that at the hospital, darlin'. It was a terrible risk.''

The honesty in his confession made her blush ferociously. "Well, I'm fine." She was completely healed from the birth.

He softly murmured, "Frankie, I'm not trying to embarrass you. I'm just trying to—"

"Be nice and wonderful," she said, finishing his sentence. All this time, he'd been every decent thing she didn't want him to be. It made him so easy to be with—*too* easy. She suddenly wondered how long she'd been standing next to where he and Astrid sat on the bed, simply gazing down into his eyes. "I…guess I really don't mind you coming to see Astrid. I mean, when I'm here, instead of Mama. But you really can't stay here, Doc. All my life people have stayed with me and protected me. I've been doing fine alone with Astrid. I need space. To…"

"Grow up."

Why did he have to understand that, too? Most men wouldn't. Since her transplant, she felt as if she'd had a growth spurt, and her emotions had never really caught up to her twenty-seven-year-old body. Her eyes drifted wistfully over Doc again. She knew if she insisted, he'd leave. But her own emotions were defeating her now. No matter how wrong it was, she wanted him to stay.

Her eyes suddenly widened. Was she playing this all wrong? What if she took Doc on as a challenge? After all, she was her own woman now. Free and independent. Healthy and unfettered. Why, she could do whatever she pleased with a man, couldn't she? Absently, feeling vaguely preoccupied, she surveyed him. Maybe she could actually make Doc fall in love with her. Not that he would, of course. But she'd been around so few men, and this could be an excellent opportunity for practice.

Oh, granted, she didn't have much to work with in terms of assets. Not that she was down on herself, but she was a realist. Everything Doc had so painfully pointed out to her during her adoption interview was still true. She'd had health problems in the past. She had no career, no money, and next to no experience with men. Her father was currently paying her rent. But then, she was fundamentally an optimist. Over and over in life, she'd picked herself up, dusted off her knees, and gone on. All the romances with which she'd occupied herself during her bedridden youth had drummed one thing in her head—happy endings did exist.

Her eyes lighted on Astrid. *Doc and I do have her in common.* That was a start. So was the way Frankie made Doc feel in bed. Instinctively, she knew he'd been with smarter, prettier women. Nevertheless, for some strange reason, he really couldn't keep his hands off her. Not that she'd be easy. No, she'd simply tease Doc, pushing him to the point of no return until he begged. Then, of course, she'd have to turn him down. After all, this was only practice. It would be foolish to open herself up and get hurt again, as if this were the real thing....

Doc's gaze had turned wary. "I hesitate to ask what bright idea just popped into your head."

Frankie arched her eyebrows innocently. "Idea?"

He chuckled softly, nodding. "Yeah, idea."

She merely smiled. "I think I just figured out how to handle you, cowboy."

"Oh, Frankie." Doc threw his head back and laughed a deep, hearty laugh that made him feel like a million bucks. Had it really been less than a year ago that she'd yelled at him to stop and smell the flowers, while his mental wheels spun in an angry tirade?

She skipped into the room. Her eyes positively glittered with mischief, shining as bright as those of a frisky mare who'd just been corralled with a prize stallion. "What, Doc?"

You're impossibly cute, baby doll. That's what. How he could sleep in the same bed with this woman without losing his mind, Doc couldn't say. She'd emerged from the bathroom in a boxy, high-necked white flannel gown. Thick socks. A little knit sleeping cap with a hole in the crown, and one of those ridiculous, old-fashioned pink sleeping masks from the five-and-dime slung around her neck.

"Honey," he said, "you look so strange, I somehow think that outfit could use a snorkel and flippers."

"Well, when you insisted on staying here with me tonight," she declared, checking the temperature of Astrid's bottled milk against her wrist, "I immediately realized I had better dress for my own protection."

"Now, that's real smart thinking, Frankie." Except all her efforts were wasted on Doc. One look, and he wanted to cuddle her against him and nuzzle off that silly cap. "Where did you get that outfit? A nunnery?"

Lifting Astrid from his arms, Frankie smothered the baby's face with kisses. "A nunnery? If memory serves me correctly, you ruined my chances of ever getting near one of those!''

He chuckled. "Touché."

"Told you I know how to handle you, cowboy."

Yeah, and if she kept skipping around him like an elfin nymph, Doc might confess that moving into her apartment had never even occurred to him.

Hell, he'd been headed to the Hamptons.

Starting tomorrow, he was taking some vacation so he could see more of Astrid and make sure Frankie decided not to pursue the legal complaint against him. As well, he wanted to check on his summer house, between his rental tenants' stays. Mama Luccetti—a firm believer in the adage that it takes a village to raise a child, and who also just plain wanted her grandbaby to herself—had suggested that Doc try to talk Frankie into going. They could leave Astrid with Mama, just overnight, and he and Frankie could have a much-needed, serious talk about finances and child support.

Of course Frankie wouldn't have agreed; she could barely stand a trip to the fridge without Astrid in tow. So, when she assumed he was moving in, Doc had decided to press the advantage. His eyes were still slowly traversing her head-to-toe garments. "You know what else you could use?"

Frankie nestled into a deep corner of the couch, not answering for a moment, but merely rocking Astrid in her curved arm as she situated the bottle. Doc felt his heart swell, filling with more emotion than he was used to. Emotion. Dammit, every time he got near Frankie and Astrid they tied him in knots. They were so hopelessly...cute. Frankie—in that crazy outfit. And Astrid—her pink mouth furiously working, suckling the bottle's nipple. Frankie wasn't breast-feeding because of the drugs she took for her own health, but Doc knew how badly she'd wanted to. Now he wished she could. And that he could watch. He'd love to see his sweet little slice of sugar pie, all curled up in her blanket, safe and warm and suckling Frankie's breast.

He started to get up and head for the couch, suddenly wanting to crush both Frankie and the baby against his chest in a hard, protective embrace. But he'd already decided he wouldn't get overly physical with Frankie. He wanted her, but he couldn't offer more. Besides, the most important thing was earning her trust. Doc simply had to prioritize, put emotions above his baser male impulses. He couldn't blow it. He had to keep going slow like this, giving him and Frankie both time to feel out this situation. Already, a somewhat natural routine was emerging, one that was working for him, her and the baby. *Yeah, cowboy, it's called old-fashioned dating.*

She glanced up from Astrid. "What else do you think I need?"

My arms around you, baby doll. Doc's chest still felt tight, and he wanted to tell her how pretty she looked with Astrid. Instead, he said, "Gloves. Big thick ones. Maybe even mittens."

"I was thinking more along the lines of a chastity belt."

He mulled that over. "Chastity belts are good."

"Not that it matters," Frankie offered. "Because I'm warning you. I know judo, Doc."

He laughed. "You do not know judo, Frankie."

She didn't even crack a smile. "Well, I understand the basic principles of leverage. And with leverage alone, even a slender woman like me can send a beast like you spinning head over heels.''

''Baby doll, you sent me reeling months ago.''

''Smooth talk,'' she murmured with an airy wave of her hand. ''Nothing more.''

It wasn't, but because Doc wasn't exactly sure what it was, he didn't correct her. ''C'mon. You at least need to change your nightgown. You'll burn up.''

''Oh, don't worry. I'm putting on my skimpiest nightie.''

He struggled to keep real hope from his voice. ''You are?''

She nodded. ''Certainly. As soon as you leave.''

With a look of mock wistfulness, he leaned back on the bed and propped himself on an elbow. ''Now, that wouldn't happen to be the skimpy black nightie you don't actually own, would it?''

''Only if that's the kind you like most.''

''Forget the nightie,'' he said decisively. ''Just wear stockings. Black to match your hair, with a seam up the back. High heels. A sexy little garter belt. Teeny-weeny thong undies. Black push-up bra...''

Frankie groaned in horror, her cheeks flushing as she carefully dabbed a soft cloth against Astrid's milk mustache. ''How disappointing to find you have such a truly impoverished imagination. Doc, that one's straight out of *Penthouse*.''

''You read *Penthouse*? Truly, I'm shocked, Frankie.''

She shrugged. ''My brothers always hid them under their mattresses. I admit, I did look. Only once.'' She shot Doc a smile. ''For research purposes, of course.''

''Research?''

"To see what men of your ilk want from a woman."

Doc chuckled appreciatively. "The plot thickens. Do feel free to show me anything you learned."

Frankie almost smiled. And then every trace of humor fled her face. "Doc—" Her voice caught sharply. "Come here. Astrid feels hot."

Doc frowned, quickly rising and crossing the room. He pressed his lips to Astrid's forehead; she was a little warm. "Don't worry," he said, heading for the thermometer in his black bag. "If she's got a temperature, it's low. Still, with babies this age, it could spike."

Frankie's voice was sharp. "Don't be so negative."

"Sorry," he said, meaning it. He didn't want to worry Frankie. Softly cooing endearments, he turned the baby over his knees and inserted the thermometer. A moment later, he said, "It's a degree above, that's all."

"A degree? You're sure? That's all?"

"C'mon, don't worry." Doc took in how Frankie's eyes were riveted on his, how her hands were tightly clenched. The urge to offer comfort was so strong that he was completely powerless to mask the huskiness of his own voice. "Tonight you and Astrid have got the one thing you need."

"What's that?"

"A doctor in the house."

And if it killed him, he wasn't going to make a lover's move.

EVERYTHING FELT WARM. In the dream, she could feel the sun beneath the chill spring air—touching her cheeks, dancing in her hair, glinting off the red hood of the convertible. Feeling as strong as the cool wind, the bright white sunbeams touched on the roadway as she bore down, pushing the gas.

Just ahead was the grassy, triangular median with the tall, whitewashed fork. And for the first time, she noticed two cardinals perched on the wire fence next to the road.

Doc was definitely part of this dream. Frankie knew that now. Was she driving the red convertible to visit him? Or was she driving away from him?

She didn't know. All she knew was that she loved the feel of this glorious wind in her hair, and the familiarity of this road, which she'd driven so many times. She was in Pennsylvania, she knew. Just around the bend was the high school, and to the left was the white church with its steeple and Mr. Cranson's apple orchard, where she'd first been kissed.

But that was all wrong.

Frankie's first kiss had occurred when Johnny Tomassino kissed her under a rose arbor during a sixth-grade field trip to the Brooklyn Botanic Garden.

She groaned softly in her sleep.

Then the confusion lifted—she was racing in the red convertible again. Her eyes lifted to the rearview mirror. Far behind her in the distance was a reptile-print scarf, whipping around in the air like a real live snake. Had she been wearing the scarf? Had it come untied from her neck and blown away?

She wasn't sure. Suddenly, her eyes shot to the road again. The fork was so close now! Too close! She had to decide which way to turn! A kaboom deafened her. Suddenly the steering wheel was vibrating so hard her arms shook. Metal screeched and a spray of red sparks paddle-wheeled up from the asphalt.

A blown tire. That's what it was. Her eyes shot to the rearview mirror... *Which way? Which way?* she murmured.

"Frankie?"

She roused. In the darkness she blinked, and realized Doc was in bed with her, gently shaking her shoulder. Fleeting images darted through her mind, and when she caught them, they were sharp, almost as if she'd been remembering, not dreaming.

"Doc?" she murmured.

"Right here beside you, baby doll. What do you need? Want me to hold you?"

It was clear from his voice he'd do anything she asked, and that alone made her feel warm and safe. "No." She sat up, her heart hammering. Unceremoniously, she clambered over him, heading for the window. Puffing her cheeks to blow, she exhaled, then shook her muzzy head.

What felt like a second later, Doc was beside her. One of his huge hands squeezed her shoulder as he pressed a glass of water to her lips, saying, "Here." She sipped gratefully, letting the cool water slide down her throat, and she didn't fight when he urged her to lean her back against his chest. He molded his hand around her head. Raking his fingers up from her nape, he ruffled her curls.

"Bad dream, Frankie?"

Her voice was a raspy croak. "No. Not bad, really. It just woke me up. I'm a strange sleeper." She glanced up, with a fleeting smile. "Deep dreams. This one's kind of weird. I've had it more than once. It started after my transplant surgery."

His teeth were a quick flash of white in the dark. "Must be all your hidden, subconscious desires."

And not so subconscious, Frankie thought, glancing over her shoulder at the bare chest that had been warming her back. Even in the dark, she could see the trail of hair narrowing down to where his loose sweatpants rode low on his hips. For a second, as he leaned closer, she thought he was going to kiss her, but he didn't. Too bad, because right now she would have let him.

She'd been so sure his presence in her bed would make her tense, unable to sleep. Surprisingly, he'd simply felt big and warm next to her. Comforting. Safe. Sure, Frankie said she wanted to be on her own. But if the truth be told, she'd lived in a crowded household her whole life, and getting used to this apartment was still difficult, even if having Astrid helped. Most of the time, she felt lonely.

Now Doc chuckled softly and brushed at a lock of her hair. "Well, I hope some of these deep dreams of yours are about me, darlin' girl."

She frowned. "Actually, I do think you were in the weird one." She turned toward him, fighting the urge to nuzzle her face in his chest hair. "Like I said…it's this dream I keep having, over and over. I'm in a car, driving really fast, and…" Her voice trailed off. "Well, if I write out the whole thing, maybe you could help me analyze it sometime."

"Glad to."

She sighed. "Let's check on the baby."

As they went to the crib together, the dark, silent night closed intimately around them. Gripping the crib rail, Frankie felt more grounded. Her dreams might be elusive, but the wood beneath her palm felt solid and real. As her eyes adjusted more fully, she could see the apartment's familiar interior. Outside was the Woo Long bakery, with its strange mix of fortune cookies and wedding cakes. And Mott Street, at which she'd stared a million times before, with the lights of Chinatown beaconing in the distance. Doc was grounding her, too. Sometimes he seemed so incredibly familiar, as if she'd known him far longer than she actually had. Somehow, he seemed to belong here, in her home. Just like the bed, the curtains, the flowers, and Astrid.

"Isn't she just as cute as a button?" Doc whispered. He nestled closer, sliding behind Frankie, both his arms circling her waist. She leaned against his chest, looking down at their handiwork, the dream now forgotten.

"I love her so much," Frankie whispered back.

"So do I, baby doll. I appreciate your letting me be here through a night. It's special."

Smiling, Frankie dangled a hand into the crib and grazed Astrid's cheek. And then she gasped, whirling toward Doc and grabbing his strong body for support. "Oh, Doc, she's burning up!"

THE FEVER LASTED TWO DAYS.

And Doc never left. Handling crises, it turned out, was his forte. He cared for Astrid—giving cool sponge baths and periodically checking her temperature. He fixed meals and assured the relatives that everything was fine. Sometime during the first twenty-four hours, with a soft sigh that said he was breaking some silent rule he'd set for himself, he started trying to kiss Frankie again, too. And since her resistance was running as low as her daughter's, she let him. After that, he kissed her often. And for those fleeting seconds, Frankie actually forgot to be worried sick about the baby. It was a tremendous relief. Frankie didn't know what she would have done without Doc.

"Frankie," he said, after a particularly long, hair-raising bout of Astrid's feverish wails.

"Hmm?"

Doc looked faintly bemused. "You had a heart attack, baby doll. This is just a fever."

Frankie had never felt so frazzled. "True. But that was me," she explained as she gathered up the baby's soiled sleepers. "And this is Astrid. I admit I worried some during the pregnancy, Doc, since there were odds against us. But when we came through with flying colors..." Frankie paused, then sounded surprised. "Well, I guess I simply don't think much about healthy people getting sick."

His eyes were kind. "Kids get sick, Mama," he said softly. "But she'll be fine. In fact, we should think of this as her golden opportunity to build antibodies." He smiled. "Now, about your antibodies, ma'am."

Frankie blinked back tears, since every one of Astrid's wails had cut right to her heart. She glanced toward the crib. "Mine?"

"Yeah, now that Astrid's sleeping again, you look like you could use a big ole fat hug and a kiss."

Knowing Doc was right, Frankie simply snuggled into his arms while he plopped his cowboy hat playfully on her head. Then she let him hug her so tight she thought her bones would crack. "How's this building my antibodies?" she asked, her voice coming out husky.

"Right now," he assured her, touching his lips

gently to hers, "your entire body is busy, fending off my germs."

Her body was busy, all right. Buzzing and tingling with his sweet, sexy kiss. He hadn't shaved, and as he leaned closer, she could feel his prickly golden whiskers graze her cheek. A second later, she felt the hint of his mustache on her upper lip as his coaxed hers apart again, deepening the kiss, his mouth moving on hers with soft, tender pressure that made the whole world seem very fuzzy and far away.

"Uh-huh," she whispered against his skin, molding her hands around his powerful shoulders and indulging him. "I am feeling better, Doctor."

"But I feel I must examine you further," he said in return, trailing kisses down her neck. "Here. Here. And way down here," he whispered, not even stopping when she leaned so far back that his hat tumbled off her head.

Such sweet moments as that carried Frankie through until Astrid's fever broke, and when it did, Frankie said, "Your being here, helping me, really meant something, Doc. I mean that."

He shrugged, his eyes filling with emotion. "I hate that Astrid's been sick. But I liked being here. You know, Frankie, I'm exploring this situation, too. How we might feel about each other."

"Well, you turned out to be the voice of reason."

He lifted a golden eyebrow. "Me? The voice of reason?"

"I guess that is a pretty scary thought," she teased.

And then, for the first time in days, they had a good laugh. It was full of relief over Astrid, but it held something more—the unspoken connection of a deeper bond they were coming to share. With a breathy sigh, Frankie said, "I'm just so glad you were here, Doc."

His voice was low. "Let me stay another night, Frankie."

"Why? Astrid's better...."

For a long moment he was silent, considering. "Because I want to sleep the way we have been. Me in your bed."

"Even if we don't..."

He nodded. "Yeah, even if we don't."

So much for her bright idea about practicing feminine wiles on this man. He'd managed to twist her around his pinkie again. She just wished she knew more about men, so she'd know what was really going on here. Her instincts told her Doc was good with smooth talk, maybe not so good with deeper emotions, since he was still hurting from his fiancée's death. But Frankie wasn't about to flatter herself by thinking Doc was falling for her, even if he did seem to want more intimacy than he could admit to. Maybe she was simply the closest available female. And they did share the love of their child. Surely, that was the reason for his attention.

"Frankie?"

"I'm thinking."

It would certainly be helpful if she could ask the most approachable of her aunts—Aunt Sophia—for advice. But then, so far, her advice had not been particularly illuminating. Sighing, Frankie gazed deeply into Doc's eyes. Even though she feared him breaking her heart because he'd never make a commitment, and even though she wanted the freedom to explore her new life, he was the one who seemed fragile at this particular moment. Her breath caught. "All right, Doc. You can stay."

THE HONORABLE JUDGE T. Winslow was envisioning the secret philanthropists who financially backed the Big Apple Babies adoption agency. All were relaxing in well-appointed rooms in Manhattan's toniest neighborhoods: Central Park, Sutton Place, Wall Street. Judge T. Winslow, of course, was in the Bahamas.

"Tilford, you scared me to death!"

Judge Winslow winced. The speaker was his best friend, who was ninety and in poor health. "That's why I'm making this conference call. I would have phoned sooner, but I had no idea—"

"No idea!" a second voiced exploded. "You've served nearly a century on the New York family court bench. Your heart attack made the six o'clock news."

"And worried us all sick," put in another aged male voice.

"Please," Judge Winslow reminded the Manhattan movers and shakers. "The main point is that I'm in excellent health. I do assure you, it doesn't get much better than this." As if to prove his point, Judge Winslow was reclining by the swimming pool, and he retied the sash to his huge white terry-cloth robe around his rotund girth. He smiled as a bikini-clad waitress handed him a large fruit drink with an umbrella swizzle stick.

"Well, I'm just relieved you're all right, Tilford." The soothing female voice held a hint of Southern roots, but the identity of the speaker was a mystery to all the others. Most saw one another socially; only this woman insisted she could never meet face-to-face.

"Next time you fake a heart attack, Winslow," said a Wall Street tycoon, "please call first. I failed to purchase some very lucrative stocks because of this. And to think my son was actually in the courtroom when you pulled that stunt. Was Jake all right?"

Judge Winslow sighed. "Was Jake Lucas all right? *I* was the one who supposedly had the heart attack, remember?"

"Yes, yes," came the Wall Street baritone.

The judge heaved a laborious sigh. If he wasn't careful, these people would instill enough guilt to ruin his much-deserved vacation. Especially since Jake Lucas was a problem. The poor young man had been searching for his biological parents for the past year, and while he'd confided in the judge about the failed search, ethics demanded Judge Winslow keep his mouth shut.

Still, it was the judge's friendship with Jake's biological father that had led to the start of the Big Apple Babies adoption agency in the first place. Back then, Jake was a young, burnt-out hotshot prosecutor for the family courts, so Jake's biological father had come to the judge, wondering how he could secretly, anonymously help his son. Judge Winslow suggested they—and some others—pool their money and start an adoption agency, making Jake the head executive. But now, Jake, with the blessing of his adoptive parents, was looking for his biological father. And his biological father did not want to be found. Judge Winslow frowned. In a year, he'd gotten nowhere with helping along that family reconciliation. Stirring from his reverie, the judge realized his friends were still discussing his heart attack.

"Tilford," chided Grantham Hale. "You really should be more thoughtful."

"I am. I'm thinking of ways to help that friend of Jake Lucas's, Doc Holiday." The judge sniffed self-righteously, even though he wasn't really angry with Grantham Hale. At least not since the judge had sentenced his own most unmarriageable great-granddaughter, Phoebe Rutherford, to spend time with the man. Of course, Phoebe had turned out to be marriageable after all, and she was now Grantham's wife. Even the case of Jake Lucas and Dani Newland paled by comparison, when he had practically forced Dani to declare her love for Jake right on the witness stand.

"Phoebe," Grantham suddenly yelled. "Could you get Lyssa and Kirby out of that potted plant? I'm on the phone."

"If that's Granddaddy," yelled Phoebe, getting the kids under control, "tell him I'm furious. For ten horrible minutes I thought he'd had a *real* heart attack."

Judge Winslow sighed. "Working in family court is always high risk."

Grantham chuckled. "Only if you're the world's most unconventional judge."

There was a long pause. Then everyone sighed. After another moment of chitchat, they began ringing off. Grantham was last, of course, since Phoebe got on and said hello.

When Judge Winslow finally hung up, he leaned back, sipping his umbrella drink and pondering his latest case. Doc Holiday and Frankie Luccetti seemed terribly unsuited. Still, his instincts told him that his unconventional courtroom antics might have helped bring together yet another man, woman and child....

Chapter Nine

Frankie glanced over her shoulder as she dimmed the
lights to soothe Astrid, then she lifted the baby onto
the changing table. "Don't forget to take that brown
bag home with you, Doc. Mama packed it for you."

"Don't you worry about me, baby doll," Doc said,
sliding the last of the leftovers into Frankie's fridge.
"I ain't leavin' my goodies here for you and that
devilish little munchkin to gobble up. I'm just trying
to hide them until I'm ready to go home." He chuckled. "Hell, as much home cookin' as they had at the
party, every man in Manhattan could have had leftovers."

"With some to spare," agreed Frankie. "The party
was great, huh?"

"Yeah." Mama and Papa Luccetti's fiftieth wedding anniversary party had taken place in Aunt Sophia's backyard in Long Island. Doc had helped bar-
becue the ribs, then he and Uncle Big Sal had rolled
out a mammoth anniversary cake topped with spar-
klers. He'd danced with Frankie to countless big band
tunes, and watched with merriment as her four brothers took the stage with Astrid and crooned Sinatra
songs.

"Fifty years of marriage." He sighed now, shrugging out of the black suit jacket and loosening the western-style tie he'd worn for the party. "And they still look happy."

"They are happy." Frankie finished powdering their daughter's behind, then glanced at Doc as he relaxed in a corner of the couch. "Hat," she said simply.

"What? Am I in the presence of a lady?"

"At least one."

"Which one of you two *isn't* a lady?"

Frankie shot him a saucy smile. "Guess."

Laughing, Doc swept the hat from his head, casually tossing it to an end table. "Just 'cause you kiss good doesn't mean you're not a lady, Frankie," he remarked, his eyes returning to her and the baby.

"Do I kiss good?"

Doc tried to look dumbstruck. "Gee, baby doll, I forgot. Guess you'll have to come smooch me before I can answer."

"I'll think about it."

Smiling, Doc watched Astrid squirm fussily; she'd been cooed at for hours and was long past due for her crib. As Frankie wrestled with the baby, the hem of her short black skirt, which was printed with tiny flowers, swished against the backs of her bare thighs. She wore a simple white blouse tucked into the elasticized waistband and strappy black sandals.

"Well, Doc, I take it you're not leaving yet?"

"Not until I get a long kiss good-night."

Lifting her gaze, Frankie caught the frank admiration in his eyes and flushed a deep rose. As she started wriggling one of Astrid's arms into a sleeper, her voice lowered. "You could stay, you know."

"Hmm." He nodded, wondering exactly how she meant the offer. After Astrid's fever, he'd stayed three more nights, but then he'd had to leave. Sleeping together without having sex had simply gotten too hard for both of them. Still, they'd long been missing the comfort of each other's arms. Most nights, Doc woke and found himself remembering how Frankie's head felt curled on his chest and how her breaths warmed his bare skin, and how, even while she was sleeping, her fingers toyed with his chest hair. He wanted to be here to comfort her when she awoke with that strange, deep dream, the one they kept meaning to interpret together but never did because they always had so much else to talk about.

That seemed especially true since they'd starting spending time with Doc's friends from Big Apple Babies, attending events as a couple. They'd gone to the Hamptons, too, in order to close up Doc's summer house. Even now, Frankie refused to leave Astrid, so Mama Luccetti decided to accompany them, as chaperone and baby-sitter. Of course, since Mama was going, Papa had to. Then Aunt Sophia and Uncle Big Sal. Which meant Frankie's brother, Mickey, had to be invited because he had a large van they could all fit into.

They wound up staying a week.

It was the best vacation of Doc's life. Members of the Luccetti clan came and went. It was hot enough to swim, cool enough that the tourists had all gone home; the nights were perfect for cookouts, bonfires and long walks on the beach. Doc and Frankie had played with the baby, and at night, they'd collected shells under the light of the pale moon, talking about nothing and everything.

"The party really was something," he murmured now. "And the food. I can't believe how your family eats."

Frankie carried Astrid to the crib. "The way *we* eat? You don't do too bad yourself. Uncle Big Sal now calls you the Mysterious Inferno, because he can't figure out how you burn off all the fat."

"I like to stay lean and mean."

A silence fell. Doc's eyes strayed to the kitchen, and when they landed on Frankie's calendar, his heart pulled. Nearly a year ago, that same calendar was nothing more than big blank blocks, marking off empty days. Now, the calendar was a mess of scribbles. There were notes about Frankie and Astrid's doctor appointments. Reminders for Frankie's hair and nails. A parenting seminar. Two evenings blocked off for taking Astrid to the restaurant, where Frankie was again working the cash register for her parents. On Wednesdays, she made volunteer phone calls on behalf of the animal humane society. And she'd gotten a diaphragm. The day after Doc had mentioned it, she'd noted the appointment in bright purple ink that was as good as a neon sign.

It was the kind of thing Frankie did—not always speaking directly, but letting Doc know things just the same. Of course, she could be verbal. Like last week, when he'd invited her and Astrid to his fenced-in roof garden for a cookout. It was one of the few times she'd been at his place.

"Hmm," she'd ventured. "You were going to share this apartment with Marta...I guess you got rid of her things."

He had. Most of Marta's artwork had been sold, though some was in storage. "Well, there are still some clothes in that closet." He'd shrugged a little helplessly. "I guess I should have gotten rid of them, but they were too expensive to throw out and I wasn't sure where to donate them. Even now, I don't like to think about them."

"Even now?" Frankie said. "You miss her even now?"

He'd squinted at Frankie. "Well, sugar plum, my feelings have changed. I don't feel the kind of grief I once did."

Frankie's lips had pursed. "This closet?"

Doc's warning flags had finally started going up. "Yeah."

The next thing Doc knew, Frankie had flung open the closet, and her eyes—momentarily appreciative—had roved over the clothes. She'd looked so enamored of the garments that he'd foolishly said, "You're welcome to have them. They're great clothes," he'd defended carefully when he saw her stunned expression.

Frankie merely sniffed. "Well, I can certainly understand why you'd want to keep your fiancée's things. Because of the expense and everything. But since you wanted to remove them and couldn't, I suppose I could offer to help you."

Staring in bemused stupefaction, he'd watched as she riffled through the garments, raking hangers across the rod. To him, the clothes were just that—clothes. So he wasn't the least bit offended by Frankie's pique.

"She wore a lot of cashmere," Frankie had remarked, tossing item after item to the floor. "Silk."

She'd paused only once, holding up a sexy red lace bra. She stared so critically at the cups that Doc half expected her to comment on the fact that Marta had been admirably endowed—at least until he realized Frankie was biting her lower lip to keep it from trembling. When she flung down the bra, he'd felt terrible. Especially when it was followed by a matching red lace girdle that obviously hadn't been designed for flattening a woman's tummy.

Doc's heart had lurched so painfully he could barely breathe, and he suddenly felt strangely defensive on Frankie's behalf. "Frankie," he'd said softly. "You're you. And Marta was Marta. She's gone now."

"Yes, she is, isn't she?" Frankie said dismissively. Then she glanced over the clothes. "Well, almost."

With that, Frankie had gathered the clothes into her arms. Grabbing Astrid, Doc had followed her—all the way down the hallway, into the elevator. "You're going to throw her clothes into the street?"

Frankie merely raised an eyebrow. "Just to help you out, since I really don't want them." Outside, on the sidewalk, she'd raised her voice like a street hawker. "Expensive leather coats for free! Cashmere sweaters. Lace lingerie."

Businessmen turned to stare. SoHo artists who were used to scavaging secondhand wear circled closer, and gallery art buyers who'd been gazing through large plate-glass windows headed for the doors. By the time Frankie came down with a second load, a crowd had gathered. One classy-looking blond woman actually tried on a pair of Marta's slacks under her suit skirt while conferring with a friend about the fit. Doc guessed he couldn't blame the woman; the slacks were Versace originals. In the end, he'd wound up grinning. Hell, it was a scene that Marta, with her own impulsive nature, would have appreciated. Besides, Frankie's jealousy warmed him from the inside out.

Upstairs, he'd hauled her into his arms. "You have no idea how adorable you are."

She'd gulped guiltily. "Was Marta very beautiful?"

"Oh, Frankie," he said, sighing. "Yes, she was. But you need to understand some things." And then he'd straightened her out. He'd loved Marta and would have lived his life with her. But she'd been married to her art and feared commitments to anything else, including kids. Doc knew it, and he'd been prepared to live that way.

"And now?" Frankie had asked.

"Now," he'd said huskily, "I know I would have been settling, that there could be so much more." He stopped, but Frankie understood. She was capable of giving to Doc in a way that Marta never could have, not even if she'd lived forever. And having admitted that to Frankie, Doc knew he'd finally let Marta go. He'd put his fiancée to rest, and was moving on with the woman who'd given birth to his child. He just wished he knew where they were moving to. Now he got up and followed Frankie to the crib.

"Here," she whispered, pressing Astrid against his chest.

He held her for a moment—shutting his eyes, feeling her smooth skin against his rough whiskered cheek, smelling the lotion and baby powder. She was so small, so innocent. And the love that swelled in him every time he held her was so powerfully strong he knew he'd never get used to feeling it. "'Night, my sweet little slice of sugar pie," he whispered, laying her down.

A moment later, after Frankie further dimmed the lights, she joined him on the couch. "My," she said, "don't you look serious. What are you thinking?"

He draped his arm across her shoulders. *About all the emotions I feel nowadays.* "Not a thing, baby doll."

"I hate secrets."

He drew her closer for a quick kiss. "If I get too secretive, sugar plum, I promise I'll give you the high-tech Doc-decoding device. It's real flashy with lots of extra gadgets."

She smiled against his lips, sighing in relaxed self-satisfaction. "So, what should we talk about?"

"Ah. Well, we could interpret those dreams of yours."

She glanced up, her dark eyes sparkling with mischief. "Okay." She made a point of getting comfortable, squirming against Doc. Slipping off her shoes, she drew her feet beneath her on the couch, then rested her hand casually on his thigh. "My dreams," she teased. "What if I was dreaming about you right now, Doc?"

Her body heat made him feel heavy and relaxed, as if he were drugged, and the weight of her hand on his thigh was maddening. "Dreamin' while you're awake?"

"Dreaming you'd kiss me."

"Then I'd be the man who makes dreams come true." He settled his mouth over hers, and her pliant, moist lips opened readily. For a moment, their tongues tussled, then she drew away, raking a finger down his cheek.

"Whiskers," she murmured.

He hadn't shaved since this morning. "You've got a way of bringing out the hairy beast in me, Frankie." And with that, he crushed her against his chest, not giving her an inch to move. He felt her needy response—in the swift surrender of her parting lips, in the loosening of arms that wreathed his neck. Under her white blouse, he felt the hard, tight buds of her nipples, and without dragging his mouth from hers, he slid a hand over her breast. As he kneaded her softly, the tips became stiffer. Moaning, he imagined how her firm, pert breasts would look with those aroused tips wet from his lips; reddened and hard, they'd glow like golden nuggets of rose fire. The sudden desperate need to see her naked shook him.

The thought alone made the weight of his groin unbearable, and the persistent ache got heavier when he heard Frankie's breath catch with desire as she moved her hand on his thigh. Deepening their kiss, he slipped his hand over hers. Ever so slowly, he guided it upward, along the threadbare inner seam of his jeans. Each inch was the worst kind of torture, the flesh beneath Doc's soft, well-washed denims quivering in anticipation of her touch. Gasping, he slid her hand right over him. And she must have wanted that because she molded her palm to him with an unpracticed squeeze that made him go out of his mind with need. When her fingers stiffened, sliding up and down the length of his fly, he could take no more. "Oh, Frankie," he moaned. "Baby doll."

The throaty sound she uttered wasn't quite a chuckle, but she was obviously pleased with making him so insane and helpless. "Yes?" she asked, panting softly, her voice all mock innocence as she squeezed him again.

"I forgot. You sidetracked me."

"Sidetracked you? Where were you trying to go?"

"Here." Doc shifted his body, lifted her skirt and pulled her on top of him in one swift gesture, so she was straddling him with nothing between their aroused bodies but his jeans and her panties.

Her cheeks were flushed bright pink with excitement, and her dark eyes glittered like a starlit black night. "This is a good place to go."

"I was hoping you'd enjoy the trip." He was caught between laughter and a desire that was dead serious, so he merely covered her mouth with his again, delivering a sweet, slow kiss that sparked real fire. Because the way she was straddling him threatened to make him explode, he shifted her to his side and glided a splayed hand from her knee to her breast. The hem of her flirty skirt lifted, and the blouse came untucked from the elasticized waistband. Neither of them were laughing now. Especially not when his hand slid into her panties.

He loved how she quit kissing him then. Her jaw went slack, and she leaned back her head in ecstasy as he dipped his fingers between her legs, gently parting her cleft and stroking only once, gathering honey. While his tongue dived deeper into her mouth, demanding her response, he made a fuss of withdrawing his touch, then neatly straightening the waistband below, as if he wasn't the least inclined to touch her intimately again.

Her whimper of needy protest was everything Doc wanted to hear. But the time for teasing had passed. Now he needed her so bad it hurt. His hands slid

between them again, sliding down from the collar of
her blouse, quickly flicking open the buttons.

But something was wrong. Through the haze of his
desire, Doc realized she was shifting away. She was
leaning back, looking flustered and embarrassed.
Quickly, Frankie rebuttoned her blouse, her eyes
glazed with a confused mixture of concern and
thwarted passion.

"Just not my shirt, okay?"

Doc leaned up on an elbow and stared. Only her
vulnerability kept him from exploding. He found her
hand and twined his fingers through hers. "Frankie,
it's not okay. Look, sugar plum, if we're gonna make
love, I want to see you. All of you. Complete surrender. No withholding."

Her voice was low. "Last time I didn't take off my
shirt."

He bit back a sigh of pure male frustration. He
wanted her so much. But damn if he was going to
take her like this. It hurt him that she didn't trust him
to see her fully naked. His ragged voice steadied a
bit. "I want you, no holds barred. The bed we share
has got to be a place where anything goes."

She was staring downward, high color in her
cheeks. "But last time…"

His gaze caught and held hers. "This isn't last
time, Frankie. This is now." Gently, he raised her
hand to his lips and kissed the fingers. "Aw, darlin',"
he said, sighing. "Try to understand." He trailed his
finger down her blouse, over her chest, still feeling
the dull ache of his readiness to love her. "I…know
you're afraid of getting hurt, and I think you're afraid
I'll be turned off by your scars, which I won't. I
promise." Vaguely, he realized he'd done what he

didn't think he could—started making promises. His throat ached with both emotion and frustrated desire, so he paused, swallowing hard. "I've also known you long enough to know you go to mass every Sunday with your mama, come rain or shine. So I know you don't lightly give yourself to a man."

She started blinking rapidly, as if she might cry. Those silky eyelashes cast shadows on her cheekbones in the dim light, and as he watched them flutter while she battled her unshed tears, Doc's heart nearly broke. "I accept you just the way you are, Frankie," he said softly. "I want you, just the way you are."

She nodded, digesting that.

"Now, c'm'ere, honey." Sitting up, he hugged her against him, then cupped her nape, tenderly ruffling the curls. "I told you I was going to settle once for not having all of a woman. But I won't do it with you, Frankie."

"It's all or nothing, huh?"

He nodded.

"I guess I'm just not ready," she said in a small voice.

If the truth be told, he wasn't sure he was, either. He knew what he thought he wanted, but what if he hurt her? "That's okay."

For a long time, they merely sat there, nestling together on the couch while desire slowly ebbed. "The night's still young," he finally said. "Now, why don't you tell me about those dreams of yours?"

"Okay..." She frowned. Her cheeks were still flushed with slight embarrassment over how close they'd come to making love without doing so. "Come to think of it," she said softly, "I guess some weird things started happening after my transplant surgery."

There was a long pause. Frankie didn't talk much about her surgery. She didn't like to dwell on the past. She was simply grateful for today, for all the gifts she'd been given—life, comparatively good health, and most of all, their baby girl.

"Weird?"

She nodded. "Like…this sounds so silly, but I started…" She suddenly giggled, lightening the mood between them. "Well, I started eating two bananas every morning for breakfast and watching the nightly business report on CNN."

Doc started to say that wasn't so weird. Marta had been a big fan of morning bananas and the nightly business report. Doc himself liked to watch the news. Many very normal Americans did.

"Anything else weird?"

She shook her head. "No."

He chuckled. "Gosh, Frankie, if you get any weirder, I'm not sure we can still be friends."

She shot him a shy glance, reminding him they'd become so much more than friends. Since her eyes were meeting his for the first time since she'd stopped their kiss, Doc smiled back, then he snuggled her closer in the crook of his arm, leaned over and gently, tenderly brushed his mouth across hers.

Her smiled gentled as she wiggled, getting more comfortable. "Well, it *was* weird, because I never paid attention to the news before, Doc. And I didn't have this recurring dream, either. I guess it has to do with the new freedom I have to make choices about my life."

He nodded. "Okay. I'm with you, baby doll."

"Well," she continued, "in the dream, I'm always driving. I'm in a bright red convertible, speeding down a long, straight stretch of road. It's a two-lane country road and...and I think it's in Pennsylvania.'' She must have noticed his face, because she suddenly said, ''Doc, is something wrong?''

''Nothing.'' But a shiver had wended down his spine. It wasn't at all unpleasant, but it was a shiver, nonetheless. ''Uh...what's the road look like, darlin'?''

She frowned, trying to visualize. ''Hmm. It's one-lane, as I said. There's wire fencing on either side, and a grassy median in the distance. The median has a pole with a fork on top that points in two different directions.''

''And you're in a red convertible?''

She nodded. ''An apple red one.''

Doc's pulse was drumming so loud he barely heard the last words. He knew an intersection that was just as she described. But when he'd visited it, the red convertible had been wrapped around the pole.

He told himself the notion forming in his mind was crazy. An impossibility. ''Frankie,'' he said. ''What was the exact date of your transplant surgery?''

She squinted, unable to follow his logic. ''Why?''

He wasn't saying anything until he thought this through further. ''I just wondered.''

Frankie told him the date.

And Doc's breath caught. Because it was the exact date of Marta's death.

''DID YOU TELL FRANKIE what you suspected?'' Jake Lucas reclined in a swivel chair, running a hand through his thick black hair.

Doc had been staring through the frosted glass of Jake's shut office door, at the block lettering that read

Jake Lucas: Director. Now he shook his head. "It's such a crazy thought. I mean, the whole idea that maybe Frankie wound up with Marta's heart." He frowned. "But I got such a strange feeling that first day I went to Frankie's apartment, as if Marta was there. And I know Marta donated her organs. I was with her when she filled out the card. She always kept it in her wallet, next to her insurance cards."

Shane, who was lounging against the wall, took off his black Stetson, rested it on top of a file cabinet and toyed with the brim. "Might be better to let sleeping dogs lie this time, little brother," he said in a drawl that mirrored Doc's.

Doc smirked. "Yeah, well, I happen to have a scientific background. I lack your talent for living with mysteries."

"I'm an ex-cop," reminded Shane. "*Ex* being the operative term. There are no more mysteries in my life."

"Well, I know about living with mysteries." Jake sighed.

Doc guessed Jake was thinking of how he'd met his wife, Dani. Years ago, Dani had given up a baby for adoption, and Jake had been the lawyer who handled the case. Much later, Dani had insinuated herself into Jake's life under false pretenses, to find out what had become of her child. "If you're talking about Dani," Doc said, "that's a mystery you solved, Jake."

"If you call marriage a solution," said Shane dryly.

"For a cop, you sure are gun-shy," chided Doc.

Shane shrugged. "Ex-cop."

"Actually," Jake said, "I was thinking about my

current search for my biological parents.'' He paused, tweaking his dark mustache thoughtfully, rolling the end between his thumb and finger. ''A few months back, I was so close to finding them, then the leads dried up. If I didn't know better, I'd think my parents caught a whiff of the search and set up roadblocks. It's almost as if they heard I was looking for them and don't want me to find them.''

Doc's heart went out to his boss and friend. For years, Jake had wondered about his biological parents. Recently, with some prodding from Dani and his adoptive folks, he'd finally started to search, so he could put the mystery of his past to rest. Doc knew Jake feared rejection. He feared he'd hear those horrible words he'd always dreaded: ''We just didn't want you.''

''What about that guy you went to med school with?'' Jake prodded now, not giving up. ''You know, the one you said you tutored and who now works in the transplant unit?''

Doc sighed. ''Steve Hill. Asking him to check the records is pretty unethical.''

Shane studied the brim of his Stetson. ''True, but if you're really curious…''

Doc shot him a wry glance. ''And this from a cop.''

''Ex-cop. Besides—'' Shane defended himself ''—to catch bad guys, you've got to be a little bad yourself.''

''Wow,'' said Jake. ''What if it turned out to be true? I mean, it would be like…having proof there's something beyond. As if a small piece of Marta's memory lived on, in her heart, remembered by Frankie as a dream...."

A sudden rush of excitement overcame Doc, and the scientist took over. "You guys are right," he said decisively, thinking about his strange initial attraction to Frankie. "This is such an amazing thing. I've got to know."

"I OWE YOU, DOC. And I trust you'll never divulge where you got the information. But can you tell me why you want to know what happened to Marta's heart?"

"I'd rather keep that to myself."

"Well, okay. Hang on."

Doc kicked back in the office next to the infirmary, adjusting his hat, shoving the phone receiver between his jaw and shoulder, and propping his boots on a desk. If his suspicions were right, it really was downright exciting. Not that anything would come of this...

Hell, just the fact that it had taken more than a week to reach Steve Hill, who'd been on vacation, wasn't a good omen. Now Doc thought of Frankie, a bemused smile coming to his lips. She'd invited him over for dinner tonight, which was hardly unusual, since she often cooked for him nowadays. But tonight sounded special.

Frankie sure was. Doc's chest tightened with emotion. He wished she was ready to deepen their relationship, to take the next step and become lovers again. For him, it was past time. Hell, if the truth be told, he already knew becoming lovers again wouldn't be enough for him. With Frankie, he kept taking a step—only to find out he was ready for another. Inside him was a big bottomless hole that Frankie made bigger just by filling him.

Yeah, he was starting to want the whole enchilada. Or stuffed shell pasta, he mentally corrected himself with a smile. They'd been dating awhile. And in the near year since they'd met, they'd traversed some pretty strange territory. Stranger still, if this wild hunch of his turned out to be correct. Which, he reminded himself again, it wouldn't. Anyway, the main thing was that he, Frankie and Astrid had slid into a kind of familial routine that was better than anything he'd ever imagined.

Shane was happy, too. Just last week, Doc and Shane had been hanging out on the roof garden with a couple of cold ones. "I like her," Shane had announced, right out of the blue.

"Seeing as you're the king of understatement, I guess that means you think I ought to marry her."

"I thought so at first," Shane admitted. "But only because of the baby."

"And now?"

"Now I think she's right for you, little brother."

"Yeah," Doc had agreed. "Strange as the idea seemed to me at first, I think she is, too."

He and Shane had shared a long glance, both of them thinking over their parentless childhood in Texas, of the devastating flood that had destroyed their family farm and taken their parents' lives, of being separated in childhood and raised by different aunts.

"Feels nice to have a family again," Shane said softly.

"Sure does." Mama Luccetti had taken in Doc and

Shane as surely as if she'd given birth to them. The last time Doc had visited Mama, she was busy sewing new buttons on one of Shane's ratty old shirts.

The phone clicked back on. "Doc?"

His heart lurched. "Yeah?"

"Just checking on you. Hold one more second."

The phrase sent excitement racing through Doc again. What if he was right? What an amazing, wonderful and strange thing that would be. He was a doctor. A pragmatic, practical man of science. To him, the body was simply a biological system. It was intricate, endlessly fascinating and wonderfully economical, but it wasn't mysterious. The human heart—no matter what storybooks said—was nothing more than a pump. The discovery that it was something more could challenge Doc's whole world view. It could make him believe in such things as God and a spiritual afterlife…things that Frankie was somehow able to believe in without proof, on nothing more than faith alone.

"Doc?"

His heart hammered with anticipation. "Yeah."

"Marta's heart was donated. And the recipient was a New Yorker, a woman named Francesca Luccetti."

Doc barely knew what he said next. Hanging up, he leaned back in his chair, his mind reeling. He blew out a long, awed sigh as his eyes went to the window. Between buildings, the sky was wide and blue and seemed to stretch forever, making the world seem bigger and more mysterious than ever. He remembered that strange feeling he'd had the day he met Frankie, as if Marta was somehow there. This was proof there was something beyond man's mundane existence.

Doc had to tell Frankie. He picked up the phone, then his hand stilled. No, this was so over-the-top fantastic, he needed to tell her in person.

He'd do it tonight.

Chapter Ten

When Frankie asked Papa Luccetti for an advance paycheck from the restaurant, saying she wanted a new outfit for a dinner date with Doc, Papa had readily agreed. Of course, Papa had been thinking of a conservative dress....

Which was why Frankie flushed guiltily now. "C'mon," she urged softly, knowing Doc was on his way.

Her fingers, the nails of which were French manicured, trembled on the small pink silk flowers that covered each garter as she slowly, painstakingly attached them to black silk stockings. In the mirror on the back of the bathroom door, her eyes trailed critically from the black high heels, all the way up the decorative seams on the stocking backs, to the black lace garter belt itself, and finally to the silk thong-style bikini panties that weren't exactly comfortable, but were what Doc had said he liked.

Turning, Frankie stared critically at her breasts; they were barely covered by a matching black push-up underwire bra. A discreet pink flower nestled between the transparent lace cups, hiding the bra's front catch. The underwires, which actually gave her cleavage, were about as comfortable as the panties.

"It's no wonder men designed these outfits for women to take off," Frankie murmured with a flustered sigh. "No self-respecting woman could stand to wear such a thing very long." She wiggled her behind, trying—to no avail—to get comfortable with the thong. Still, she felt a sudden rush of excitement. What was a little discomfort, compared to how she hoped this affected Doc?

Oh, Frankie, just hurry up and finish dressing. Doc'll be here any second! She quickly ran down her mental checklist. She'd already taken Astrid to her parents. As much as she missed the baby, even for a second, privacy was an absolute necessity for her plan. The veal and salad were prepared, the lights dimmed, the table set. She'd just lit the candles. And, of course, the tape in the boom box was queued up with jazz for the striptease.

Her breath caught in anticipation. "Doc did say he liked sexy black underwear," she assured herself anxiously.

She just wished she felt more confident. Of course, she'd read about a couple of stripteases. In *Lassoing Louie,* there was a description of one by the cowgirl heroine, Savannah. Still, Frankie was so nervous right now; if she quickly changed into jeans and a T-shirt, Doc would never even have to know what fantasies she'd been planning to put into action.

But she desperately wanted to please Doc. He loved Astrid so much. He'd never said it, but Frankie thought he might be coming to love her, too. Oh, she'd pretended she was merely using him to practice her wiles on the opposite sex, but only because she'd feared his rejection so much. Frankie could admit that now. She knew it was past time to take this risk, to let him know how much she appreciated him being in her and Astrid's lives, and how ready she was to share herself. As far as her own independence was concerned, Doc had proved himself reasonable. He saw her as her own woman.

"But I just don't know." She sighed.

Her eyes settled on the long deep pink scars that crisscrossed her chest and ran all the way down her belly.

So many times, she'd tried to pretend that fear of rejection had nothing to do with her refusal to remove her blouse for Doc. But it was a lie. She was terrified. Could Doc really see these scars as she did—as battle scars, hard won in her struggle to survive?

She blinked rapidly, fighting back hot tears. She'd never felt sorry for herself, and she wasn't about to start now. "Quit it," she warned aloud, impatient with her own self-doubt. "You'll just ruin your makeup."

Cousin Gina had done her hair, nails and makeup. Faint rose blush and pink lipstick, a hint of liner and mascara drew attention to her fine complexion and dark eyes. Tiny buds of pink baby's breath were scattered through the dark curls of her hair.

"Don't you dare chicken out," Frankie warned her reflection. She couldn't. Not now. She'd come to want Doc with the same fierce longing she'd wanted their baby. That he was such a good man counted more than his sexy handsomeness. In fact, Frankie found it unsettling when women openly gawked at him, then sized Frankie up as if she were competition. Frankie just wanted the inner man. He was patient, kind and loved Astrid the way she did. He'd taken the time to court her family, too—eating Mama's food when he wasn't even hungry, listening for hours on end to Aunt Sophia's hypochondriacal aches and pains. At Doc's urging, Shane had even reworked the security system at the restaurant for her parents, free of charge.

I'm not losing this man, she thought.

Her hands still trembling, Frankie reached and slipped the new dress from a black velvet hanger; it was a sleek, ankle-length, round-necked gown of pink silk. Side zippers ran from beneath each arm to her upper thighs, leaving two long, sexy side slits. She'd barely gotten into it when a knock sounded at the door. Her pulse leaped in her throat as she heard Doc open the door with his key, letting himself in.

"Frankie?" he yelled. "Baby doll?"

His soft drawl sent a prickly tingle of awareness undulating through her. Like the rippling shiver of an ocean wave on a sunny day, it left her hot all over. She mustered her most casual tone. "Be right out! Why don't you take a seat on the couch and pour yourself a glass of Uncle Mario's homemade wine? The bottle's open. I left a glass for you there on the end table."

"Everything smells great," he called. "And the table's really something special."

She told herself she might lose her nerve if she looked before she leaped, but she cracked open the bathroom door, anyway, just to peek at him. Unaware she was watching, he casually grasped his hat by the brim and tossed it beside him on the couch. When it came to him removing the hat, Frankie thought with pride, she'd definitely gotten him trained.

After he poured some wine, he ran a broad hand over his head, ruffling the golden curls that had been trapped beneath his hat. Loosened, the waves spilled through his fingertips, catching the reddish candle-light, then fell to the collar of a tan suit jacket he wore over a black T-shirt. Black cowboy boots peeked from beneath tan slacks; the soft fabric draped over legs so powerful that Frankie's own suddenly got weak. Relaxing, Doc stretched a long arm across the sofa back.

She mustered a coy tone. "Are you sitting down yet?" Her own knees still felt so weak she wanted to sit down herself. She hadn't even begun to dance for him—wasn't even sure she really could go through with it—but just looking at him, she'd started throb-bing, aching for him sexually.

"Yeah. Just poured myself a glass of wine. You coming out of there or not?" As if only now sensing something was up, Doc added, "Hey, what are you doing in there, anyway?"

"Ready or not," Frankie whispered, "here I come."

No amount of Uncle Mario's homemade red wine could have prepared Doc for Frankie or soothed his dry throat. Not when Frankie's long-legged strides brought her breezily into the living room. As she passed the kitchen counter, she flicked on music, a saxophone's bluesy wail. Doc had meant to tell her about the discovery he'd made today, but when he saw what she was wearing, all words failed him.

He could merely stare. Already, without Frankie, the apartment oozed sensuality tonight. Not twenty feet away, in the sleeping alcove, the white tie-back curtains framed her bed in the archway; the dust ruffle was freshly pressed and the bedspread folded far back to reveal sumptuous pink satin sheets. The air was thick with scents—homemade bread, basil and garlic. Fragrantly burning slender rose tapers flickered in the dim light, throwing dancing shadows against the wall. A lace cloth and linen napkins were on the table, with china plates, crystal glasses and a vase of pink roses.

And then there was Frankie.

She was stunning as she swirled around—a vision of pink—and took up a position, not ten feet in front of him. "Oh, Frankie…" Doc started to rise, feeling overwhelmed she'd done all this for him.

"Please. Don't get up, Doc." Her voice was a prelude to something more—it held a hoarse hitch of excitement, as bluesy and low as the music.

His throat suddenly ached from dryness; as he reseated himself, he felt…big. Too tall for this delicate room, too broad for the fragile rose of a woman who was before him. He realized his fingers had grown too tight around the globe of the wineglass and loosened his grip. "You don't want me to get up?" he drawled persuasively. "Not even if I'm feelin' the need to wrap my lovin' arms around you right now, baby doll?"

"No."

Why not, Frankie?

And then Doc had his answer. His breath caught

as her sweet hips swayed from side to side in a slow, jazzy rhythm. His eyes trailed over her hair that was as ink-black as her stockings and shoes; the tiny pink flowers nestled in the curls were the color of her dress. He watched her move, turning in circles now, the deep slits of her pink gown brushing her ankles, offering him tantalizing peeks at legs that seemed as long and sexy as the wail of the saxophone.

On the wall behind her, she cast a shadow as tall as a goddess, and the candlelight glimmering on her skin enhanced its natural duskiness. As his eyes slowly lifted from the spike heels, up the stocking seams, he suddenly imagined her long, straining legs clutching around him. *C'mon, dance with me in another way, Frankie,* he'd whisper as those high-heeled shoes crossed on his bare behind.

And then he remembered how she'd been dancing alone with the mop the day they met. Her eyes had been shut tight, her mind alive with the fantasy of dancing with a man. And now, Doc couldn't help but feel he was that man, since she was dancing for him again. Arousal surged through him, deep waves of it. It was as strong, pungent and full-bodied as the red wine. And like the wine, he felt, with each sipping glance of Frankie, a slow, fiery drip of dark, liquid heat that slid down, puddled in his belly, and got dense and thick and hard like something left too long untended. His groin tightened almost painfully, taking his breath. Lifting his glass, Doc took a deep draft of wine as he watched her dance, letting the blessed liquid follow the path of dark heat she'd engendered, soothing his raw throat.

She'd done something to her eyes. They looked

darker than usual, deeper and more mysterious. Tiny strokes of liner in the corners made them tilt seductively. Hell, if he didn't know any better, Doc would swear she actually meant to strip. But no, Frankie was such a good girl. She was barely more than a virgin. She didn't know about such things. Surely, she would never—

She whirled around again, rolling her hips and delectable backside for his benefit. His heart hammered as she leaned to the side, one of her long French-manicured nails reaching beneath her armpit for the top of a zipper she slowly pulled down, inch by inch. *Oh, Lord, have mercy,* Doc thought, feeling utterly unbalanced, *she's really stripping for me. She's going to do this.*

As that first zipper came down, as he waited for the dress to open, the slow, dripping heat in his groin started burning with real fire. He shifted on the couch, forced himself to ease back on the soft cushions. If Frankie meant to do this for him, he was damn sure going to enjoy it. More than just physically arousing, this touched him beyond compare. She'd never tried anything so risky. He knew she was scared. And this dance was all for him. She was telling him he was her fantasy man.

He slowed his breaths because, like butterflies, they'd turned fluttery, hard to catch. Swirling his wine in the goblet with sensual slowness, he sipped, imagining the taste on his tongue was the taste of her most intimate honey.

But Doc's eyes never left Frankie.

Her skin was flushed now, awash in the dark, dusky rose of exertion and excitement. She inched down the second zipper in an excruciating, slow tease calculated for nothing more than arousing the animal in him.

And arousing it she was. With both silk edges of her gown unhinged, she toyed with him so mercilessly he had to bite his tongue not to beg her to quit. With her glimmering catlike eyes fixed on him and her legs looking as long as a showgirl's, she sashayed closer to him. And closer. And closer. But never so close he could reach out and pull her to him.

Then she sashayed away again.

And with each step, she caught another dainty handful of pink silk, lifting the gown, exposing lightning-quick flashes of silken finery beneath that quickened Doc's breath. He strained, seeing something creamy…something black…a little pink flower….

With a sudden flash of dark stocking top, he imagined his fingers sliding beneath and teasing her bare cream skin until she was every bit as distracted as he was getting. He'd take the sweet pink flowers that covered the garters between his strong teeth, and, unsnapping them, one by one, he would—

His own gasp took him by surprise as her slender, magical fingers, now heavy with bunched folds of silk, lifted once more, letting him look his fill at the puffy lace triangle of pink silk panty in front.

It, like the garter belt, had side ties, just rose silk strings with long trailers. All he had to do was pull, and the scrappy panty would float to the floor. It had been so long—nearly a year, which now felt like the worst kind of hellish eternity to Doc—since he'd stroked the sleek dark pelt he knew was hidden beneath. He couldn't hold back the low husky groan that rumbled deep in his chest.

She whirled around.

And his breath stopped altogether.

His darlin' girl's creamy backside was bare. She was wearing one of those thongs, just a strip of pink lace string snuggled between her cheeks that appeared only long enough to vanish under the garter belt.

Oh, in the worst way, Doc wanted to beg her to stop.

And then he wanted to beg her to dance forever.

He could no longer stand to watch. He had to touch. To feel her touching him back. To feel her fingers—raking through the golden curls of his head, twining in his thick chest hair and pulling, digging deep into the hard muscles of his shoulders as she whimpered his name.

His eyes raked over her, his eyelids dropping heavily while her every high-heeled step further drugged and entranced him. His thighs naturally loosened, and he felt vaguely self-conscious. There was no mistaking what she was doing to him. His dress slacks, less confining than his usual denim, couldn't hide it.

She'd slowed her pace—her breath becoming a soft panting, her dark eyes half closed upturned slits. Now she was less nervous, and her movements became dreamy. She was weaving a silk web and he was willingly flying into it. Then soaring, as she smoothed the pink silk gown around her breast, molding the fabric so he could see her black transparent bra cups.

Didn't the woman know he was already out of his mind with longing? Didn't she mean to put him out of his misery? Her eyes, so dark and hungry with desire, saw his unmistakable response. But still she danced on.

She was all woman and willing to explore her power over a man. Over him. She was doing it with such class, too. This woman, the mother of his child, was more amazing than anything he'd ever known. Or seen. Or touched. Or talked to.

He suddenly realized why she hadn't gone further. And his heart wrenched inside his chest. Stretched to breaking, it hurt with more emotional ache than he'd never known. Couldn't Frankie go all the way for him? Couldn't she trust him to fully share her full nakedness? *Oh, please. Please, baby doll. You can do it. C'mon, do it for this cowboy.*

He wanted it for him.

Even more, he wanted it for her. He could never prove his trustworthiness, not unless she gave him this chance.

She glided smoothly to the left, then the right. And then, with a sudden sharp intake of breath, Frankie grabbed her gown by the hem and swept it over her head. The fabric swirled so gracefully to the floor that her dancing body could have still been in it.

And then she quit moving.

Oh, she tried to keep on. She took one sudden jolting, almost staggering step that nearly caused her to trip over her high heels. Her face fell even if her body didn't. And then she was simply at a standstill, ten feet in front of Doc, clad only in the skimpy underwear, the large, dark, vulnerable pools of her eyes looking scared and uncertain as her hand flew to her scarred chest.

"Frankie—" Doc's drawl was thick with desire, deep with emotion. He barely made it across the room to her. He was so hot for her it hurt to walk. So breathless with emotion he couldn't talk. So moved by this woman he loved that he could do nothing more than pull her right into his embrace and hold her tight, willing his warmth and strength into her, wanting her to feel his soul-deep love.

He began kissing her—slowly, tenderly—her neck, her face, her lips, and raggedly whispering, "Oh, Frankie, I love you. Don't you know I love you? Haven't you guessed that yet?"

She was rapidly blinking back tears. "You do?"

Never had he felt such deep emotion mixed with such strong, aching arousal. In answer, he hugged her tighter, squeezing her against his chest and pressing his hips gently to hers, making her feel in his hardened length just how much. "You hear me, baby doll?" he whispered fiercely. "I love you." He stepped back a fraction, and his heart thudded dully as he watched her cross her arms over her chest again. He mustered all the gentleness in his soul. "No, Frankie," he said huskily, prying loose her fingers, moving her arms aside. "Please let me see you, Frankie."

Her breath caught sharply as he splayed his broad hand between her breasts, then traced it downward, touching her scars and yet heedless of them, taking in the beautiful whole of her. When his eyes returned to hers, they were cloudy with desire and emotion. His voice broke. "Aw, honey, don't you know you're the most beautiful woman I've ever seen?"

A tear splashed down her cheek. Doc's own eyes stung. "So beautiful," he assured her again, touching her breasts tenderly through the bra cups, leaning and pressing warm kisses to each of her bare shoulders. "You've got to believe me," he murmured.

Her voice caught. "I do. I really do."

The certainty in her words was all the further aphrodisiac Doc needed. Swiftly leaning, he grasped the small pink flower between the cups, unclasped the bra and lavished all his love on her breasts. Oh, this was so much more than any sex he'd ever known. Because these were breasts Frankie had shown him. Breasts of a body she'd never shared with any other man but him. She was offering herself, her whole self, so boldly up for his touch....

And he took her gift. With all his heart. With the pad of his tongue, he bathed the sweet, hardened rosebuds of her nipples and traced searing circles around them, suckling tenderly as he had so many times in his imagination. He trailed kisses down her chest that had never felt a man's lips. With each new kiss that initiated the age-old dance of love he assured her he didn't just accept her body. He needed it. Craved it with a lover's addictive want for the woman he loved.

He couldn't believe the climax that shook her just from him touching her. As she shuddered, whimpering senselessly in his arms, he slid his hands between them, felt her pulse through the damp silk of her panties. It was more than he could bear. He wanted her more than any man had ever wanted a woman.

He wanted sex with her. Marriage. To raise their child together. He wanted absolutely everything Frankie could give. With a low moan, Doc lifted her, carrying her to the bed. Throwing the spread farther back, he lay her on the sumptuous pink satin sheets.

His eyes trailed over her body, took in how the candles flickered over her skin; his every glimpse of her scars made him ache—body and soul—with doubled devotion. She'd been so scared, risked so much to have their baby. Risked so much now, to share her whole self. Every single scar was a reminder of the trust Doc would never break.

Standing by the bed, he very slowly removed his jacket and shirt, folding them as carefully and deliberately as he meant to make love to her now. Only when he reached his belt did she stop him. Raising his hands slightly, Doc let her undo the buckle. Her fingers were shaking because this wasn't at all like the first time. Oh, they'd explored each other then. But this was different.

This time, so much love was flowing between them.

The ache of his body was nothing next to the ache of emotion as she inexpertly folded back his belt, loosened his fly and finally, blessedly released him. He watched as she pushed his slacks and briefs down his hips, and then he suddenly murmured, "Frankie, baby. Oh, no, you don't have to..."

But already she was brushing her dark curls on his belly and kissed him...there. Silkily taking him between her lips and filling him with such a crushing, bone-deep longing his eyes stung once more. Groaning, he gently brushed a hand over her cheek, smoothing her hair. All those tiny sweet pink flowers she'd worn in her dark curls fell, spilling over his hand. He'd never experienced anything so brutally sexy.

Knowing he'd never last, he tenderly urged her up,

until she was kneeling on the mattress. Tugging loose the bows at the sides of her thong, he removed the silk, huskily promising, "I'm gonna love you all night, Frankie." And then he shook his head, gazing deep into her dark eyes and correcting himself. "No, I'm gonna love you forever."

Her voice trembled like her hands on his shoulders. "Then love me, Doc. Starting right now, I want you to love me."

He began opening her garters, rolling down the hose and removing the shoes. Then, when she was naked, he urged her down, his body covering hers, and his tongue stretching between her lips, deep and languorous and wet. Each openmouthed sigh of need heated their skin, until they burned in a tight embrace.

"Please," she whimpered. She'd already whispered that the diaphragm was in place, and now his gaze paused on her beautiful face, the slits of her onyx eyes, her lips that were parted in ecstasy, her dark curls spread on the pink pillow. He'd never imagined making love could feel so akin to worship. But he'd come to worship her. To cherish her like the greatest of gifts. Kneeling, he reached for the condom she'd laid out. As he carefully put it on, his heart squeezed again at his own need to protect her and make her safe, at his fear of a pregnancy that could harm her in any way. Sensing his emotion, she reached for him and held him close.

"I'm so afraid of ever hurting you," he whispered.

"You could never hurt me."

She was so right about that. He'd sooner die. Her eyes were so round and black now, so vulnerable and trusting. He slid between her thighs, one arm straining as he guided himself to her, stroking her with that ready part of him.

They both cried out as he pushed—so slowly, so gently—inside. Everything was pure silk—the sheets, her stockings, the tantalizing garter belt he'd left in place. And most of all—her. She was so moist, hot and tight. So small and beautiful, like all the tiny pink flowers she'd worn for him. Oh, yes, she was small and delicate. But there was no torture involved in this. No ache now. Just a slow opening of their bodies to each other.

His heart swelled with love for this woman who was opening for him like petals unfolding. The mother of his daughter who'd flowered for him, over this year, blooming so beautifully into a woman.

Frankie was completely naked, so completely his. He moved on her, shifting slowly from side to side, stretching and filling each time, marching with his knees and climbing higher inside her with each deeper thrust. Even as they sighed and cried together, he kept climbing that ladder to heaven.

"I—I—" Her whimper was almost lost, her voice gasping. "I love you, Doc. Did I mention that? Did I tell you? Did I forget? I love you."

With broken words, Frankie climaxed again. And the virginal tightness of her came back then, squeezing and holding Doc so he couldn't move inside her. It pulled a cry from him he didn't recognize as his own as he shuddered and spilled, answering her words with his own needy sensual murmurings. He was trying to tell her he was the man she'd been dancing with in her fantasies the day they'd met. And he was begging her to keep dancing with him always, saying she had to live forever, because he could never stand to lose her.

He simply loved her too much.

When he could finally say something coherent again, something she could understand, what he said was, "Marry me, Frankie."

Chapter Eleven

Frankie draped the satin sheet across her and Doc's waists, then rested against him with her head on his chest. Nearby, on the dining table, the once-tall tapers burned low and the linen cloth was spread with food. "My plans for tonight went better than I ever imagined," she murmured.

He chuckled softly. "What? You're going to hold me to that marriage proposal?"

She smiled. "You bet."

"Good thing, baby doll. 'Cause I won't feel comfortable until we dot all the diamonds and cross the bouquets."

Frankie cuddled closer. The scents of his aftershave, shampoo and soap were long gone, leaving nothing but the musky male scent of him—a delicious elixir that went right to her head. "Isn't that dot the i's and *toss* the bouquets, Doc?"

She wasn't sure, but she thought she felt him stiffen slightly against her. "Frankie, what do you think of having a small wedding?"

Doc never talked about his wedding plans with Marta, and it was one area where Frankie hadn't pressed. The other woman aroused her fiery jealousy, and the less Frankie knew about her, the better. "A small wedding?" she gently prodded, suspecting his mind was on the wedding he'd planned with Marta. "You're kidding. With the Luccetti family?"

"Hmm." Doc finally ruffled her hair. "Okay. A big wedding it is. With a dress for a princess. Big band. Food galore." After a moment, another of Doc's soft chuckles warmed her. "I do have one serious confession to make, though."

"Hmm?"

"You know that judge, Tilford Winslow? Well, baby doll...you see, he's kind of crazy. And he knows Jake, so in an effort to play matchmaker, I'm afraid he faked that heart attack in the courtroom."

"Yes, well, Doc," Frankie returned with an indulgent smile, "you seemed to forget I've *had* a heart attack and spent my formative years in cardiac units. Personally, I have to say it was the singularly most fake heart attack I have ever witnessed, discounting those in the movies, which was why I immediately called the family. Obviously, for some strange reason, you were going along with his ploy."

"I should have guessed you'd know," Doc murmured.

"Well, his great-granddaughter, Phoebe Hale, kindly explained the whole situation to me—saying her relative was merely eccentric to a fault, not sick. So, we started chatting, and she told me the history of Big Apple Babies, explaining how the judge is a financial backer, and she said she knew you and Jake and Dani Lucas. Anyway, when she invited me over, I baked that plate of cookies...."

"The ones I almost ate after your parents' anniversary party?"

"Uh-huh." Stretching lazily against him, Frankie arched like a cat, reveling in the feeling of well-used warmth at her womanly core.

Doc stroked her backside through the satin sheet, his voice throaty. "Get any good gossip from Phoebe?"

"About you? Lots."

Leaning, Doc dropped kisses on her forehead. "That's what I love most about you, Frankie. You're always one step ahead of me."

"Then you won't be mad," she said, "when I bring up this other matter."

"Ah...now she reveals her hidden agenda."

"Well, I was just thinking. If I did happen to have a doctor husband with a good salary—especially one who also has connections at Big Apple Babies— might that improve my chances of becoming an adoptive mother?"

Doc's glance of mock reprove didn't last. Too quickly, his eyes sparked with appreciation and desire. "I can see you had all this planned," he murmured. "But you know, baby, it would be easier for us if you'd consider a child that wasn't...perfect."

Her breath caught in surprise. "I'm not perfect, Doc. Nobody is."

"I think you're perfect, Frankie."

"Well, all babies are perfect," she agreed. Then she sighed wistfully. "You're right. Who could be better than us to parent a special child? All my life I've dealt with medical red tape, insurance forms, ridiculous doctors—"

"Gee, thanks."

"You know what I mean. Besides—" she rolled her head back, to better stare into his luscious eyes "—maybe all that in-hospital training made it easier for me to snag you." She smiled. "Now, about the baby…"

He was rubbing tantalizing circles on her naked back; now he ducked his hand beneath the sheet, exploring her satiny bottom with a warm, liquid-silk caress. "Just a second ago," he said huskily, "this was all theoretical.…"

She smiled meaningfully, thinking of Astrid's conception. "A lot can happen in a second. And Astrid can't be alone. Besides, you seem to forget I'm Italian. Mama and Papa will be sorely disappointed without more grandchildren, especially since my four brothers don't seem to be settling down."

Right before Doc leaned in for another kiss, he said, "You'll get no argument from me about more babies, Frankie, just so long as we keep you safe."

"Speaking of munchkins," she whispered against his lips, "should we pick up Astrid at Mama's?"

"Not yet. Believe me, you're distracting enough without my needing to hop up and heat a bottle." A strong, broad hand splayed on the small of her back, pressing her against him, so she could feel just exactly how distracted he was. His eyes smoldered under the heavy lids, saying he had a hidden agenda of his own, to love her a little longer. "Oh…" he murmured. "I completely forgot. I had something to tell you."

She smiled. "Guess I stripped you of your memory," she teased with a raspy chuckle. She pushed a lock of hair from his face, watching how candlelight licked in the waving strands. He was the picture of sensual luxury, reclining on the sumptuous pillows, the sheet draping his lower body, outlining the bold curve of masculinity between his thighs.

She blew out a dreamy sigh, her own memory getting hazy. "What were you saying?"

"Well...prepare yourself. It's kind of intense."

She made a point of snuggling closer. "I'm ready."

"Well, you know that dream you told me about?"

"Yeah."

"Well...it was familiar to me." Doc's thick drawl cleared a fraction with excitement. "I mean, everything. The median, the kind of road, the fence, the fork."

Frankie's fingers stilled on his chest and her ears pricked up. She felt strangely unsettled, as if something she couldn't put her finger on wasn't quite right. She fought the urge to press a finger against his lips to stop him from speaking another word. He was waiting for her to make some response. "Familiar?" she said.

He emitted a deep sigh of emotion. "I never told you. But Marta was driving a red convertible when she died. It was in Pennsylvania. She crashed the car into a pole, a fork in the road that was just like the one you described."

Her heart thudded dully, as if the blood it pumped had suddenly gotten thick and muddy. *Just don't react, Frankie. Wait. Think it through. Don't freak out.*

"Anyway," he continued, "it was strange. And so, I got this wild idea. Like what if you were actually the recipient of Marta's heart? And so I called this friend of mine...."

A shiver went down her spine. *No, oh no! This couldn't be!* But she already knew what was coming. Hadn't she noticed new habits since her surgery? New personality quirks? Doc rushed on, his words catching with excitement, oblivious of the fear that was gripping her, freezing her stiff. The heart inside her no longer seemed to pump blood at all; her veins felt packed with hard, cold, solid ice.

"Anyway," Doc concluded, "can you believe it? It's really true. You turned out to be the recipient."

Frankie watched in horror as Doc shook his head in bemused stupefaction, shooting her a quick, lopsided grin and gushing some craziness about how this changed his whole world view. He was no longer a pragmatic man of science, but he had begun to actually believe in a life beyond what he could see and touch.

"It explains so much," he drawled. "Don't you think? Like my immediate attraction to you. And the feeling I had when I first came here, as if Marta were right here in this room. I looked around—for a scent, an object, some music—something that might explain the strange sensation, but there was nothing. Frankie, maybe it was you...." Suddenly, he stopped and said, "Frankie?"

She stared back. Her eyes wide, her lips pressed together. She couldn't move. Couldn't think of anything to do or say. She was in complete shock.

His voice was deeply concerned. "Frankie?"

This time the voice got her moving. Her pulse started racing. Blood whirred in her ears—propelled by the heart of the woman this man was going to marry in the past. With a sudden jolt, Frankie sat back, snatching handfuls of the sheets against her chest, trying to cover her nakedness because she felt so painfully exposed.

Her voice was raw. "I see. You sensed her in the room when we met. You mean you fell in love with me because I'm really her."

Doc moved toward her. "That's not what I said, Frankie. You're not listening."

"Who could listen to this?" Her eyes flashed angry fire, and the hot tears suddenly came, splashing down her cheeks. She was still so shocked, she didn't know what she really felt or what she was saying; she simply lashed out. "I should have known! I should have guessed! Why else would you fall in love with me?" Grabbing the sheet, she elbowed past him and ran to a closet. She quickly donned a robe, not dropping the sheet that hid her body until the belt was firmly fixed around her waist. She kicked the sheet away, leaving it on the floor.

She was just about to turn around when she felt Doc's hands on her shoulders. Even now, when she least wanted him near her, her traitorous body reacted to the warmth of his hands. He leaned close, his persuasive drawl carrying his breath to the bare skin of her neck. "Apparently, I wasn't thinking, Frankie."

Apparently. She whirled around. "Why would you want me, anyway? Woman stare at you on the street. Marta was beautiful. Now I understand."

His widening eyes said she'd lost her mind. His tone was careful. "I don't know what you're talking about, baby doll."

She didn't bother to answer. Her black eyes murderous, her fists packed tight, she simply lunged like
a she-devil, throwing a rounded right that smacked
his naked shoulder. He leaned, deflecting some of the
blows with his open palms, while others bruised his
shoulders. He jerked back, just before a particularly
violent punch connected with his face.

"Whoa there, Frankie, would you listen?"

She kept swinging. "How could you tell me this?"

"How could I not?" he suddenly exploded, grabbing her wrists. He yanked her so close she became
torturously aware of his nakedness. "Dammit, baby
doll, I realize now how wrong I was, but I swear I
thought it was a good thing. That it proved this was
fate and that we were meant to be together. It was
such a strange way to meet. An interesting story to
tell Astrid one day. Be reasonable. Please. It's just a
heart, Frankie. Like Marta's clothes are just clothes
to me."

She was shaking with terror and rage. "Just a
heart? I don't think so! Not if I'm dreaming about the
way she died!" Her teeth almost chattered from the
shudder that shook her. She suddenly gasped, "It's
like…it's like Astrid is Marta's baby."

His voice warned her not to pursue the line of rea-
soning, and he spoke with a calm that didn't meet his
eyes. "That's crazy, Frankie."

When he loosened his grip on her wrists, she
snatched them away. She crossed her arms over her
chest, her eyes pleading with him. "Don't you understand? I'm not myself anymore! The heart beating
my life blood is from some other woman whom you
loved."

"Marta," he countered. "Her name was Marta."

"I never wanted to know her name! I didn't want to know anything about her. Not where she lived or what she did for a living. Or what she did for fun. Definitely not that she and I shared a man."

"Shared? As in past tense?" He was now biting back temper. "Why deny this? Why not just accept it? Like I said, I really thought you'd see it as a positive."

She felt her own face contort, screwing up with more pain than she'd ever felt. She felt positively ill. Scared. As if something strange and foreign had crawled right inside her and taken up residence. Another chill washed over her shoulders, prickling her neck.

And then she felt the hurt. Maybe that's what she felt most of all. She stared at him. "Can't you understand what it's like, not to be loved for yourself?"

His breath had quickened. He sounded taken aback, hurt. "I love you more than anything. I can't lose you, Frankie. Of course I love you for yourself."

"I don't even have a self."

"A self? You're—" He stretched out his arms, unable to find the words. "You're so unique. There's no one like you in the world."

Why couldn't he understand that she was like the Tin Man in *The Wizard of Oz?* With no heart of her own. Empty inside. She hugged her arms to herself. "This is just too strange for me," she managed to croak. "Just too weird. *Way* too weird."

Doc's eyes were wary, his drawl calculated to soothe. "Now, c'mon. Listen to me, baby doll. We're gonna sit right down and straighten this whole thing out.''

"Straighten this out?" Suddenly losing control again, she uttered a howl. He was the one who'd lost his mind! She thought she'd come by his love fair and square. Doc was so good for her, so perfect. She'd loved him and he'd started loving her back. They even shared a child. And now she found out his attraction might be based on her connection to a past love.

"Please, Frankie," he murmured.

She stared at him. He wasn't even aware he was standing there stark naked. Everything was so easy for him. He was like a golden god.... And he'd been everything she had ever wanted.

"Dammit!" she exploded with a rare curse. It just wasn't fair. All her life, she'd been visited by nothing but pain, illness and loneliness. Didn't she deserve one glimmer of hope? Of peace? Of love? What had she ever done that was so wrong as to deserve this? She could never accept it. The pain simply wasn't to be borne. She deserved something that was her own. This was her newfound independence? Ha! She pressed a hand to her chest, as if she really could rip out her own heart.

"Get out, Doc. I want you to leave."

"I'm not leaving until we talk."

That he wouldn't heed her command just enraged her further. Telling herself she had no choice, she swiftly grabbed the phone and punched 911. "There's a man in my house," she said into the receiver. "And I want him out. Now."

The police came immediately.

Only when Doc resisted and was threatened with arrest, did he leave. Frankie didn't even look at him. Then, not having words to explain the depth of her confused feelings to anyone, only knowing that she loved Doc but could never bear to so much as see his face again, Frankie flung herself onto the bed where he'd just loved her so thoroughly, pulling the bedspread all the way up to her neck.

And then she cried herself to sleep.

WAS SHE GOING TO MARRY DOC or not?

There were only seconds left to decide. The grassy triangular median was in front of Frankie. One of the two female cardinals on the fence leaned into the wind and took flight. *You have to find those silk flats,* she thought.

Unzipping the black leather jacket she was wearing over her wedding gown, she reached across the seat. Her bare feet felt cold, but her toenail polish was probably dry. "Where are those shoes?"

Gripping the wheel with one hand, she raked through an overnight bag on the passenger seat. Digging deep, she felt something silk.... But it was only a narrow snakeskin-print scarf. Just as she tried to stuff it back into the bag, the scarf was whisked away, whipping around in the wind like a snake about to strike.

She glanced up. The fork in the road was so close! Turning left meant going to the white-steepled church where Doc was waiting. Turning right meant a long drive back to New York City. Alone. *Hurry up and decide! You don't have much longer!* She was already an hour late. Doc was pacing in front of the altar, sure she'd chickened out....

Tossing and turning, Frankie moaned into the satin pillow. "Are you going to marry Doc?" she murmured in sleep. "Marry him...or not? Marry him... marry him..."

A loud *kaboom* deafened her.

Frankie glanced up, her ears ringing, and she tried to hang on to the vibrating steering wheel of the red convertible. What had she just heard? A blown tire?

Her fearful eyes shot to the rearview mirror.

But the face in the mirror wasn't her own!

A blond stranger stared back. Hair blew wildly around the other woman's face, and her china blue eyes were wide with a terror as deep as that which struck Frankie's mortal soul. Where was Frankie? Where was her own reflection in the mirror? Did she have a self anymore? *Wake up, Frankie! Wake up!*

"Wake up!" Frankie murmured. "Oh, please, wake up!"

Bolting upright in bed, she clutched the spread to her chest, no longer even sure who she'd been trying to warn—herself or the other woman, who was about to wreck. Her voice squeaked with fear. "Oh, no...no," she said, realizing she was drenched in sweat, that her pulse was surging. She suddenly realized something else Doc had never said. He'd never really known whether Marta planned to marry him. He didn't know if she'd been driving to the wedding or out of town when she crashed.

"Oh, please, no," Frankie whispered again. Because for the first time, she couldn't deny it. This wasn't a dream at all. Or even a nightmare. It was a piece of Marta Straussberg's memory.

DANI LUCAS SAT PERCHED on the edge of Doc's desk in the Big Apple Babies infirmary. "Oh, Doc, I take back all the things I've ever said about cheering on the woman who brings you to your knees."

Leaning in a swivel chair, Doc simultaneously bounced Astrid against his chest and caught his hat by the brim, tossing it to the desktop. With a free hand, he grabbed Dani's fingers, giving them a soft squeeze, just needing to feel a woman's comfort. Right about now, he felt awful glad Mama had dropped by with Astrid, so he could see his sweet little slice of sugar pie for a few minutes. "How could I have been so insensitive?" he drawled. "I just wasn't thinking, Dani. I swear, it never even occurred to me that she'd react that way."

He felt like such a fool. Every time he shut his eyes, he was tortured by the memory of Frankie's face twisting in pain. And the way she'd come at him, pummeling him.

Dani shook her head. "She called the cops."

Doc's chest constricted with emotion. They'd hauled him out to the street, and she hadn't even looked at him. *Damn.* He sighed. "For a second, Dani, I thought everything was going to work out. I mean, Frankie and I have got something real special, like you and Jake have got."

"You can get her back."

Smiling ruefully, he merely surveyed Dani—her coal eyes, her no-nonsense ponytail. She was on a lunch break from Saint Vincent's, so she was wearing her nurse's uniform. "You know I've tried everything," he said, leaning and nuzzling Astrid's cheek. Hell, the other day, he'd almost banged down Frankie's door. He talked to the Luccettis daily, all of whom were doing their best to talk sense into Frankie. His brother Shane was no help. In the middle of all this, Doc's wedding-shy brother had announced a surprise quickie marriage to Lillian Smith, a woman Doc hadn't even heard of, much less met. It didn't make a lick of sense. Not that Doc could worry about Shane now. All he could think about was Frankie.

He sighed again. "I do see her point of view now. But I really didn't feel the way she does. To me, I swear, the whole thing was like a nice revelation. Proof there's something more in life. But now I know it's hard for her. She doesn't feel complete in herself. She's so conscious of being reliant. She knows in such a bone-deep, life-and-death way that you can't survive without other people."

Dani patted his shoulder. "Doc, everybody knows that."

Doc shook his head, defending Frankie. "Not like Frankie does. I mean, the very essence of her life, her heart, came from somebody else…and then she finds out it's from a woman she sees as a rival in her love life."

"Don't be so hard on yourself."

"Hard on myself? Hell, Dani, I hate myself right now. I did the one thing I vowed I'd never do—hurt Frankie." He'd lost her, too. No woman looked at a man the way she'd looked at him—and then came back. Hell, he was no wimp. He'd break down her door and make her listen to reason if he thought it would help. But he knew his mere presence would cause her more pain. And that he'd never do. He'd hurt her enough. He wouldn't hurt her any more, not if it killed him. Sadness wrenched inside him and his fingers clenched tighter through Dani's.

"I'm just a simple man," he continued. "I just didn't know…" And now he was paying. Dying inside from never seeing her; he'd never see Frankie hold Astrid again because the three of them were never together. He only saw Astrid with Mama Luccetti. "Do you think I should have told her more about how different she is from Marta? More about what makes her so special—"

"Doc," Dani said.

"Hmm?"

"You're cutting off my circulation."

"Oh." He loosened his fingers. But he knew Dani didn't really mind. Hell, she knew how bad it was for him right now. If he didn't have his friends and his baby girl to hang on to, Doc didn't know what he'd do. Especially since Shane was unavailable. Hadn't Frankie realized he was just as reliant as she? That he needed her? That he'd come to count on having her and Astrid in his life?

A shout sounded down the hallway. Just as Mama Luccetti stepped inside Doc's office and took Astrid, footsteps pounded from farther away. Doc merely sighed. No emergency could compare to the crisis in his personal life.

"Doc! Doc! Hurry up! Get out here!"

The urgency of the voice finally pulled him to his feet. Then a beefy hand grabbed the doorjamb, and Doc's co-worker, James Sanger, rounded into Doc's office, puffing air. "Hurry!" he gasped. "Jake's been shot."

Dani clutched Doc. "Jake? My husband?"

"Mr. Lucas?" echoed Mama Luccetti, in shock.

"Hurry! He's on the street. He was on the sidewalk. I don't know what happened. I think a car rounded the curve. It sounded like a gunshot...."

Doc heard none of the words. Already, he'd grabbed his physician's bag and was long gone.

DOC WAS LEANING AGAINST the wall in the hospital corridor.

Frankie paused, clutching his hat in one hand and Astrid in the other. Blanketed in soft pink, Astrid was sound asleep in the safe cradle of Frankie's arm, pressed against her chest. Even if Mama hadn't been on the scene, Shane had tracked Frankie down, saying Jake Lucas had been shot, hours ago, outside Big Apple Babies, and that Shane thought Frankie might like to know. Misunderstanding, Frankie had gotten the baby, then gone to Big Apple Babies first, where she'd found Doc's hat on his desktop.

Now that she'd found the man himself, she was having grave doubts about coming here, though. First, she didn't even know Jake very well.... And second, she and Doc could never go back to the way things were before. Not knowing what they knew now about her connection to Marta. Still, she loved him. She felt compelled to be here for him, too, and wanted to help in any way she could.

So did the countless people associated with Big Apple Babies who'd assembled in the lobby: Phoebe and Grantham Hale. A woman named Rosita de Silva, who was watching Dani and Jake's kids. James Sanger. Ethel Crumble. Frankie had even glimpsed a suntanned Judge Winslow commiserating with Dani's parents. Shane was still conferring with the police about what had happened.

So far, it seemed that Jake was a victim of random violence. He'd lost a lot of blood, which had looked bad, since his was a rare type. Earlier though, his biological father, who had the same type, had stepped forward, offering the blood that helped save Jake's life. After filling Frankie in, the large assembled group had directed her to where Doc stood vigil outside Jake's door. Now, watching him, Frankie suddenly realized she couldn't approach Doc, after all. It hurt too much.

He was leaning against the wall, his shoulders hunched and his hands shoved deep into his jeans pockets. Though they'd gotten the news Jake would be fine, Doc looked wrung out, sad and worried. He'd been the first to reach Jake, and Frankie had been told Jake never would have lived if not for Doc. She fought a crushing desire to go and hold him. Doc had suffered so many sudden losses. His parents in childhood. Marta.

But Jake Lucas was going to be okay.

A nurse appeared. "You can come on in, Doc."

As he headed inside, Frankie cradled Astrid closer and edged toward the door, wishing something—some word or touch—could help her accept what she'd found out about her connection to Marta, wishing she knew what to say to Doc now. Lord, it was so hard to be in love with a man you couldn't be with. Not wanting to disturb his time with his friend,

Frankie came to a standstill and merely gazed in on the scene.

"He'll be fine," a man with a deep baritone was saying.

Jake was propped up on pillows, looking ashen and weak, but generally well, despite his bandages. Dani was seated next to him on the bed, and Doc was standing, turned away from Frankie. He shook hands with the man who'd spoken. "So, you're Jake's father?"

The man nodded. His well-tailored gray suit made him look wealthy, as did his head of thick salt-and-pepper hair. "His biological father, yes. I'm Jefferson Lawrence."

Frankie's lips parted in surprise. Jake's father was Jefferson Lawrence? Judging from his expensive attire, he was *the* Jefferson Lawrence, too. Everyone had heard of the Wall Street tycoon. A savvy investor, he helped cut every slice of the Big Apple's pie.

Doc's hands still covered the man's. "I'm glad you've come forward." He glanced at Jake. "Glad you've found each other. And I want to thank you personally for being a private backer for Big Apple Babies. We do a lot of good work there, if I do say so myself, sir."

Jefferson leaned, resting his hand gingerly on Jake's shoulder, his deep baritone voice resonating in the room. "Maybe I should have come forward before...."

Jake patted his father's hand. His voice sounded weak. "You have now. I wasn't about to give up searching for you."

No, from what Frankie had heard, Jake had long

carried his father in his heart, and he'd wanted to meet him for a long time. Frankie edged an inch closer, fascinated, listening to Jake's low voice, as he explained the cause of the estrangement to Doc with Jefferson Lawrence filling in the blanks when Jake felt too weak to talk.

As a young man, Jake's father had little to offer Alicia Hollander, the woman he loved. So he'd joined the army, hoping to find a living with which he could eventually support her. Instead, he'd fought in Vietman, and during a long internment in a POW camp, was believed to be dead. When he finally returned home, he found Alicia had died, giving birth to his child.

Instinctively, Frankie drew Astrid closer, thinking of the risks involved in her own pregnancy. They'd been so lucky, so blessed. She dropped a kiss on Astrid's forehead, then she tilted her head, continuing to listen.

Jake was saying that when his father found him, he'd already been adopted into a loving home. Feeling he still had little to offer, knowing his child was safe and grieving for the girlfriend who'd long thought him dead, Jefferson Lawrence was more determined than ever to make good in a world that had given him so little. He'd gone to school on the GI bill, studied finance, and he'd eventually taken Wall Street by storm.

All the while, Jefferson had remained in Jake's life, anonymously watching over him. It was Jefferson who had approached Judge Winslow, and the two men had gathered the handful of secret private investors who had started Big Apple Babies. Jake was given a wonderful career as the head executive for the adoption agency, and the rest was history.

"Doc," Jake chided weakly, when he was finished with the tale. "You look like you've sunk about as low as it goes. My friend, you saved my life today. And that was supposed to be a story with a happy ending."

Doc nodded. "I know. And it is. But I just wish Frankie…"

Frankie edged closer, almost to the threshold of the room. These past weeks, Doc had missed her. Her parents swore they feared for his health because she was breaking his heart. And to hear him now, bringing up her name, talking about her with his friend who'd nearly died…

"You wish…?" Jake prodded softly.

Doc shrugged again. "Oh, I don't know. Just that Frankie would realize we're all in this together."

Dani said, "What do you mean, this?"

"Life."

Frankie *was* thinking about it. About Jake's father who was both a stranger to Jake, and yet not a stranger at all, and who had stepped from obscurity, giving blood to save his son's life. And about Marta, whose heart had saved hers. And about Doc, who'd saved Frankie from sheer loneliness by giving her this wonderful baby they shared. As she squeezed Astrid tighter, thoughts of her pregnancy came racing back. She remembered those months Astrid had grown inside her—utterly helpless and totally dependent. Suddenly, Frankie wasn't at all sure where one life ended and another began. Right from conception, on the most physical level, people needed one another to survive. And emotionally? So many people had touched Frankie's life she couldn't count them. Hadn't each of her relatives given her a piece of their heart as surely as Marta had? Hadn't Doc? *Frankie, maybe we're nothing more than the sum total of the people who touch us.*

"No one stands alone," Doc was saying now. "And Frankie and I have a child now, a life. I just wish she could take love at face value, realize things aren't black and white. Life can't be boiled down to science, as I once thought. If she could just realize that and forgive my insensitivity."

Her heart wrenched, and Astrid stirred in her arms. In her mind's eye, she saw a fork in the road. One side seemed to point to life, the other to emotional death. Maybe living or dying was a choice people made every moment. Frankie wanted to live as much as she could, to embrace whatever life offered.

It's supposed to be a story with a happy ending. Jake's words played in her mind. How odd that Jake's words, those of a near stranger, would be just what Frankie needed to hear right now. Funny, because they *were* all in this together.

Tears threatened at her eyes. "Doc?"

He turned slowly.

Holding Astrid, she took another step, almost crossing the threshold, and gazed deeply into the silver-blue eyes that had never seemed like clearer windows into Doc's soul. All the love in the world was right here, waiting for Frankie. Smoothing Astrid's blanket with a trembling hand, she managed to say, "Mama told me...and Shane called."

"Oh." Doc waited.

She swallowed hard, her throat tight. "You know how I said I wanted to be loved for myself? Well, I—I was listening to you...and to Jake. And I just realized that I'm not just myself. Maybe no one is." She glanced around, thinking of all the people who'd come to Jake's aid. "We're all connected, Doc."

Doc was moving toward her, his gentle drawl raw with emotion. "Even you and me, Frankie?"

"Especially you and me, Doc."

"And this...thing with Marta?"

"It's okay," she whispered. "She's a part of us, too."

"C'm'ere, baby doll." As Doc drew her and Astrid into his arms with an all-encompassing hug, Frankie had never felt so complete and right. So healthy and whole. So reliant and yet so much an important part of the world around her.

Doc angled his head downward, his breath mingling with hers, his words husky. "Can we make this union of souls legal?"

She lifted his hat, settling it on his head, where it belonged. "Are you asking me to marry you again?"

A glimmer of the old Doc returned—a twitch of his lips into a wry smile, the hint of a sparkle in his eyes. His gaze never leaving Frankie's, he said, "Dani Lucas, you'd better get ready to cheer on this woman, 'cause she's lassoed me and brought me to my knees." With a smile, he cupped Frankie's face in his hands. "Frankie, say you'll marry me."

She smiled through tears she could no longer fight. "You know I will, cowboy."

Somewhere in the background, Frankie heard her mother and Aunt Sophia utter in unison, *"Grazie*

Dio!" as they arrived, bringing covered dishes for Jake's family. Seemingly from a million miles away, she heard Mama take charge, and even though she didn't know Jake from Adam, Mama started saying, "Mangia! Mangia!" begging Jake to eat and build up his strength.

"To a Luccetti," Frankie whispered, squeezing Astrid into Doc's arms, then putting her own around his waist, "there's only one thing more important than food, you know."

"What's that, Frankie?"

"Loving one another."

Mama waved her broad hand whimsically in the air, murmuring, "Eat, eat!"

And then Frankie lifted her mouth to Doc's, kissing him with quick, passionate hunger, knowing he was the only man who could feed her, body and soul, and that only his nourishing love could fuel the lives of the family they would share. As he shifted Astrid and his embrace tightened around Frankie, she knew no fiction could ever compare to the fantastic reality of the love they'd found. And as Doc deepened their kiss, parting Frankie's lips wider and delving his tongue deep, she knew it would never again matter whose heart beat inside her.

All that mattered was the power of its love.

Epilogue

Frankie stood at the window, staring out into the dark, moonlit night. The iridescent pearl moon was pale and round, exactly like the one the night they'd first made love. Frankie had never looked more beautiful, clad only in a transparent white robe that was meant to be worn over something far more substantial than her bare skin.

Silently watching her, Doc was barely capable of taking a breath as his gaze settled on the shimmering light that rippled on her tantalizingly naked back through the gossamer fabric. From outside, waves crashed against the shoreline. Inside, the room was musky with the scent of love.

It had been a long day, with a fairy-tale wedding. Friends and family had arrived from both here and abroad, and many guests had attended, including Doc's aunts. There was an orchestra at the reception. Dancing. And above all, food. Since Frankie and Doc didn't want to leave Astrid, and since they were anxious to move into their new apartment, they'd decided to take this honeymoon weekend on the Cape, with Astrid in tow.

Silently, Doc now tossed back the covers, rose from the bed and checked on his sweet little slice of sugar pie, who was peacefully sleeping in a crib. Then, crossing to the window, he gazed down the length of Frankie's body, gently pulling her against him. His voice was husky. "Come on back to bed. I'm so cold without you, baby doll."

Her voice was deep with drowsiness. She'd awakened in the night, and he knew she'd be back to sleep in minutes. Her half-closed eyes and the slackness of her kissable mouth attested to it. "You're warm," she murmured.

With a soft smile, Doc merely grasped her hand and led her back to the bed and beneath the covers with him, where she belonged. Only then did she murmur, "I had the dream again."

"Oh, baby doll…"

Frankie pressed a finger against his lips. She looked barely able to keep her eyes open, and her voice was a whispery croak. "It's okay." Her hand dropped and cupped his cheek. "In fact, it was beautiful, Doc." Sighing, she gazed at him deeply from beneath her heavily lidded eyes. "Marta was going to marry you. I know that now."

He was surprised to feel his gut clench. To realize, that even now, he'd still needed to know. "You think so?"

"I know so." A smile curled Frankie's lips. "I remembered everything this time." Tears suddenly glossed her black eyes—they were of sadness, and loss for the woman Frankie had come to accept as a part of her. A woman to whom she owed the very gift of life.

"Doc," she began gently. Her eyes, so full of sleep, found his in the darkness. "Marta was turning, going to the church...to you. She'd decided. But then the tire blew. No matter how hard she tried, she couldn't turn. Even when she knew she was in trouble, she tried to turn, hoping you'd know which way she was headed. And after she wrecked her car at the fork in the road, everything went black...."

Doc inhaled sharply. Wrapping his arms tightly around Frankie, he drew her close in protection.

Solemn, hushed awe stole into her voice. "But then there was suddenly light again. A blinding white sunburst. And then all my fear—or Marta's—was gone. Just like that. There was only a rush of warm relief and joy." Frankie trailed a finger down Doc's cheek. "All along, I think that's what she was trying to tell me. She just wanted you to know she was going to marry you. And that she was in that place of pure white light now, completely at peace."

Doc nodded and hugged Frankie tight. "She's gone now, Frankie," he whispered.

"I do believe she is," Frankie whispered back, her sleepy voice barely audible.

Gently urging Frankie closer, Doc tenderly arranged the covers around her shoulders. As he watched his wife's eyes drift shut and listened to the uninterrupted rise and fall of her breath, he simply held her, safe and sound in his arms as she slept on through their wedding night, dreamlessly.

More BIG APPLE BABIES are
headed your way soon!

This July don't miss
American Romance #733
AKA: MARRIAGE
Another book in Jule McBride's exciting
Big Apple Babies miniseries!

AKA: MARRIAGE

Don't miss the action when Big Apple Babies security guard Shane Holiday goes undercover—as a husband! Marriage-shy Shane has no intention of really helping his new wife adopt a baby—he's just out for his own personal revenge. But a taste of love and family life can do strange things to a lone wolf and renegade....

* * * * *

AKA: MARRIAGE

by Jule McBride
July 1998.

Only from American Romance!

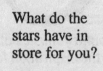

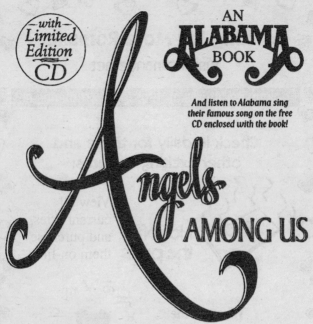

Don't miss these Harlequin favorites by some of our bestselling authors!

HT#25721	THE ONLY MAN IN WYOMING by Kristine Rolofson	$3.50 U.S. $3.99 CAN.	☐ ☐
HP#11869	WICKED CAPRICE by Anne Mather	$3.50 U.S. $3.99 CAN.	☐ ☐
HR#03438	ACCIDENTAL WIFE by Day Leclaire	$3.25 U.S. $3.75 CAN.	☐ ☐
HS#70737	STRANGERS WHEN WE MEET by Rebecca Winters	$3.99 U.S. $4.50 CAN.	☐ ☐
HI#22405	HERO FOR HIRE by Laura Kenner	$3.75 U.S. $4.25 CAN.	☐ ☐
HAR#16673	ONE HOT COWBOY by Cathy Gillen Thacker	$3.75 U.S. $4.25 CAN.	☐ ☐
HH#28952	JADE by Ruth Langan	$4.99 U.S. $5.50 CAN.	☐ ☐
LL#44005	STUCK WITH YOU by Vicki Lewis Thompson	$3.50 U.S. $3.99 CAN.	☐ ☐

(limited quantities available on certain titles)

AMOUNT	$ _____
POSTAGE & HANDLING	$ _____
($1.00 for one book, 50¢ for each additional)	
APPLICABLE TAXES*	$ _____
TOTAL PAYABLE	$ _____
(check or money order—please do not send cash)	

To order, complete this form and send it, along with a check or money order for the total above, payable to Harlequin Books, to: **In the U.S.:** 3010 Walden Avenue, P.O. Box 9047, Buffalo, NY 14269-9047; **In Canada:** P.O. Box 613, Fort Erie, Ontario, L2A 5X3.

Name: _____

Address: _____ City: _____

State/Prov.: _____ Zip/Postal Code: _____

Account Number (if applicable): _____

*New York residents remit applicable sales taxes.
Canadian residents remit applicable GST and provincial taxes.

Look us up on-line at: http://www.romance.net

HARLEQUIN®

AMERICAN ◆ ROMANCE®

COMING NEXT MONTH

#729 WANTED: DADDY by Mollie Molay
Jeremy and Tim knew exactly what kind of father they wanted, but
nothing they did made their mom go out and find him. The boys had no
choice: they had to take matters into their own hands and kidnap a dad!

#730 THE BRIDE TO BE…OR NOT TO BE? by Debbi Rawlins
Showers

Kelly was looking forward to her button-down small-town life with ol'
reliable Gary in their soon-to-be-built new home. So why, then, was the
sexy carpenter igniting her with his searing glances that threatened to
burn down her white picket defenses?

#731 HUSBAND 101 by Jo Leigh
Shy Sara Cabot was assured *Thirty Steps to Sure Success with the Opposite
Sex* would work for anyone. Then she tried them on a hunky ex-navy
SEAL. The steps were guaranteed…but to do what?

#732 FATHER FIGURE by Leandra Logan
Charles Fraser was used to doing his father's bidding, so how bad could
becoming a father figure to his five-year-old nephew really be? But then
he met the boy and his hard-to-resist mom….

AVAILABLE THIS MONTH:

#725 DIAGNOSIS: DADDY
Jule McBride

#727 A BACHELOR FALLS
Karen Toller Whittenburg

#726 A COWBOY AT HEART
Judy Christenberry

#728 A LITTLE BIT PREGNANT
Charlotte Maclay

Look us up on-line at: http://www.romance.net